THE WASHINGTON ULTIMATUM

A Novel

Lee Gimenez

RRP

River Ridge Press

VALERIE,
BEST WISHES,

The Washington Ultimatum
by
Lee Gimenez

THE WASHINGTON ULTIMATUM.
Copyright © 2013 by Lee Gimenez. (www.LeeGimenez.com)

Printed in the United States of America.
Published by River Ridge Press.

First edition.

Cover image: Copyright Jason Stitt, 2013; used under license from Shutterstock.com
Cover design: Judith Gimenez

ISBN-13: 978-0615819655

ISBN-10: 0615819656

Other Novels by Lee Gimenez

Blacksnow Zero

The Sigma Conspiracy

The Nanotech Murders

Death on Zanath

Virtual Thoughtstream

Azul 7

Terralus 4

The Tomorrow Solution

THE
WASHINGTON
ULTIMATUM

Chapter 1

December 3
Honolulu, Hawaii

Angelica "Angel" Stone glanced at her watch and realized the thousands of people crowding the area would be dead in an hour.

Angel was sitting in the outdoor cafe at the rear of the Westin Hotel in Waikiki Beach. The cafe fronted a wide stretch of the famous beach, which was packed with bikini-clad women, unruly kids and overweight men in garish Hawaiian shirts. Waikiki, with its crowds of Asian and American tourists, was the number-one sightseeing destination on the island. That's why she'd chosen the location.

The initial explosion would kill thousands. Better yet, the effects of the dirty bomb would last for years, the low-level nuclear radiation making the area unlivable for a radius of two to three miles.

Calmly sipping ice-tea, she brushed perspiration from her forehead. It was a perfect day, with temperature in the seventies. The sky was a cobalt blue, with no clouds. But the mid-day sun was hot and she had been at the table for an hour, wanting to make sure the concentration of the tourists was at a maximum. Her lightweight cotton dress was beginning to cling.

A muscular guy with bleached-blond hair weaved his way through the crowded cafe and approached her table. He was wearing a tank top, baggy trunks and flip-flops.

"Buy you a drink?" he slurred. The man stunk of booze – had probably been drinking all day.

Angel stared up at him, gave him a hard look. "No," she said, her voice cold.

He placed a hand on the table to steady himself. "Buy you a drink, honey? My name's Dan." He laughed. "Dan the man."

Angel was used to getting hit-on. Surfer-dude swaying in front of her was the third man to approach her that day. She was a sultry-looking woman, with classic high cheekbones, a slender but curvaceous figure, and long black hair. If she hadn't gone into the CIA years ago, she could have made decent money as a model.

"Get lost, asshole," she hissed.

A goofy grin crossed his face. "Why so grouchy? Sounds like somebody needs to get laid in a bad way."

Angel was repulsed by the persistent drunk, but she didn't need any complications. Not here. Not now.

Instead of kicking him in the balls like she wanted, she pasted on a phony smile.

"I've got a meeting in a couple of minutes," she said. "But I'm staying here at the Westin. Room 326. Come on up in say, half an hour. We'll party, have some laughs." She wasn't staying at the hotel and had no intention of shacking up with this clown.

"Now you're talking, sweetheart," he said with a leer. "You won't regret it. The girls I hook up with, they can never get enough of Dan the Man."

"Yeah, I bet. Now run along. I'll see you in a bit, okay?"

He gave her a grin and a mock salute, and weaved away through the teeming cafe to the bar.

Angel looked at her watch again, then out to the beach. It was time.

Standing, she pulled a twenty from her pocket and dropped it on the table. Slinging her tote bag over her shoulder, she turned and headed out of the place.

The parking lot was next to the high-rise hotel and she found the blue Ford cargo van a moment later. Her accomplice had parked it there the previous night as planned.

A control freak, Angel had the urge to check the contents in the back again, make sure everything was set. But she didn't want to attract attention in a parking lot full of people. Anyway, she had already checked it twice.

Walking past the cargo van, she reached Kalakaua Avenue a moment later. The wide boulevard was choked with traffic – sightseeing buses, honking cars, and vans with surfboards strapped on top.

She hailed a taxi near Duke Kahanamoku's statue. The cab pulled to the curb and she got in.

"Airport," she told the driver.

The heavyset man had a droopy mustache and stained teeth. "Any luggage, lady?"

"Just drive."

She settled on the lumpy back seat of the worn Chevy Impala. The taxi smelled of stale cigarette smoke and she opened the side window. Fresh air streamed in, cooling her face.

The driver headed west on Kalakaua, reaching the high-rise canyons of downtown soon after. She had been to Oahu many times, and the sights and sounds of the crowded city held no interest for her. They drove through Kalihi and reached Honolulu International a while later.

After taking the airport complex's on-ramp, the driver turned his head and faced her. "Which airline, lady?"

"Private," she replied.

He nodded, and drove past the main terminal building. The airport was teeming with cars, mostly cabs, dropping off tourists laden with multiple suitcases.

At the end of the terminal the crowds thinned. The taxi slowed in front of a smaller building and pulled to the curb.

Angel paid the fare and walked through the entrance designated for private planes. Going through airport security, she made her way to the tarmac on the lower level. After showing her forged ID one last time, she walked out into the bright sunshine. The wide tarmac smelled of jet fuel.

Rows of private jets were parked along the concourse. She spotted hers right away and strode toward it. A Gulfstream G500, the sleek twin-engine jet was painted black and had no markings save the tail number.

As soon as she reached it, its engines whirred on to a low-pitched whistle. The cabin door opened and her accomplice looked out and lowered the metal ladder. She nodded to him, then turned back to the terminal building.

Reaching into her tote bag, she pulled out the burner cell phone. She dialed the memorized number, held the phone to her ear. Hearing a loud click, she knew the bomb's detonator had worked.

She put away the phone and strained to hear over the whine of the jet.

Then she heard it. A deep rumble, from far away.

The airport was ten miles from Waikiki Beach, but the sound was unmistakable. The dirty bomb had exploded.

Angel breathed a sigh of relief. Phase One of the operation was complete.

With a smile, she climbed the steps and went into the plane.

Chapter 2

Atlanta, Georgia

J.T. Ryan was startled awake by a buzzing sound.

Instantly, he reached for the Smith & Wesson .40 caliber resting on the nightstand. Realizing it was only a call on his cell phone, he laid the gun down and picked up the phone.

The info screen said FBI and he held the phone to his ear. "Ryan," he said groggily, as he sat up on the bed.

"It's Erin."

He recognized the voice. Erin Welch was the Assistant Director in Charge (ADIC) of the FBI's office in Atlanta. Ryan, a private investigator, had done consulting work for her before.

He rubbed his eyes with his free hand. "What time is it?"

"3:20 a.m."

"Jesus. This better be important, Erin."

"It is," she said. "Where are you now?" He sensed the urgency in her voice.

"My apartment."

"I need you in my office, J.T."

"When?"

"Now."

Turning on the bedside lamp, he said, "Sounds serious. What's going on?"

"Are you living under a rock? It's been all over the news since late yesterday."

"I was working under-cover and got in late. What's up?"

"There was a bombing in Hawaii. Appears to be terrorism."

"Any leads?"

"Just get over here."

He heard a click and realized she'd hung up.

Putting the phone down, he went in the bathroom. He took a quick shower and threw on his usual clothes – dress slacks, a button-down shirt and a navy blazer. Running a hand through his close-cropped brown hair, he scanned his reflection in the mirror. His rugged appearance stared back at him, with a 5 o'clock shadow. He'd shave later.

Going back in the bedroom, he placed the S & W in the hip holster and clipped it to his belt.

***

A few minutes later he was driving south on Peachtree Street. There was almost no traffic at this time of night and he stepped on the gas, the Acura TL hitting sixty.

His thoughts churned on what Erin had said. A terrorist attack in Hawaii. Visions of the twin towers and 9/11 crossed his mind.

The FBI building was in downtown Atlanta, and as he pulled up to the structure, he noticed most of the lights in the windows were on. In contrast, the nearby buildings were dark.

Parking in the underground garage, he went through the two layers of security, was handed a visitor's badge, and took the elevator to Erin's floor.

The fourth floor was bedlam. The rows of cubicles were all occupied, by mostly male FBI agents, talking loudly on the phone or working feverishly on laptops. Other agents rushed about. Ryan had been there many times before, but had never seen the place so frenzied.

Erin was sitting behind her desk in her corner office and as soon as he stepped inside she stood and they shook hands.

"Grab a seat," she said, closing the glass door to her office. The noise from the bullpen dropped to a murmur.

The woman sat down behind her desk. She was wearing a stylish Armani suit with a white blouse, but the clothes were wrinkled, and she had black smudges under her eyes. Her long, blonde hair was pulled into a ponytail.

"How bad is it?" he asked, sitting across from her.

A frown crossed her sculpted good looks. "Bad. Really bad. They estimate 2,000 dead and 3,000 wounded. And that's probably a low number."

Ryan's heart began to race. "Damn. You said it was a bomb?"

She grimaced. "Yeah. That's the worst part. It wasn't just a regular explosive."

He leaned forward in the seat. "What do you mean?"

"It was a dirty bomb."

A feeling of dread settled in the pit of his stomach. As a former Army Special Forces officer, Ryan was well versed in all types of weaponry. A dirty bomb, although not as deadly as a nuclear weapon, was nevertheless highly feared for its capability to cause damage and create widespread panic.

"That's been confirmed?" he asked.

She nodded. "Yes. The FBI is on the scene, as is Homeland Security, along with the local cops. They've checked radiation levels. They're high, within a radius of three miles of the blast zone."

"Christ. Have they been able to figure out what type of explosive was used?"

"They're working on it. Looks like they used plastic explosive – C-4 or Semtex – to create the blast. They don't know the source of the radioactive material yet – could be medical waste from a hospital, or some other source. But most likely, the bomb was stored in a car."

"A suicide bomber?"

She shrugged. "It's possible. The car and the surrounding area were vaporized."

"What was the location of the blast?"

"Waikiki Beach, in Honolulu. The explosion took place mid-day, their local time."

"And I bet the area was packed with tourists."

"Absolutely," she said. "They timed it on purpose to cause the most casualties."

Ryan nodded. "This wasn't done by amateurs. It was a well-planned operation. Pros."

"I agree, J.T."

"What are the local authorities doing?"

"The governor of Hawaii has declared a state of emergency. The state's National Guard has been deployed in Oahu to assist the police. They're containing the situation. But, remember, it's an island, and there's only two ways out – by plane or boat. People are panicking – the tourists want off the island, ASAP. All the outbound flights are jammed full."

She stood, strode to a corner of the large office and turned on a wall-mounted flat-screen TV.

The screen came to life – the TV was tuned to CNN, the sound turned low.

The images from the live news broadcast were chilling. It was nighttime now in Honolulu and the images must have been from a plane, because it was an overhead view of the Waikiki Beach area. Although the fire from the explosion had been extinguished, the district was ablaze with light. Crisscrossing searchlights from police and fire departments bathed the area.

The view zoomed in and Ryan could see men in bulky Hazmat suits scurrying everywhere. Emergency vehicles and squad cars surrounded the blast area, which consisted of a collapsed building and damaged structures all around. Dead bodies littered the wide beach. They were being bagged and put on gurneys by emergency personnel, but there were so many it would probably take days to complete.

Erin pointed to the screen. "That demolished structure at the center was a large hotel. The bomb must have gone off close by."

Ryan watched without saying a word, sickened by the sight. He recalled the searing images of 9/11 once again, reliving that day in his mind. He would never forget the twin towers. He would never forget today.

Erin turned off the set, returned to her desk and sat down behind it.

He leaned forward in the chair. "I want in. Anyway I can help, I'll do it. I won't charge you a cent – I'll do it for free."

The agent crossed her arms in front of her. "Bullshit. You'll be paid like always." She paused. "You're on the case. Starting right now."

He was about to object, tell her again he didn't want the money.

Erin waved him off. "The thing is, J.T., I need you. Your expertise. You did a hell of a job on the Sigma case."

He nodded, recalling the counterfeiting case he helped solve a couple of years ago.

"As the person in charge of this office," she said, "I have a lot of agents working for me. But the truth is, I need someone who can cut through the bullshit, the procedures, and get their hands dirty."

Ryan grinned. "And maybe break a law, now and then, to get the job done."

She pointed a stern finger at him while suppressing a smile. "Enough said. You get my drift."

"I do."

"The FBI Director in Washington," she continued, "has issued an alert to all the field offices across the country. This bombing case is all-hands-on-deck. Solving it is our top priority. Our only priority."

"I understand," he replied. "Whatever you need, I'll do it."

"Good. I knew I could count on you."

Just then the laptop sitting on her desk emitted a loud chirping noise. Erin turned toward the computer. "This can't be good."

"What is it?"

She lifted the lid on the laptop so she could read the screen. "It's a code one alert from the Director in D.C. It's a high-priority e-mail to all the FBI offices." She tapped on the keyboard.

As Erin began reading the screen, the color drained from her face.

She said nothing, instead turned the computer so Ryan could see it.

He read it quickly. It was an e-mail from FBI Director Michael Stuart. It said,

The following text message was just received from a source we have not been able to trace:

HAWAII WAS JUST THE BEGINNING.
THE MAINLAND IS NEXT.

ALLA HU AKBAR. (This line was in Arabic, but Ryan knew it meant, "God is Great.")

AL-SHIRAK

Chapter 3

Paris, France

It was a cool, breezy day and Angel Stone zipped up her windbreaker.

From her vantage point on the balcony of her 6th story penthouse apartment, she had a breathtaking view of the Seine River, the Tuilerie gardens, and the Champs-Elysee. In the distance rose the Eiffel Tower, what the locals referred to as the "iron lady". Located on the boulevard St. Michel, the exclusive apartment had been a present to herself years ago.

Angel sat at a glass-topped table and sipped hot tea, idly watching boat traffic on the river. Still jet-lagged from the trip from Hawaii, her thoughts drifted, recalling her checkered past.

Once a rising star at the CIA, Angel had never been shy about breaking rules to get the job done. But she'd pushed it too far on her last field mission, her CIA partner had been killed, and Angel had been banished to a desk job. An adrenaline junkie, she chafed at the tedium in Langley. Bitter from the demotion and her new job's modest pay grade, she waited for something better.

Wanting more, much more, she made a fateful decision and seven years ago struck out on her own. Initially selling CIA secrets to raise cash, she eventually hired out as a mercenary, then turned to the illegal arms trade, selling stolen weapons on the black market. A particularly lucrative deal selling Stinger missiles in Africa paid for this apartment.

A gust of wind blew and she tucked her swirling long hair behind her ears.

Taking a sip of tea, Angel contemplated her current operation. More ambitious than anything she had attempted before, it necessitated bringing in a new partner into her group of accomplices. But she knew it was unavoidable. Bigger jobs required more resources. A tinge of fear crossed her mind, but she pushed that away. When had she been afraid of anything?

She smiled, knowing the payoff would be worth it.

Glancing at her watch, she realized it was time.

Standing, she opened the tall French doors and stepped inside the apartment. The high-ceiling living room was decorated with Louis XV furniture. Intricately carved armchairs and brocade-fabric sofas sat on gleaming wood floors. An elaborate roll-top desk made of cherry wood and inset with gold leaf took up one corner of the room. Original, iconic paintings hung on the walls.

She went into her study, which was lined with floor-to ceiling bookcases, all filled with priceless books. Walking to the bookcase that covered the left-hand wall, she removed one of the books, a Bible, and pressed a recessed tab that was hidden by the book. A portion of the bookcase popped out from the wall, and she slid it aside, using the built-in casters. On the wall where the bookcase had been was a closed metal door, with a retinal-scanner panel next to it.

Pressing a button on the scanner, she leaned close, letting the device scan her right eye. Hearing a click, she pulled open the heavy door and walked inside.

The windowless, simply furnished 'safe room' contained little – a metal desk, an ergonomic chair, and a tall, steel cabinet. On the desk sat several computers – a couple of laptops, and a desktop unit with a large monitor.

Setting down the cup of tea, she took off her windbreaker and sat behind the desk.

She turned on the desktop computer and input her series of lengthy passwords. Next to the computer was a small hand-held device and she turned it on. In the unlikely event that the soundproofed room was being monitored, the device would disrupt any recording of her conversation.

The monitor screen flicked to life.

As she expected, her accomplices were already on the secure video conference call. The split-screen showed three faces. On the left was her longtime and trusted associate, Frank Reynolds. Frank had been her go-to-guy for years – a hands-on operative with no scruples – her kind of man. His blond hair and boyish good-looks belied the fact that he was a cold-blooded killer. Like her, Frank lived in Paris, but in a modest one-room flat.

In the center of the screen was Carlos Montoya, her Spanish partner. The swarthy-looking man with a long, hooked nose and short beard had been with her for two years. A native of Seville, he now lived in Madrid. Carlos was a banking and communications expert. His ability to launder money through dummy corporations and multiple banks was invaluable.

Angel greeted each of these two, then turned her gaze toward the third man, her new partner. His thin, pock-marked face filled the right side of the screen. Doctor H. Heiler. The German scientist wore round, wire-frame glasses and had an inscrutable, ice-cold smile he flashed at odd moments. The seventy-five year old man had a shadowy past; called brilliant by some and insane by others, he had worked for the East German government before the reunification of that country. He lived in Berlin, had a secret lab there, and hired out to the highest bidder.

The scientist gave her the creeps, but she had no choice about including him in the operation. His knowledge of nuclear radiation and weaponry made him an intrinsic part of the group.

"Dr. Heiler," she stated flatly, "how are things in Berlin?"

The man laughed. "It is December. Cold, as you would expect, *Fraulein* Stone."

She held up a hand. "We've known each other for six months, Doctor. Why don't you call me by my first name."

"As you wish."

"By the way, what is the H. stand for in your given name?"

He flashed a cold smile but said nothing.

Angel shrugged. "Let's get on with the meeting, then. As I'm sure you've seen in the news, the incident in Honolulu went off exactly as planned. You're to be commended, Doctor. The casualties exceeded even my own expectations."

"I aim to please, *Fraulein.*"

The ex-CIA agent took a sip of her now lukewarm tea. "I'll wire you the initial payment today."

The scientist nodded, said nothing.

She leaned forward in her seat. "You're sure, Heiler, that the next explosive is set to go?"

"Yes."

Her voice took on a hard edge. "I hope so. I have a lot riding on it."

"As we all do, *Fraulein.*"

Angel turned to Carlos Montoya. "Carlos, you've got the bank deposit side covered?"

"*Sí,*" the Spaniard answered. "Everything is in place. The authorities will never be able to trace the money back to us."

"Excellent."

Carlos rubbed his beard with his palm. "I also sent you six new burner cell phones. The messages from those will be untraceable."

"Yes," she said. "I received the package. Good work, Carlos."

Lastly she turned and faced Frank Reynolds, her long-time accomplice. "You have things arranged for our arrival?"

The blond man nodded. "Got it covered, Angel."

"Good." She leaned back in the chair and finished the rest of the tea.

"Well, gentlemen," she continued, "it appears all is on schedule. Frank and I will be heading to the States tomorrow. If you need to reach me, only use the encrypted laptops or the phones Carlos supplied. Never call or e-mail me on an unsecure device." She lowered her voice. "Our lives depend on it."

Each of the men nodded solemnly, realizing the gravity of her words.

She flashed a warm smile. "Next time we all meet in person, we will be extremely wealthy."

After a quick wave, she turned off the computer.

Then her thoughts turned to her upcoming trip to the U.S.

Phase Two of the operation was about to begin.

Lee Gimenez

Chapter 4

Atlanta, Georgia

J.T. Ryan was in his mid-town office doing paperwork, when a rap at the door caused him to glance up. FBI agent Erin Welch was standing in the open doorway, a grim look on her face.

Ryan pushed aside the report he was reading. "Grab a seat. Want some coffee?"

Erin made a face. "No. I want to live." She sat on one of the client chairs in front of his desk.

Ryan chuckled. "I forgot. You've had my coffee before."

"Cut the crap, J.T. I'm not in the mood."

The attractive woman appeared worn out – there were bags under her eyes and she wore no makeup. She was wearing a stylish suit, but it was wrinkled.

"No sleep, huh?" he asked.

"No time. I've been living at the FBI office since this damn thing started."

He pointed to the thick stack of folders on his desk. "I've closed out all my other cases. I'm ready to work on the bombing full time."

"I appreciate that," she said in a tired voice.

He took a sip of coffee. "Been watching the news about Hawaii. The explosion caused quite a panic. It's going to take a long time for their tourism industry to recover. But I noticed there was no mention of the terrorist threat we received. You guys have done a good job of keeping it out of the media."

Erin's blonde hair was pulled into a ponytail and she tucked a loose strand behind her ear. "The Director wants it that way, until we know more. No sense in creating more panic."

"What have you found out about this Al-Shirak group?"

She frowned. "Nothing yet. They're not showing up on any database – FBI, NSA, Homeland Security, CIA, Mossad, Interpol ... nothing there. We've been scrutinizing the internet chatter from the usual suspects – Al-Qaeda, Hezbollah, and others. But this new group doesn't appear to have any connection to them. We've been at it for three days, but still nothing."

"That's odd."

"I think so too. But the world of terrorism is shadowy – and fluid. There's new bastards popping up all the time."

Ryan nodded, said nothing.

"While we're on the topic of bad news," she said, her voice grave, "I've got more."

He leaned forward in the seat. "Tell me."

"The Homeland Security guys have pretty sophisticated equipment," she said, "and they've been monitoring the radiation levels in Waikiki. What they found is disturbing. At first we suspected the explosion was caused by C-4. We also suspected the radioactive material used was most likely medical waste from a hospital or lab in Hawaii. But we now realize this bomb was much more sophisticated."

"How so, Erin?"

"The blast was too large for regular C-4 to have caused it. The bombers used something to magnify the explosive power. And there's one other thing that's even worse."

"What?"

"After a few days, the radiation levels at the blast zone are higher than you'd find from medical waste. And it's spreading faster than we anticipated."

Ryan was confused. "How's that possible?"

"We now think the bombers used some type of sophisticated accelerant that augments the spread of the radioactivity."

He shook his head. "Christ. These guys are definitely pros."

"Yeah. That kind of technology is leading edge."

The detective leaned back in the chair and processed this new information. "Who has that kind of technology?"

"In theory," she said, "the U.S., Russia, China, a few others, although no country would admit to it. In any case, there's no need for the major powers to use this technology – they already have large stockpiles of regular nuclear weapons, which have greater destructive power." She paused. "But we never thought terrorists hiding in caves in Afghanistan could develop something like this."

"So," Ryan said, "it's possible a country like North Korea or Iran, could have given Al-Shirak this technology."

Erin crossed her arms in front of her. "We're checking on that angle, but so far, we've come up empty."

"From what you've told me," he stated flatly, "so far you've got nothing."

Her eyes flashed in anger, and her lips pressed into a thin line. After a moment, she took a deep breath and simply said, "Yeah. You're right."

She pointed to the coffee maker that sat on top of the filing cabinet. "I'll take that cup after all."

He grinned. "Sure you want to risk it?"

She nodded.

Standing, he reached for the coffee urn and poured her a cup. After handing it to her, he went to the office window and sat on the sill. His 20th story office overlooked other high-rise buildings in mid-town. It was a cloudy day, but the skyscrapers of downtown Atlanta were clearly visible.

Ryan turned back to the agent. "I told you I'd do whatever you need. And I meant it. But I need something to go on, some lead to follow. So far, all you've got are ghosts."

She took a sip of coffee and grimaced. "God, this *is* awful." She placed the cup on his desk.

Ryan smiled. "Yeah, but it's hot."

Erin ignored the remark, then rubbed her temple with her hand, as if she had a headache. "I agree, J.T. We don't have much to go on. I've got twenty agents working their informants. Every other FBI field office is doing the same. So far, zilch."

"Tell me more about the text message that came in from the terrorists."

"Okay," she replied. "It was exactly as I showed you on the computer the other day. The text was sent to the cell phone number of FBI Director Stuart. Neither we, nor the NSA have had any luck tracing it. Like you said, it's like chasing a ghost."

Ryan rubbed his jaw. "Interesting that the message went to the FBI. If the terrorists wanted publicity, why not send it to the media – CNN or the New York Times?"

"We can't figure that out either."

He took another sip of coffee. "So. What's next?"

Erin frowned. "We keep trying to trace the source and try to figure out who the hell this Al-Shirak is. And we wait for the second message."

"Not much of a plan, is it?"

"It's all we've got."

Chapter 5

Savannah, Georgia

The Gulfstream jet touched down with a thump, then rolled down the private airstrip before turning left and parking next to a row of other small planes, mostly twin-engine props.

Angel Stone unfastened her seat belt and glanced out the oval window of the passenger cabin. The airfield consisted of a one-story building and a small hanger, with a parking area next to that. There was no one about, save an overweight rent-a-cop in a tight uniform, patrolling the grounds. In the distance, she saw farmland and rolling countryside.

"There's nothing out here," she said, turning to Frank Reynolds, who was sitting on the seat across from her.

"That's why I picked it," he replied, standing up. "We're ten miles from the city – a good place to base our operation."

She nodded, grabbed her tote bag and coat, and followed him out of the plane.

Angel waited on the tarmac by the foot of the jet's stairs as Frank helped their pilot unload the bags from the plane.

It was a cold, drizzly day and she was glad she had brought her black parka. Putting it on, she zipped it up and grabbed her duffel from Frank.

"The car's over there," he said, leading the way.

She followed him to the mostly empty lot and found the Toyota Camry a moment later. Painted a non-descript gray, the sedan was as plain as a paper bag.

They stowed their gear in the trunk, and he started the Camry. Pulling out of the lot, he waved to the rent-a-cop, who flashed them a smile.

"Friend of yours?" she asked.

"I gave him a couple of hundred," Frank said, "last time I was here. Told him to keep an eye on the car, and the plane, once we landed."

She nodded, satisfied Frank was on top of it.

They found the lightly-trafficked state road and made their way through the rolling countryside. A short while later Frank took a gravel side road that led to a two-story wooden farmhouse. The house had a sagging front porch, peeling paint, and looked old – probably built in the 1940s. A rusted-out pickup truck sat up on blocks next to the house. The place appeared deserted and the nearest neighbor was probably a mile away.

"I like it, Frank," she said, as the car came to a stop in front of the house.

He turned off the engine. "I rented it for two months – but we'll be done well before then."

They climbed out, unloaded the bags and went inside the ramshackle place. The living room had plank floors, a wood-burning stove, and was filled with dusty, early-American furniture. The room smelled musty, as if it hadn't been lived in for a long time.

She dropped her bags on the floor. "Where's the stuff?"

"Out back, in the barn."

"Let's see it," she said.

"I thought we'd unpack first, grab a bite. I stocked the kitchen with some supplies."

"Screw that," she replied, her voice hard. "We'll do that later. I want to see them first."

He nodded, set down his bags.

They went through the kitchen and out the back door. The large back yard was overgrown with weeds and scrub. A wooden barn was set back about fifty feet, a black Dodge cargo van parked next to it.

They crossed the yard and reached the barn.

Duct taped to the barn door was a printed sign that read:

WARNING!
ELECTRIFIED ALARM SYSTEM
WILL CAUSE DEATH
DO NOT ENTER!

She noticed a latticework of wires draped across the door. A large padlock, obviously new, hung from the door handle.

Next to the barn door was a keypad; a light on the keypad glowed red.

"You set this up?" she asked.

"Yeah," Frank said. Approaching the keypad, he tapped in a code and the light turned green. Then he removed the lattice of wires from the entrance.

Unlocking the padlock, he opened the door and they stepped inside.

The high-ceiling barn had the faint smell of hay and manure. Bales of hay were stacked five high and ten across in a corner of the dimly-lit area, but other than that the place was empty.

Frank turned on the light switch and the naked light bulbs hanging from the pitched roof glowed yellow.

He crossed the barn, and without a word, grabbed one of the bales of hay, lifted it by the bailing wires, and hoisted it aside. He grabbed a second bale and pulled it out of the way. He was big and strong and made it look easy.

It was obvious the devices were behind the stacks and she joined him. Picking up one of the bales, she hoisted it and slid it aside, grunting from the effort.

"Son-of-a-bitch," she muttered. "these things are heavy."

He laughed, said nothing and continued clearing the way.

Ten minutes later they were done.

Angel brushed the sweat from her face and struggled to catch her breath. But the sight in front of her brought a smile to her lips.

Arranged neatly against the wall of the barn were seven of the bombs. Dr. Heiler's creation.

Each of the devices was about the size of a very large suitcase. The rectangular, box-like devices were painted a dull black, with no markings. On the top of each was a small control panel with a keypad.

She crouched by one of the bombs, ran her hand over the ceramic casing. She felt a tingle of excitement, an almost sexual jolt from the touch.

"They're beautiful," she said as she lovingly caressed the bomb.

Frank laughed. "Only you would say that. They're deadly, that's for sure."

She stood, turned toward the blond man. "Any problems getting them here?"

He shook his head. "They came in by private freighter to the port of Savannah. They've got security there, but Heiler hid the bombs inside a shipment of other machinery. And he did a hell of a job masking the radioactivity."

Angel crossed her arms in front of her. "Show me."

There was a small hand-held device on top of one of the bombs and Frank picked it up. Turning it on, the device emitted a slight crackling sound.

"Let me see," she said.

He showed her the readout on the radiation detector. The reading was well within the normal range. The bombs were not emitting any radiation.

"How about the C-4?" she asked. "That can be picked up by gamma-detector scanners."

"Heiler shielded for that too." He pointed to another readout on the hand-held detector. "See?"

Finally satisfied, she said, "Good."

He put down the detector. "I'll go get the van, drive it in here so we can load it."

"Okay," she replied.

A minute later the cargo van, its back doors open, was parked in the rear of the barn.

She pointed to the bombs. "I remember these things are damn heavy."

"Oh, yeah," Frank said. "They weigh a lot." He reached into the van and lowered to the ground a rolling hand-jack. Sliding the jack under one of the bombs, he cranked the jack so that the bottom of the explosive device was raised to the height of the van's floor. Then he pulled the jack next to the van and pushed the bomb into the van.

"The bombs have casters on the bottom," he reminded her. "Otherwise we'd have a hell of a time doing this."

"Heiler thought of everything."

"Yeah. That German bastard was quite a find, Angel."

He closed the van's doors.

She glanced at her watch. "It's too late to do anything today. We'll leave early tomorrow morning." She paused, gave him a hard stare. "And no drinking tonight. I need you with a clear head. We've got a long drive ahead of us."

He gave her a mock salute. "You got it, boss."

She turned, began walking out of the barn.

"Angel," he called out from behind her. "We still have to restack the hay in front of the other bombs."

"That's your job, Frank," she replied, without looking back.

***

Rummaging through the farmhouse's dusty, old kitchen Angel found canned Spam and stale bread. She made a sandwich, ate it standing up, and washed it down with a Coke.

Curious as to what else Frank had stocked, she continued rummaging thorough the cupboards. Hidden behind a bag of sugar she found a quart bottle of Smirnoff. Shaking her head slowly, she poured the vodka down the drain and threw out the empty bottle.

Afterwards, she grabbed her bags from the living room and climbed the squeaky wooden stairs to the second story. Finding an empty bedroom, she dropped the bags on the floor. The room smelled of mildew and she went to the window and opened it, letting in cold, fresh air. Next she pulled the Sig Sauer automatic from her tote bag and placed the pistol on the nightstand.

She inspected the adjoining bathroom, which had a claw-foot tub, something she hadn't seen in years.

The tub's faucet made a strange howling sound when she turned it on, as if the water hadn't been used in a long time. Eventually, cold water spurted out. Well-water, she guessed, but at least it looked clean.

Stripping off her sweaty clothes, she took a quick shower as best she could, using the hand-held faucet extension. After drying herself with a scratchy towel from the rack, she threw on sweatpants and a sweatshirt.

Pulling the covers off the bed, she stretched out on the lumpy mattress, shifting and turning, trying to get comfortable. It was only early evening, but she knew she had to get as much rest as possible. Tomorrow would be a tough day.

Setting her mental alarm clock for five a.m., she closed her eyes and was asleep in minutes.

***

Startled by a loud cracking noise hours later, Angel bolted from the bed and grabbed the handgun.

Scanning quickly around the dim bedroom, she saw no one. Faint moonlight came in through the open window.

Holding the handgun in front of her, she padded out of the room on bare feet. Walking down the corridor, she inspected several empty rooms before finding the source of the noise in a well-lit bedroom. She should have guessed.

Sprawled on his back on a four-poster bed was Frank, snoring. He was still dressed in his clothes from the day before.

On the wood floor next to the bed was a broken bottle of Dewar's scotch. A small puddle of liquid lay among the cracked pieces of glass.

"Jesus, Frank," she muttered. "What the hell did I tell you?"

Placing the pistol on a side table, she sat on the bed and stared at the sleeping handsome man. Once, a long time ago, they had been lovers. But his heavy drinking had driven them apart. Now they were just business partners. Probably better that way, she mused. Mixing sex and business was a bad combination.

She slapped him, hard, across the face.

He yelped, awake now, and tried to sit up. But instead he fell back on the bed.

"What the fuck ...?" he mumbled, seeing her for the first time.

"You were drinking," she stated flatly.

"Just a couple of pops ..."

"Bullshit! Looks like you had the whole bottle."

Frank was about to protest, but she slapped him again, harder this time.

He reared back, his eyes full of anger, and his hands formed into fists.

"You going to hit me?" she asked quietly. "I told you not to drink."

The anger left his eyes. "I just ... got carried away."

She caressed the red mark on this cheek with the palm of her hand. "I know, hon." Standing, she glanced at her watch.

"It's almost four a.m.", she said. "Why don't you take a shower, Frank. I'll make some strong coffee. As soon as you sober up, we'll hit the road."

He sat up on the bed, rubbed his eyes. "Okay."

She picked up the Sig Sauer, stuck it in the waistband of the sweatpants, and left the room.

Padding down the stairs, she went into the kitchen and began to brew a large pot of coffee. There was no tea for her, so she would have to make do.

She heard water running from an upstairs bathroom, and then the coffee maker made a beeping sound.

Pouring herself a cup, she sat at the chipped Formica kitchen table. There was a window that looked out to the heavily wooded side yard. Hazy moonlight lit up the quiet, rural scene outside.

Sipping the hot coffee, she thought about what the coming day would bring. She was excited, but nervous too.

It would be a big day for her. And an even bigger day for the country.

Lee Gimenez

Chapter 6

Atlanta, Georgia

J.T. Ryan was on the 400 freeway, driving to his apartment when his cell phone buzzed. Pulling it out from his blazer's pocket, he read the info screen. It said FBI.

He held the phone to his ear while keeping an eye on the heavy northbound traffic all around him.

"It's Erin," he heard the woman say.

"What's up?"

"We just caught our first break," she said excitedly.

"Yeah? Tell me."

A semi to his right and just ahead edged toward his lane and he tapped on the brakes and leaned on the horn.

"The local cops in Chicago," Erin said, "were alerted about a box in a Greyhound bus station."

"So?"

"The box contained a burner cell phone and a Koran. On the first page of the holy book was scrawled the name Al-Shirak."

"That is a big break, Erin. They know who's it is?"

"Not yet. The box had been left under a bench at the station. The cleaning crew found it — their supervisor thought it was suspicious and called the cops."

"Where's the box now?"

"The FBI guys in Chicago have it. Their forensics people are checking it for prints and trace evidence."

"Good."

"Where are you now, J.T.?"

"Just left my office – I'm driving home."

"I'd like you to go out there and help with the investigation. Can you fly out tomorrow?"

Ryan glanced at the Acura's dash clock. "It's seven p.m.," he said. "I'll be home in a couple of minutes. I'll pack a few things, drive to the airport and take the next flight to Chicago tonight."

A BMW cut in front of him and he leaned on the horn again.

"Thanks," Erin said. "I'll let the FBI guys know you'll be coming."

He disconnected the call and stepped on the gas.

***

Ryan's flight landed at O'Hare airport at one a.m. Chicago time.

He rented a Chevy Impala and took the lightly-trafficked Interstate 90 to downtown. Having been to Chicago many times before, he had no problem finding the FBI offices on West Roosevelt Road.

It was well past two in the morning by the time he got there and the nearby office buildings were dark. But as in Atlanta, the FBI offices were a hive of activity.

After going through security, he was handed a visitor's badge and escorted to a large cubicle on the third floor. The cubicle was occupied by an Asian man in his thirties wearing a gray suit. The agent, a short, muscular man, stood and extended his hand when Ryan stepped in.

"I'm Special Agent Tim Cho," the man said. "ADIC Welch called my boss, told him you were coming."

The two shook hands.

"Good to meet you, Cho. You're in charge of the investigation?"

The agent nodded. "Let's go to the conference room."

Cho led the way to a glass-walled room and closed the door as soon as they went inside. "Coffee?" he asked.

Ryan shook his head. "No thanks. I had a gallon of it on the plane. I'm wired."

They took seats across from each other at the long conference table.

"Where's the package now?" Ryan asked.

"The forensics techs have it in the lab. They just finished checking for fingerprints, DNA, and other trace evidence."

"And?"

Cho grimaced. "Nothing so far. The phone and the Koran had no prints – looks like they were wiped clean."

"Pros."

The agent nodded. "We took the cell phone apart, checked the battery and chip. But they had been wiped also."

"What kind of phone was it?"

"A cheap burner. The kind you can buy at any Wal-Mart."

"You're checking the serial number?"

"We're working on that," Cho said. "We may be able to trace it back to a specific store location."

"And the Koran?"

"Cheaply made – printed in China, but it was an English translation, not in the original Arabic. So the group, this Al-Shirak, probably bought the Koran in the U.S."

Ryan leaned forward in the chair. "What about the inscription?"

"The name 'Al-Shirak' was handwritten on the first page in black ink. There were no other notations in the book."

"I need to see it," Ryan said.

Cho nodded, stood and walked to the phone on the credenza. He spoke into the receiver a moment and hung up.

A few minutes later a middle-aged woman in a white lab coat came in the room. She was wearing latex gloves and was carrying a heavy-duty white plastic bag.

Placing the bag on the conference table, she turned to Ryan. "You'll have to wear these," she said, reaching in a pocket and pulling out a pair of latex gloves.

"I know the drill," the detective said, taking the gloves and snapping them on.

The woman unzipped the bag, carefully took out the black-bound book and placed it in front of him.

Ryan scanned the book's cover – it was an inexpensive plastic binding. Opening the Koran, he inspected the first page. Underneath the book's title, the word 'Al-Shirak' had been scrawled in. He studied the signature, memorized the flow of the hand-written strokes.

Next he picked up the book and slowly flipped through the thin-paper pages. As Cho had said, the text was all in English – unusual, since the name of the group was Arabic sounding. But then, maybe not. There had been several cases of terrorist plots that had originated from U.S. based Islamic radicals.

In his time in Special Forces, Ryan had served in Afghanistan and Iraq, and was familiar with Korans, or Qur'ans, the Arabic name for the Islamic holy book. This one looked no different than any other he had seen.

After a few minutes, he closed the book and looked up at the woman. "Okay, I'm done with it."

She picked it up gingerly, put it in the bag and zipped it up. With a nod to Cho, she turned and left the room.

"What do you think?" Cho asked.

Ryan took off the latex gloves, dropped them on the table. "Unless you find trace evidence of some type, it's not much to go on."

"I agree."

"But," Ryan said, "on the other hand, it does tell us something important."

"What's that?"

"This terrorist group was here in Chicago."

Cho nodded. "And the first text message said the mainland was next."

"So there's a strong possibility the next attack could take place here."

Cho leaned forward in his seat. "We've already thought of that. In fact, Director Stuart is sending us extra teams from D.C., and Homeland Security is bringing in more of their people. The local PD is on elevated alert."

"Good. You're focusing on the high-value targets? Airports, train stations, the tourist areas?"

"We know how to do our jobs," Cho said, irritation in his voice.

Ryan shrugged. "Just asking."

"What are your plans? Going back to Atlanta?"

The detective shook his head. "No. I want to do everything I can to help. I'm staying."

Cho stood. "In that case, let's go back to my work station. I've got some files I want to show you. Welch said you had experience dealing with terrorist cells in the Middle East."

Ryan followed the man back to his cubicle and the agent rummaged through his filing cabinets. He pulled out four files and laid them on his desk.

Ryan pulled a chair close, sat down and picked up the first file. He began reading the contents. There were reports and photos of a local Islamic mosque. The imam who presided over the mosque appeared to have some ties to Hamas. Intrigued, Ryan continued reading.

Chapter 7

Berlin, Germany

Tucked away on a remote side street, Dr. Heiler's non-descript, concrete-block house looked no different from many others in the former capital of East Germany. The squat, gray two-story building was devoid of any decorative touches, save for the graffiti which covered so many walls of the city. Although the house was only a few miles from the famed Brandenburg Gate on Strasse Des 17 Juni, it was light years away from any of the festive tourist areas in the western parts of the city. Heiler cherished the anonymity of living there. He had chosen the location for that reason, even though he could afford something much better.

His living areas on the two above-ground floors were plain and functional. But he didn't spend much time there. Most of his time was spent in his large but packed basement. Jammed with extensive computer equipment, testing apparatus, a machine shop, and a lab, the basement was his life. He loved tinkering, loved developing new formulas. In fact, he had set up a cot in the room, just so he could take naps instead of sleeping in his bedroom upstairs.

Heiler was in his basement now, working at his computer. Currently he was revising his radiological enhancement program. He was so engrossed in his work that he almost missed the flashing red light on the wall.

The only drawback to working underground was that there was no cell phone reception; he had to take calls upstairs.

Grudgingly, he closed the computer program and climbed the concrete stairs, his arthritic joints aching with every step. It's hell to get old, he thought for the thousandth time.

There were two cell phones sitting on top of his living room end table, and the secure one was ringing. As he picked up the phone, he glanced outside through the small window. It was one a.m. and the narrow street, lit by ancient streetlamps, was deserted. The only things he spotted were parked VW and Trabant sedans, their faded paint and dented bodywork speaking volumes about their impoverished owners.

"This is Heiler," he said into the phone.

"Doctor, it's Angel."

Heiler visualized the attractive, young woman in his mind, and for a moment forgot all about bomb making.

"Good to hear from you, Angel. You have brightened an old man's day." Then he remembered the protocol. "What is the code word?"

"Black Hawk," he heard the woman say. "What's the response, Doctor?"

"White Shadow." He sat on the threadbare sofa, glad to be off his feet. "How are things, *Fraulein?*"

"Everything is on schedule."

"That is good news." He pushed the wire-rim glasses up the bridge of his nose. "How can I help you? I am assuming this is not a social call."

There was a chuckle from her end. "Afraid not, Doctor. When we talked last time, I forgot something. Something important."

"Yes?"

"I need you to send a part."

"What, *Fraulein?*"

"I want you to send some small part of the bomb, something generic, off-the-shelf. It has to be non-explosive and non-radioactive. There must be some minor part that could be used in bomb making, but couldn't be traced back to you."

Heiler thought about this for a moment. "Everything I make is specifically constructed – all of it is leading edge."

"Think. There must be something."

Then it came to him. "Yes, of course. The control panel. I buy it from an electronics store."

"Excellent," she said.

"Give me your location, Angel, and I will send it today."

"No. It's not for me. Write down the name and address I'm going to give you." She read off the information, and he wrote it down on the pad resting on the end table.

"Make sure you wipe your prints from the part, Doctor, and send it through your usual cut-outs, so it can't be traced to you."

"Of course. May I ask why you need this?"

There was a pause from her end. "It's better if you don't know. Goodbye, Doctor."

He heard a click as the call was disconnected.

Heiler sat there a moment, sorting out the conversation. The woman was inscrutable sometimes. But the money was good. Very good. And aside from the money, there was the aspect of revenge.

Giving it no more thought, he stood and shuffled back to his basement.

Chapter 8

Miami, Florida

Angel Stone disconnected the call and put the cell phone in her jacket pocket.

It was six p.m. and traffic was heavy on Interstate 95. She was driving the Camry, following the black cargo van, just ahead of her.

The Ives Dairy Road exit sign flashed by and the van's turn signal came on. She followed as the van took the exit and headed west on the jammed, four-lane local road.

Twenty minutes later they were on Biscayne Boulevard, the massive Aventura Mall towering next to the wide avenue.

There was a multi-level parking garage attached to the shopping complex and the van drove into it, with Angel right behind. The lot was full on the first three levels, but they finally found empty slots on the fourth.

Climbing out of the Camry, she walked over to the van parked a few cars over.
Frank Reynolds was leaning against the van.

"What do you think?" he asked.

"Looks good so far," she replied. "Let's go inside."

She led the way, crossing the covered terrace way into the complex.

The upscale mall was packed with shoppers, the wide aisles full. It was only weeks until Christmas and most of the patrons were laden with shopping bags. Festive lights and Christmas bunting decorated the atrium and store windows.

To Angel's right was the entrance to Bloomingdales, where a pretty girl dressed as a Santa's helper was handing out perfume samples. Holiday music played on the loudspeakers, competing with the voices of the shoppers as they browsed.

"Let's find the food court," Angel said.

She pushed through the crowd, and moments later found the large, open area at the center of the mall. This too was packed, almost all of the tables in use. The pungent odor of the different food vendors assaulted her all at once and she almost gagged. Aventura might be upscale, she thought, but every mall food court smelled the same.

Glancing around, she saw Frank heading toward a Chinese food stall. Shaking her head, she spotted a Chick-fil-A in the corner and strode over.

After getting her food she found an empty table and sat. Frank joined her a minute later.

"How can you eat that crap?" she asked him, in between bites of her chicken sandwich.

He picked up a greasy eggroll and munched on it. After a gulp from a Sprite, he said, "Food is food. I'm not that fussy."

She shrugged, but knew he was telling the truth. The man would eat anything.

"So," he said, "what do you think of the place? I scouted three malls in the area – this was the best location."

"I think you're right, Frank."

"Aventura is the largest mall in Miami," he said with a gleam in his eyes. "2.7 million square feet. All the big names are here – Macy's, Bloomingdale's, Nordstrom's, Sears, JC Penny's, you name it. 300 stores, a 24-screen movie theatre, a playground for kids."

"You did good, Frank."

The blond man grinned, took a huge bite of his moo-shoo-pork.

Angel pushed aside her empty food tray and watched idly as Frank wolfed down the large platter of Chinese food.

When he was done, she said, "Want some more?"
Realizing she was joking, he smiled. "No. I'm done."
She stood. "Let's go then. We've got work to do."

***

A short while later they were back in the parking garage, standing next to the cargo van.

Frank unlocked the back door of the van, opened it and climbed inside. Angel scanned the surrounding area, saw no one nearby, and joined him, closing the door behind her.

There were no windows in the cargo compartment and he switched on an interior light.

Strapped to the floor of the vehicle was a bulky, box-shaped object, draped with a tarp. He unhooked the straps and pulled off the tarp, revealing the bomb. The black device gleamed under the lights and she ran a hand over the casing.

Once again she felt an intense, sexual thrill. Pushing that feeling aside, she said, "Okay, let's do it."

Frank went to the control panel and pressed a switch. A green light lit up on the panel and the device emitted a slight humming sound. He tapped six of the buttons on the keypad and stepped away from the bomb. "Your turn," he said. To prevent accidental detonation of the device, they had agreed long ago to put in two separate codes.

Angel leaned over the control panel and tapped in the second code.

Instantly the light on the panel switched from green to red and she knew the device was ready. One phone call was all it would take now for detonation.

Although being so close to this much destructive power excited her, it also made her nervous. She trusted Dr. Heiler and his warped brilliance. But she knew nothing was 100 per cent foolproof. He had installed back-up mechanisms, but electronics still failed sometimes. Granted, it was rare, but not unheard of.

Angel stepped away from the bomb.

"Let's get the hell out of here, Frank."

Lee Gimenez

Chapter 9

Chicago, Illinois

FBI agent Tim Cho parked in front of the mosque and turned off the Ford Crown Vic.   "This is it," Cho said.

J.T. Ryan looked closely at the building's facade. They had already visited two other mosques today, but this one, unlike the others, was run-down. Located in an impoverished area of south Chicago, the exterior walls of the place looked like they hadn't been painted in a long time.

The small building was domed, but otherwise blended in with the decrepit appearance of the rest of the neighborhood. Cigarette butts and empty beer bottles littered the sidewalk. Stained steps led up to the front entrance, where a burly black man stood, his arms folded across his chest.

Ryan climbed out of the car, glanced around the neighborhood. At the nearby corner, a group of young men clustered, smoking. Loud rap music was playing in the background.

Cho locked the car, set the alarm and strode up the stairs to the entrance, and Ryan followed.

Cho flashed his badge at the man posted at the door. "I'm Special Agent Cho of the FBI, and this is J.T. Ryan. We need to see Imam Rahim."

The guard wore a scuffed leather jacket and dark sunglasses. He had a tattoo of a cross on his neck; it was crudely done, and likely obtained in prison.

"The Imam is busy," the guard said tersely.

"This is official business," Cho replied. "We need to see him now."

"Do you have an appointment?"

The agent shook his head. "Don't need one. Listen, we can do this the easy way or the hard way. Which is it?"

The black man sneered. "What's the hard way?"

"I call in an FBI SWAT team and lock your ass in jail." Cho paused. "My bet is you're on parole, and probably packing an illegal firearm."

The guard's eyes went wide. "All right. I'll let him know you're here," he said, his voice drained of bravado.

"Thank you," Cho said.

The guard turned and went inside the building.

"Good work, Cho," Ryan said. "Couldn't have done it better myself."

The guard was back a moment later, opening the front door wide. "Follow me," he said.

They went inside and into a foyer, then down a corridor. At the end was a closed door, which the guard opened. "In here," he said.

In the small, sparsely furnished office, a swarthy man with a long, gray beard, sat behind a worn desk. He was in his mid-sixties, wore a skullcap and a long, flowing robe. From the pictures Cho had shown him, Ryan realized the man was Imam Rahim.

Cho flashed his badge again and motioned to the guard. "Imam, we need to speak with you in private."

"Jackson, you may leave us," the imam said, in heavily accented English. It was clear the religious leader was from somewhere in the Middle East.

Rahim pointed to the chairs in front of his desk. "You may sit, if you wish."

The two sat, and Ryan scanned the small room. Hanging on one wall was a flag with a crescent moon logo. Mounted below the flag was long, curved scimitar sheathed in a scabbard. Odd, Ryan thought, to display a sword in a place of worship.

"Jackson tells me you needed to see me?" the imam said. "I have prayer services in a short while, but I have time now."

"Very generous of you," Ryan replied.

The imam gave him a hard stare. "You must understand. I have been questioned by the FBI before. Many times, in fact."

"I've read your file," Ryan said, "you're no saint."

Rahim shrugged. "You people think I have ties to terrorist groups." He paused, an exasperated look on his face. "I do not. My mosque has been investigated. Nothing has ever been proven."

Ryan nodded. "Maybe you're just smarter than most."

"I resent your accusations. Why is it Muslims are always accused of radicalism?"

"9/11 comes to mind," the detective said, his voice hard.

"That was a long time ago."

"I've got a long memory. And let's not forget the other plots since then, most of them with ties to militant Islamic radicals."

The imam shrugged again. "Islam is a religion of peace. We cannot control the actions of a few."

Ryan pointed to the wall. "What's with the scimitar? Doesn't look very peaceful to me."

Rahim spread his palms in front of him. "The sword is a reminder that we struggle every day in the fight for men's souls."

Ryan shook his head. "Sounds like bullshit to me."

"Imam," Cho cut in. "We've come across new information. Perhaps you'll answer some questions."

"Ask away, agent. And I hope you're not as rude as your friend."

Cho glanced at Ryan, then back at the religious man. "My apologies, sir. We mean no disrespect."

The imam appeared mollified and placed his hands flat on the desk. "What is it you want to know?"

"A new radical group has surfaced," Cho continued. "A Muslim terrorist group that calls itself Al-Shirak."

The detective studied the imam's face carefully for any sign of recognition. But the man's expression remained blank.

"I have never heard of the group," Rahim replied.

"You're sure?" Cho pressed.

"Yes, I am."

The agent leaned forward in the chair. "We found a Koran owned by this group here in Chicago."

"This is a big city," the imam said tersely. "As I said, I've never heard of this ... what did you call it?"

"Al-Shirak."

"I am sorry, agent Cho, but I cannot help you."

"Can't or won't?" Ryan interjected.

The imam gave him an icy stare, but didn't respond. He turned back to Cho. "Is there anything else?"

"No. Not for now."

The religious leader stood. "In that case, if you will excuse me. I have prayers to lead."

***

Back in the car moments later, Cho said, "What do you think?"

"I don't know if he's involved," Ryan responded. "But he's hiding something."

Cho nodded. "I think so too." He fired up the Crown Vic. "One mosque to go," he said, as he pulled away from the curb.

Chapter 10

Madrid, Spain

Carlos Montoya was startled awake by a ringing noise. Sitting up on the bed, he fumbled for the bedside lamp and turned it on. His secure cell phone was ringing and he picked it up, held it to his ear.

"This is Montoya," he said groggily.

"Carlos, it's Angel."

He recognized her voice immediately. Still half asleep, he struggled to remember the code word for the day. After a pause he said, "True Winter. What's the response?"

"Broken Arrow," he heard Angel say.

Carlos's wife, Maria, who was on the bed next to him, placed a hand on his shoulder. *"Quien es?"* she asked.

"Negocio. Voy a hablar en el otro cuarto," he responded. *Just business. I'll take the call in another room.*

Maria shrugged and went back to sleep.

"Give me a moment," Carlos said into the phone. He stood, put on a bathrobe and went into the study of his apartment. Closing the door behind him, he sat behind his wide mahogany desk.

"Okay, go ahead Angel."

"Catch you sleeping, Carlos?"

He looked at his watch. *"Sí.* It is three a.m. here."

"Yeah. I guess it is."

"What's going on, Angel?"

"Everything is in place from my end. Just wanted to verify you're set on your side."

"*Sí.* I have it covered."

"Check again," she said, a hard edge to her voice.

He sighed. "Very well." The woman could be a bitch sometimes.

Carlos booted up his encrypted computer, and idly rubbed his short beard as he waited. After logging on to his secure banking program, he studied the account information on the screen. Satisfied, he said, "Everything is set."

"Excellent, Carlos. I'll keep you posted as things proceed."

"When are you pulling the trigger?"

"Tonight."

They were close to finding out if all the work of the last six months would pay off. "Good luck, Angel."

"Good luck to all of us."

Then he heard a click from the other end.

Carlos slipped the cell phone into the bathrobe's pocket, turned off the computer, and left the study.

Wide awake now, he went out to the wide balcony of his upscale apartment. Working with Angel for the last two years, he thought, was the only reason he could afford this place. Located on Calle de Alfonzo XII, the apartment overlooked el Parque del Retiro. At this time of night, the scenic park was dimly-lit and quiet, but still beautiful to look at. Through the trees he could make out the lake at the center of the park.

Sitting at the wrought-iron table, he hardly noticed the cold. Instead his thoughts turned to the operation. Angel was a bitch, he mused, but a bitch who was going to make him a very wealthy man.

Chapter 11

Savannah, Georgia

Angel Stone glanced at her watch, the luminous dial showing the time. Eleven p.m. Still too early to make the call. She would do it at midnight, to maximize the impact.

She was sitting alone on the front porch of the old farmhouse. After talking to Carlos, she had spent the last several hours out here, watching as the daylight faded and nighttime settled in. The smell of honeysuckle was strong, the cloying scent filling the air.

Strangely, she was becoming attached to the crappy old house, with its ancient plumbing and rustic furniture. Maybe it was the remoteness of the place, its sense of isolation. So different from Paris. But it was only temporary, she reminded herself. Another couple of weeks and she'd never see the farmhouse again.

On the rickety wooden table in front of her, her laptop screen glowed with the latest headlines from ABC News. She was surfing the net, as a way to pass the time.

She could hear the muted sound of the television from the living room inside. Frank, no doubt, watching some mindless program.

Angel clicked through the headlines, searching for the most recent stories about Hawaii. The explosion there still dominated the news, the crisis in that state receiving worldwide media attention.

Just then the front door of the house opened and Frank stepped out into the porch. He was holding two filled glasses, and he handed one to Angel.

She took it and placed it on the table. "Hope it's not bourbon."

Frank chuckled. "Naw. Just Pepsi. I learned my lesson."

"I hope so."

He sat at the table, pointed to the computer. "Anything new?"

"Honolulu is still the lead story. That should make our job a lot easier."

Frank took a sip of Pepsi. "That's a fact. You need me to do something? I'm restless, just watching TV."

"No, Frank. There's nothing for you to do right now."

The man stood up. "In that case, guess I'll get some shut-eye." He paused a moment. "You know, I've got a big bed upstairs. When you're done with the call, why don't you join me?"

Angel gave him a cold stare. "In your dreams. Those days are over."

"Can't blame a man for trying."

"No, I guess not." As he turned to go back in the house, she added, "And stay off the booze, Frank."

Angel read the clock on her computer screen. It was almost time.

Pulling out her cell phone, she placed it next to the laptop. She opened the Word program on her computer and clicked on the correct file. She had worked on the message for days, wanting the statement to be perfect.

Tapping the keys on the cell phone, she transcribed the message, copying it word-for-word from the file.

She felt her adrenaline pumping as she hit the send button on her cell.

Chapter 12

Chicago, Illinois

J.T Ryan glanced out the passenger window of the Crown Vic. They were on the Loop, heading back to the FBI offices.

Ryan was exhausted. He hadn't slept for days, working with agent Cho non-stop, investigating the ever expanding list of mosques in the city, each with possible ties to radical groups.

He was also frustrated as hell.

The glacial pace of following FBI procedure was getting on his nerves. He was used to working on his own, one of the many reasons he had never wanted to join the Bureau.

Ryan turned to Cho, who was driving the car. "What's next?"

"I've got to finish writing up reports," the agent said.

"That's crap – we need to move on these people. Now."

Cho shook his head, but kept his eyes on the road ahead. Traffic was heavy on the Loop. "Got to follow procedure."

"Bullshit, Cho. We've got at least three good suspects."

The agent gave him a sideways look. "We still have to give them due process."

"Listen, Cho, nobody gave the victims of 9/11 due process."

"I know that, damn it. Still, we can't just arrest these imams. We have to be careful how we treat the Muslim community."

Ryan's jaw clenched. "I hate that P.C. shit. Grow some balls, will you?"

Cho grimaced and his face turned red, but he stayed quiet.

"Talk to the District Attorney," Ryan said. "Have him issue search warrants. I'll bet we'll find something."

The agent said nothing for a long time. He got off the freeway, then took a right at the end of the ramp. "Okay, Ryan. I'll talk to the DA. We'll get the warrants."

"Now you're talking."

Chapter 13

Atlanta, Georgia

ADIC Erin Welch was on the phone in her FBI office when her laptop chirped loudly. Knowing it was a code one alert from the director, she quickly lifted the lid on the computer and scanned her e-mails.

"I'll call you back," Erin said into the phone and hung up the receiver.

Clicking open the e-mail from FBI Director Stuart, she began to read, her heart pounding after the first sentence.

At 12:03 a.m., I received the following text message on my cell phone. We have not yet been able to identify the source of the call.

DIRECTOR STUART:
AS WE TOLD YOU EARLIER, THE BOMBING OF HONOLULU WAS JUST THE BEGINNING.
IF OUR DEMANDS ARE NOT MET, FOUR ADDITIONAL U.S. CITIES WILL BE BOMBED. YOU WILL DEPOSIT ONE BILLION U.S. DOLLARS INTO OUR ACCOUNT PER THE FOLLOWING SCHEDULE:

YOU WILL PAY $250 MILLION WITHIN 24 HOURS OF RECEIVING THIS MESSAGE OR THE SECOND AMERICAN CITY WILL BE ATTACKED. AFTER THAT YOU WILL PAY AN ADDITIONAL $750 MILLION IN INSTALLMENTS OF $250 MILLION, OR THE THIRD, FOURTH AND FIFTH U.S. CITIES WILL BE ATTACKED. THE FIFTH CITY BOMBED WILL BE WASHINGTON D.C.
WE WILL NOTIFY YOU OF THE BANK ROUTING NUMBERS FOR THE WIRE TRANSFER AS WE APPROACH THE FIRST DEADLINE.
IF YOU DO NOT MEET OUR DEMANDS, WE WILL NOT HESITATE TO CARRY OUT OUR THREAT.
THE BOMBING OF HONOLULU PROVES WE ARE DEADLY SERIOUS.
ONE BILLION DOLLARS IS A LOT OF MONEY. BUT IT PALES WITH THE SUFFERING THE PALESTINIAN PEOPLE HAVE ENDURED FOR 60 YEARS.

ALLA HU AKBAR.

AL-SHIRAK

Erin read through the text message again, then stared at her watch. It was 12:16 a.m., less than 24 hours before the next attack.

Chapter 14

Chicago, Illinois

J. T. Ryan, sitting in the passenger seat, glanced at the car's speedometer. The Crown Vic was doing eighty. But it was 4 a.m., and there was little traffic on the highway.

Agent Tim Cho was driving, the man's eyes glued to the road ahead. Following right behind the car was an FBI van carrying a heavily-armed SWAT team.

Just then Ryan's cell phone buzzed. He pulled it from his jacket pocket and held it to his ear.

"It's Erin Welch," he heard the woman say.

"What's up, Erin?"

"No doubt agent Cho told you about the message from Al-Shirak?"

"Yeah," Ryan replied. "In fact, that helped us get the search warrants expedited."

"Where are you now, J.T.?"

"We questioned a lot of Muslims, but only a few of them stood out. They may be involved. We're on our way to one of them now."

"That's good, J.T. Because we only have 20 hours before the next attack takes place."

Ryan watched as Cho got in the left lane and blew past a couple of slower moving cars. "Any chance the U.S. will pay the ransom?" he asked into the phone.

"No way," Erin replied. "The American government doesn't do that. It's policy."

"That's what I thought."

"All the FBI field offices are on full alert, as are the local cops around the country."

"Yeah, Erin. But it's a hell of a big country. Fifty states, and over 300 million people. How many cities could be the target?"

"There are 725 cities in the U.S. Of those, 285 of them have populations over 100,000."

"Christ," Ryan said, shaking his head.

There was a pause from the other end. "J.T., we've got a lot of people working on this, but you guys out there may have our best lead."

The sign alerting him to the right exit flashed by and Ryan said, "Got to go. I'll keep you informed." He hung up and put the phone away.

Cho crossed three lanes of traffic, slammed on his brakes and exited.

Ten minutes later the Crown Vic pulled up to the curb in front of the darkened mosque; the SWAT team van was right behind.

The small, domed building looked deserted, as did the rest of the neighborhood. Ryan scanned the front of the religious building. The shabby facade was dimly lit from a nearby streetlamp.

Cho and Ryan climbed out of the car and the agent opened the trunk. Cho pulled out a Mossberg shotgun, a Ruger revolver, and two bullet-proof vests. Handing the revolver and one of the vests to the detective, the agent said, "The gun is for self-defense. You're not FBI. We'll do the shooting, but only if absolutely necessary."

Ryan nodded as he strapped on the vest.

By this time, the SWAT team had piled out of the van and was taking positions in front and toward the rear of the mosque. The team was dressed in black fatigues, carried assault weapons, and wore helmets with lights attached.

Cho pointed toward the front door and four of the SWAT guys climbed the steps, followed by Cho and Ryan.

The lead SWAT agent knocked loudly on the door. "FBI!" he shouted. "We have a warrant to search this building. Open up!"

There was no answer and he yelled again.

After a moment, Cho said, "Break it down."

One of the SWAT guys carried a battering ram and he hammered the door several times until the wood gave way, splinters flying everywhere.

The SWAT team, guns at the ready, rushed into the dimly-lit mosque, their boots thudding heavily. Ryan followed and watched as the men searched the foyer and went deeper into the corridors, the lights on their helmets crisscrossing rooms. The SWAT guys shouted "Clear!", as they went through the mosque.

There was a crashing noise from the back of the building, loud yelling, and shots rang out. A moment later, two of the SWAT agents emerged from a back corridor, holding a burly black man between them.

"Caught this guy trying to escape," one of the SWAT guys told Cho.

"It's our good friend Jackson," Ryan said, recognizing the man from their previous visit.

Cho stared at Jackson. "Who else is here?"

"Just me," Jackson replied. "I guard the place at night."

"We have a warrant to search the mosque," Cho said. "Where's Imam Rahim?"

"At home. He doesn't get in until nine, most mornings."

"Was he carrying?" Cho asked the SWAT guys holding Jackson.

"Yeah," one of them said. "A Saturday night special – a piece of junk."

"Place him under arrest," Cho said, "and put him in the van. This guy's on parole. No way he should have a weapon."

The SWAT guys nodded and dragged Jackson outside.

Ryan turned on the lights in the foyer as Cho said, "Okay, let's fan out. Search the assembly hall and all the other rooms. Look for anything suspicious. But put on latex gloves first. If you find something, I don't want to contaminate the evidence."

Holding the revolver in front of him, Ryan walked down the left corridor toward Rahim's office.

Turning the knob of the office door, he realized it was locked. He kicked the flimsy wooden door and it gave way. Stepping into the office, he found the light switch and flicked it on.

The room looked the same as he remembered from a few days back. There was the faint smell of hashish and incense in the air. An odd combination, he thought.

Snapping on latex gloves, the detective began to methodically search the office. He went through the desk first, then the filing cabinets. Several of the drawers were locked and he pried them open with a pocket knife.

Next he searched the closet, which was full of prayer books and boxes of religious pamphlets. Finding nothing incriminating, he unscrewed the HVAC vents and searched the wall cavities.

Turning over the office chairs, he cut open the cushions, but found nothing hidden.

Just then Cho came in the room. "Anything, Ryan?"

"No. It's clean."

Cho shook his head. "We've searched the whole building. Found nothing so far."

Ryan sat on the edge of the desk. "Rahim is no saint. He's guilty of something." Scanning the room once more, he spotted the flag and the scimitar hanging on the wall.

Walking over, he took the sword off the wall hooks and unsheathed it from the scabbard. Finding nothing unusual, he replaced the scimitar back on the wall.

On a hunch, he lifted the edge of the flag and looked behind it. On the wall he noticed another HVAC grill. "That's odd," he muttered. "Who covers up an air vent?"

Tearing the flag off the wall, he removed the screws and pulled off the grill. Inset into the wall was a closed metal box, with a padlock dangling from the hasp. "It's a strong box," Ryan said, pulling out the container.

Cho came over. "Good work. We'll take it back to the office and pry it open there."

"No time," Ryan said, placing the strong box on the floor and drawing his revolver. "Stand back, Cho."

The detective aimed the pistol and fired one shot. As the sound of the blast echoed in the room, he crouched to inspect the damage to the padlock. The lock had cracked open, and he pulled it off and opened the lid on the box.

Ryan reached in with both hands and removed the contents, then stood and placed them on the desk.

Among the items were a Glock automatic pistol, banded stacks of fifty dollar bills, and a small electronic device. Ryan did a quick count of the cash. "There's about fifty grand here," he said.

The agent picked up the electronic device and looked at it closely. "I wonder what this is?"

Ryan took it from him and studied it for a minute. "I've seen similar things before ... in Afghanistan. The insurgents used them as control mechanisms for bombs."

Cho nodded. "Why the hell would an imam need this?"

"Told you he was dirty."

"It's definitely enough to arrest him on suspicion of terrorist acts," Cho said. "Now we just have to find him."

"We'll find him."

***

After bagging the evidence, Cho called the forensics team to the mosque, and left two of the SWAT guys to secure the location.

Twenty minutes later, the Crown Vic and the FBI van pulled up to the front of a ten-story apartment building in a residential neighborhood of south Chicago.

It was 6 a.m. and still dark out, but Ryan noticed car traffic was beginning to pick up on the street.

"Rahim lives by himself on the fifth floor," Cho said, turning to the detective. "I don't want to spook him, so I'll post my men at the entrance and exits to the building. You and I will go up and make the arrest."

Ryan nodded, drew his revolver and checked the load.

"And remember," Cho added, "no shooting. We need this guy alive for questioning."

The detective chuckled. "You must think I'm a loose cannon."

"Welch told me all about you, Ryan," Cho said with a frown.

"I'm one of the good guys, remember?"

"From what I've heard, you like to shoot first and ask questions later."

Ryan laughed. "Okay, Cho. Let's go."

They climbed out of the car and after Cho conferred with the SWAT team, the two men entered the building.

Taking the elevator, they got off the fifth floor and walked down a long corridor until they found the right apartment.

Cho pressed the door bell and tapped the door with the butt of the shotgun. "FBI," he shouted, "open up!"

After a minute, they heard the locks unbolting and the door opened partway. Rahim, dressed in sleepwear, peered out from behind the doorway.

The agent flashed his badge. "FBI. Open up, Imam. We need to talk."

"What do you want?" Rahim demanded, indignation in his voice. "How dare you disturb me again. This is harassment."

Ryan lowered his shoulder and slammed it into the door, which swung all the way open, knocking the imam to the floor.

Ryan helped the man to his feet, and said, "Hands against the wall, Rahim. I need to search you."

The imam's face turned red, but he complied, allowing himself to be frisked.

"He's clean," the detective said.

Cho pulled out handcuffs and clicked them on the religious leader's wrists.

"This is an outrage!" Rahim yelled. "I want a lawyer!"

"You'll get one," Ryan said, grabbing the imam by the shoulders and pushing him down on the living room couch. "But we need to talk first." The detective turned to Cho. "Keep an eye on him while I search the rest of the apartment."

Ryan left the room, inspected the dwelling, and came back a few minutes later carrying a shoe box.

Cho pointed to the box. "What's in there?"

"Another Glock and more cash," Ryan replied. "About forty grand."

The agent turned to Rahim. "We found the bomb control device in the mosque. We know you're involved with the planned bombing."

The imam had a confused look on his face. "I do not know what you are talking about."

"Don't lie to us," Ryan said. "You're part of Al-Shirak. Admit it."

Rahim shook his head forcefully. "I told you the other day. I do not know who they are."

"If you tell us where the bomb is," Cho said, "and who your co-conspirators are, the DA may cut you a deal."

The imam's eyes went wide. "What bomb? This is insane! I'm a religious leader, not a terrorist."

"We found the control mechanism," Ryan said. "You're involved, we know that."

"No! You have made a mistake," the man responded.

Ryan pulled the revolver from his pocket and aimed it at Rahim's forehead. "Tell me now, or you die."

Cho put a hand on the detective's shoulder. "Put that away, Ryan. We need him alive."

"I know what I'm doing," Ryan said harshly, and turned back to the imam.

Rahim's face showed true terror. "I do not know anything about a bomb," he said, his voice trembling. "The woman sent me the device. She told me to keep it in a safe place. I do not know what it is for. You have got to believe me!"

"What woman?" Ryan demanded.

"The woman that gave me money. A lot of money. $100,000. Said she supported our cause. Supported the liberation of the oppressed Palestinian people."

"Who is she?" Cho asked.

"I only know her by her first name, nothing else," Rahim said, as he stared at the muzzle of the revolver. "I swear." Beads of perspiration rolled off his forehead.

Ryan shook his head. "You want us to believe a crazy story like that? Someone gives you a hundred grand and they only tell you their first name?"

"It is true. You have to believe me! I do not know anything about a bomb."

Ryan cocked the hammer on the revolver, and pressed the barrel to Rahim's temple.

The imam's face turned white.

Chapter 15

Atlanta, Georgia

Erin Welch walked in her office and slumped on the office chair behind the desk. She had just finished another round of meetings with her staff.

Dead tired from her days of sleeplessness, she opened a drawer, pulled out an energy drink and drank it down in one continuous swallow.

Just then her desk phone buzzed with a distinctive tone, alerting her to a secure call from FBI headquarters in D.C.

She picked up the receiver. "Welch here."

"Erin, it's Director Stuart," she heard the man say.

"Yes, Director."

"I'm calling the ADICs to find what progress they've made. So far, I haven't heard anything useful. I'm hoping you'll change that."

"Just met with all my teams," she replied. "We're working our CIs, but so far, none of our informants have anything."

"I don't have to remind you," he said icily, "how little time we have left."

"Yes, sir."

"Is there *anything* you've found to indicate which city may be the target?"

"Not yet, sir. As I told you earlier, one of my contractors is out in Chicago, following up on the Koran lead from a few days ago."

"I remember. Who's the contractor?"

"J.T. Ryan."

"Ryan. He's the guy that helped you solve the Sigma case, wasn't he?"

"Yes, sir."

"Okay. I've talked to the Chicago ADIC. He told me he's got a team serving search warrants on several suspects out there."

"Yes, sir. Ryan is in on that."

"Good. Call me as soon as you hear *anything*."

"Yes, Director."

"Before you hang up, I want your input on something."

"Sir?"

"Don't you find it odd the terrorists contacted the FBI directly for the ransom?"

Erin had been thinking the same thing. "Yes. And they contacted you on your cell phone number. Not many people have access to that."

"May not be anything, but I find it troubling."

"Yes, sir. Any luck on tracing the call?"

"Not yet. I've got the NSAs and CIAs full cooperation – they're using every resource, as we are – but so far, no luck."

Erin glanced at the clock on the office wall. There were only seven hours left. "Director, I know the policy, but any possibility we'll pay the ransom demand?"

"I was at the White House earlier for a National Security meeting. It's always been U.S. policy not to pay ransom, so that option isn't being considered. And in any case, this threat could be a hoax. A copycat ransom using the Hawaii bombing as cover. This Al-Shirak group, whoever the hell they are, may not have been involved with the attack on Waikiki."

"I've thought of that too."

"Okay, Erin. I've got more calls to make. Call me immediately if something breaks."

"Yes, Director."

The phone line went dead and she replaced the receiver. She stared at the clock again as a sick feeling settled in the pit of her stomach.

Chapter 16

Chicago, Illinois

"I swear on the Koran!" Rahim pleaded, his voice breaking. "I am telling the truth."

J.T. Ryan held the revolver steady, its barrel still pressed against the imam's temple as he studied the man's terror-stricken eyes. Most people in this situation, Ryan knew, would have cracked by now. Maybe, just maybe, the imam wasn't lying.

Ryan un-cocked the gun's hammer and lowered the weapon to his side.

"Thank God," Cho muttered. "You had me worried Ryan."

The detective gave the agent a hard look, then pulled up a chair and sat across from Rahim.

"You're lucky agent Cho is here, Imam," Ryan said. "Otherwise you'd be dead meat already." He pointed a finger at Rahim. "But Cho won't always be around to save your ass. Now. Tell me everything. I want to know about this mystery woman."

Rahim's eyes darted between Cho and Ryan. "I want a lawyer," he stated.

"Bullshit!" Ryan shouted. "You talk first, then you'll get a lawyer."

"I know my rights," the imam said, his confidence returning.

Ryan slapped the religious man hard across the face, the blow drawing blood from the man's lip.

The startled imam yelped, and cringed deeper into the couch.

Ryan closed his fist and pulled it back as if to deliver a punch and Rahim yelled, "Stop! I will talk!"

"I'm listening," Ryan said.

"The woman," the imam began, "came to see me two months ago, at the mosque. Said she was sympathetic to our cause. The Palestinian cause. She gave me $100,000 in cash. Told me she would contribute more, much more, in the future. But she said she wanted to remain anonymous."

"You didn't think that was strange?" Ryan asked. "Someone out of the blue gives you a hundred grand?"

Rahim nodded. "Yes, of course. But Allah works in mysterious ways. Our mosque is in an impoverished area. Contributions are meager. The money was a godsend."

Ryan studied the imam's face closely – it appeared he was telling the truth. "What's her name? Where is she from?"

"She said her first name was Sarah, but wouldn't tell me anything else. She said she wanted to keep her generosity private."

"What did she look like, Rahim?"

The imam thought about that a moment. "Tall, slender, attractive. She had a long scar on one cheek. She had dark hair tucked into a cap."

"Caucasian? Black? Arabic?"

"Caucasian."

"Did she have an accent?"

"She sounded American."

Ryan glanced up at Cho. "Call one of your sketch artists. We need to get a composite drawing."

The agent pulled out his cell phone and made a call.

The detective turned back to Rahim. "What about the control device we found in your safe."

"The woman, Sarah, called me a few days ago, told me I would be receiving a package. Asked me to hold it for her. She also said she was going to be giving me another large donation for the mosque."

"Have you gotten that money yet?" Ryan asked.

"No."

Ryan looked over at Cho, who had finished the call.

"We'll take Rahim back to the office," Cho said. "The artist will meet us there."

"Okay," Ryan replied, "but I'm not done questioning him yet."

Cho nodded. "We'll finish at the office; but we have to get Rahim a lawyer first."

"That's crap," Ryan said. "No telling what'll happen when attorneys get involved."

The agent frowned. "Sorry. But we're already pushing it, as it is."

Ryan glowered.

"What happens to me now?" the imam asked.

"You'll be charged under the Patriot Act," Cho said, "for suspicion of terrorist activities."

Rahim's eyes went wide. "But I have not done anything wrong!"

"You'll get a lawyer when we get back to the office," Cho said. "As to whether you're guilty or not, that remains to be seen."

Lee Gimenez

Chapter 17

Savannah, Georgia

Angel Stone was sitting at the farmhouse's front porch table, munching on a sandwich, when a *Breaking News* banner flashed across the laptop's screen. Putting the sandwich down, she clicked on CNN's breaking story.

FBI raises terror alert nationwide, the headline said. Taking a sip of lukewarm coffee, Angel read further. *CNN has learned that the FBI has raised the U.S. terror alert to the highest level. Our sources have been told that a credible threat has been made against an unspecified American city. The bomb threat could be similar to the recent explosion in Hawaii. Police nationwide have begun intensified patrols looking for evidence of a possible attack. Delays in airline flights are expected, as TSA agents increase searches at airports. Citizens are being asked to contact authorities immediately if they observe suspicious activities ..."*

She finished reading the rest of the story, then leaned back on the chair.

Smiling, she savored a feeling of accomplishment. They were taking it seriously, she thought. Good. Now, will they pay?

"We'll see," she muttered to herself.

It was a cool day, but the mid-day sun provided comforting warmth. She glanced at her watch. It was time.

Picking up the burner cell phone, she tapped in the memorized number. Next she wrote the text message, including the bank routing number and account codes.

She hit the send button.

Chapter 18

Chicago, Illinois

J.T. Ryan stared at the artist's sketch agent Cho had just handed him. Both men were in the conference room at the FBI offices downtown.

Ryan studied the woman's face on the sketch. Pretty face, he thought, marred with long scar on the left cheek. He looked back to Cho. "Don't recognize her."

"Me neither," the agent replied. "We're running the image through our facial recognition programs. We're searching DMV photos, passport data bases, military and criminal records. The NSA, Homeland Security, and CIA are doing the same."

"Anything?"

"Not yet."

Ryan rubbed his jaw, feeling the growing stubble there. Lately, he hadn't had much time to shave. "And the name? Sarah?"

"We're checking, but it's a pretty common name. Without a last name, it's going to be tough."

"And it could be an alias."

Cho nodded. "There is that."

"Where's Rahim now?" Ryan asked.

"He's being questioned by an FBI team. But now that he's got a lawyer, the imam has clammed up."

Ryan glared. "Told you we should have beaten the hell out of him."

Cho raised his palms in front of him. "This isn't Afghanistan or Guantanamo. We have to follow rules."

"Fuck the rules," Ryan hissed, his voice low and harsh.

The agent shook his head slowly. "It's not up to me anymore. The ADIC here is calling the shots, and he goes by the book."

Ryan glowered at him and then took a couple of deep breaths to calm down. Cho was doing his job, he realized. And that job had a lot of constraints.

Just then Ryan's cell phone buzzed. He pulled it from his jacket pocket and held it to his ear. "Ryan," he said.

"It's Erin," he heard the woman say. "The director just got the bank codes, J.T. We have less than an hour before the bombing takes place."

"Or we pay the first 250 mil," he replied.

"Out of the question. That option is not being considered."

"You've seen the sketch, Erin?"

"Yeah. We're running it through all our visual records here. Nothing. This Sarah, whoever she is, is a ghost. You guys get any more info from Imam Rahim?"

"That's a dead end, for now."

"Shit," she replied. The woman sounded tired and frustrated.

Ryan thought for a moment. "Hey, Erin. You trace the bank codes to a location?"

"Yes. It's a bank in the Cayman Islands, in the Caribbean. Grand Cayman to be exact. We're in contact with their government. But we think that once the money is wired to that account, which we won't be doing, the money would immediately be transferred to another country, probably several."

"Figures," Ryan said. "What's the FBI's plan now?"

"We keep looking for the bomb, and hope the threat is a hoax."

Ryan looked at his watch as the seconds continued to wind down. He heard a click as the call was disconnected and he put the phone away.

"Anything?" Cho asked.

"No," he replied, as a feeling of dread settled over him.

Chapter 19

Atlanta, Georgia

Erin Welch replaced the receiver and leaned back in her office chair.

The lead Ryan was working on had been her best hope. Her only hope. And now that the imam had gone mute, the prospects for preventing the bombing looked dim.

Opening a drawer on her desk, she took out another energy drink and drained it.

She massaged her temple, tying to rub away the throbbing migraine that was pounding in her head.

After a moment, she picked up the receiver again and stabbed in a number.

"Where the hell are we on identifying the woman in the sketch?" she demanded, her voice harsh.

Chapter 20

Savannah, Georgia

Angel Stone closed the lid on her laptop and stood up. Stepping off the farmhouse's front porch, she strode across the overgrown yard to an area away from the trees, wanting to maximize the reception.

Pulling the cell phone from her pocket, she dialed a number and held the phone to her ear.

"It's Angel," she said quickly into the phone. "The code word is Black Water."

"Blue Ice," Carlos Montoya replied from the other end.

"Carlos," she said, "it's an hour past the deadline. Has the money been transferred to the account?"

"I've been watching my computer all day," Carlos said. "Nothing yet."

Her stomach started churning. "Fuck. I'll show those bastards."

"What are you going to do, Angel?"

"The only thing I can do. We'll talk later." She turned off the call and watched as Frank Reynolds walked out of the house and came up to her.

"Talking to Carlos?" he asked.

She nodded. "They didn't make the payment."

A look of disgust spread across his face and he shook his head slowly.

"Start getting ready," she said. "We'll pack up after I make the call."

"I'm on it," he said. He turned and walked back to the house.

After a last glance at her watch, Angel punched in another number on her cell phone. She pressed the phone tightly to her ear, to make sure she could hear clearly.

After a moment, the call was received on the other end and she heard a loud click.

With a sigh of relief, she knew the bomb's detonator at the Miami mall had worked.

Chapter 21

Chicago, Illinois

J. T. Ryan was sitting in the FBI's empty conference room working at his laptop when agent Cho burst into the room. Cho's face looked ashen.

Without a word, the agent went to the TV set in the corner of the room and turned it on.

Ryan stood. "What's wrong?"

"Come look," Cho said, his voice grim. "The news just broke."

The detective strode over and stared at the TV screen. The set was tuned to a CBS station broadcast, the words *Breaking News* scrolling along the bottom.

Ryan's heart sank as the sickening images flashed across the screen. The view, probably taken from a news helicopter, was of a densely populated metro area engulfed in flames. Plumes of smoke rose from a large complex of buildings. The nearby roads were packed with stationary, burning cars. Ringing the complex were scores of fire trucks attempting to douse the flames. Police cars, their lights flashing, were blocking the nearby streets, diverting traffic away from the area.

Cho turned up the volume on the TV and an announcer's voiceover blared from the speakers. "... as we've just reported, a large explosion has taken place at Aventura Mall, west of downtown Miami. This shopping center is one of the largest in Florida. The cause of the blast is not yet known. But the scene is eerily similar to the bombing that took place in Hawaii recently." The announcer paused a moment, then continued, "As you can see on your screen, damage to the mall complex is extensive. Since we are in the holiday shopping season, the mall was packed with shoppers at the time of the explosion. It's too soon to give you the number of casualties and wounded, but some are estimating that number to be in the thousands."

"God damn it," Ryan uttered, bile forming in his throat. "It's Al-Shirak. The ransom demand wasn't a hoax."

"I agree," Cho said. "It's exactly the same M.O. A crowded area in a big city."

The announcer's voice continued, as more images of burning buildings flashed across the screen. "... authorities on the scene are warning everyone to avoid this area completely, until more is known. It's possible it could be contaminated with radioactivity, as was the case in Waikiki."

Ryan turned toward the agent. "I'm sure they're checking?"

Cho nodded. "A Homeland Security team from downtown Miami is on its way over there. We'll know for certain if it was a dirty bomb minutes after they arrive."

The detective stared at the screen some more, then lowered the volume of the TV. "Where's Rahim now?" he asked.

"He's being held in a cell in this building," Cho said. "Why?"

"I need ten minutes with him."

"We'll need to get his lawyer over here."

"Bullshit. I have to see the imam alone."

Cho shook his head. "No can do. You know that."

Ryan placed a hand on the agent's shoulder. "Rahim knows more. I'll find out what it is."

"Sorry. His attorney has to be present."

Ryan scowled and pointed to the TV screen. "That's going to happen again. And again. Unless we do something, goddamn it. Grow some stones, and let me at him."

Cho's face contorted in a mixture of emotions – confusion and anger. After a long moment, he nodded. "This could cost me my job, but what the hell. We're not getting anywhere unless we bend the rules. But this is your deal. If anybody asks later, I don't know how it happened."

The detective smiled broadly. "That's more like it."

Holding out his hand, Cho said, "I need your gun. No way can you see him armed."

Ryan took the Ruger revolver from under his waistband at the small of his back and handed it over. "Fair enough. I'm just going to talk to him."

"Yeah, I bet."

Cho took the gun and put it in his pocket. "Wait here in the conference room. I'll set it up and come get you."

***

Ryan followed Cho down a long, concrete-walled corridor in a basement area of the building. Harsh fluorescents lit up the space.

The imam was being held in isolation, away from the rest of the detainees, his cell at the end of this hallway. Cho had managed to temporarily disable the security cameras in the corridor and in the cell, until Ryan was done.

The two men reached the end of the hall and Cho looked through the small window on the prison cell's metal door. The agent unlocked the door, opened it, and stepped aside so that Ryan could enter. "You've got ten minutes," he told the detective.

Ryan stepped into the dank, poorly-lit room. As soon as he did, the door closed behind him, the lock clicking into place. The stink of urine and feces hung in the air.

Rahim, wearing a baggy orange jumpsuit, was sitting on the small bunk, a worried expression on his face.

"We meet again," Ryan said, still standing.

"What the hell do you want?" Rahim demanded. "Where is my lawyer?"

"Don't worry about that, Imam. We're just going to have a pleasant conversation."

"I am not talking with you," Rahim stated indignantly, "without my attorney present."

"We'll see about that."

The imam folded his arms in front of him. His face looked haggard, and it appeared he hadn't slept in days. "I know my rights!"

Ryan towered over the man. "Fuck your rights. Thousands of people died today. You tell me everything I want to know, or you'll regret it."

The imam glanced around the cell quickly, as if looking for a way to escape.

"It's just you and me, Rahim. And the cameras have malfunctioned. There's no record of this taking place."

Rahim's eyes went wide. "Please. Do not do anything rash. I told you everything last time."

"You're holding back."

"I swear, I am not!"

The detective scowled. "I don't have much time. You talk or you die."

Ryan, using both hands, gripped the man's throat and yanked him to his feet.

Then, methodically, he began to squeeze's the imam's throat, his powerful fingers tightening like a vise.

Rahim tried to push him away, but he was no match for Ryan's strength. The imam's arms flailed, landing several punches to Ryan's face, but the detective kept squeezing ever tighter.

Rahim's face turned bright red and his eyes bulged, and he emitted a rattling, choking sound.

Ryan's stomach turned, sickened by what he was doing, but he felt it was the only way to scare the man into talking.

The imam's eyes rolled white and his body convulsed, then began to sag. The detective immediately let go of the man's throat, realizing if he continued much longer he could kill him. He'd used this interrogation technique in Afghanistan and knew there was a fine line between passing out and death.

Rahim's unconscious body slumped and Ryan held on to him, laying the man down on the cot.

Looking around, the detective spotted a wash basin in the corner of the cell. Walking over and turning on the tap, he soaked the threadbare towel that hung on the rack. Going back to the cot, he patted the wet towel to the imam's face.

A moment later Rahim sputtered awake, gasping for air. His face was still red and his eyes darted about. He cringed away from Ryan, who towered over him.

"You'll talk now?" Ryan asked, menace in his voice.

The other man nodded vigorously. "Yes ... yes!"

"Good."

The detective sat down on the cot next to the prone man. "Start at the beginning. Tell me everything about the woman, Sarah."

The imam recounted his meeting with her, with Ryan interrupting often to ask for specific details of the conversation.

When Rahim was done, Ryan said, "You told me the same story before."

"Because I did not lie to you before," the imam pleaded. "Everything I told you last time was true."

Ryan studied the man's face closely, seeing only terror in his eyes. From experience, his gut told him the imam wasn't lying.

"Okay," Ryan said, glancing at his watch. He didn't have much time before Cho returned. "Describe again what Sarah looked like. What color was her hair?"

"Dark."

"Dark brown or black?"

"Black."

"How long was it? Was it curly or straight?"

"It was straight, but it was pulled up into a cap, so it was hard to tell how long."

"What kind of hat was it?"

"It was a baseball cap, and it looked too big for her."

"So her hair was probably long?"

Rahim nodded. "I think so."

"Describe her face again."

"Pretty. But she had a long scar on her cheek."

"Tell me about the scar."

"The scar?"

"Yeah. What color was it?"

"It was bright red, and long. It really stood out."

Ryan thought about this a moment. "Visualize her face again. What else did you notice about it?"

Rahim's expression scrunched in concentration. "She had a small black mark by her lips."

"A mole?"

"Yes, that's right."

"Good. Describe her eyes."

"Blue or green, I'm not sure."

Ryan raised a closed fist. "Think!"

"Green. Yes, a bright green."

"Okay. Anything else you can think of?"

The man shook his head forcefully.

There was loud rap on the cell door and Ryan turned his head, saw Cho through the small window.

Ryan stood and faced the imam. "Our talk today never happened, understood?" the detective said, his voice hard.

"Yes," Rahim replied.

The cell door opened and Ryan turned and left the room.

Chapter 22

Berlin, Germany

Dr. Heiler opened the front door of his house and stepped outside. With his back aching, he crouched down and picked up the folded newspaper on the porch.

It was cold and damp this morning, and he tightened the sash on his bathrobe as he stepped back inside.

Going to the kitchen, he put the newspaper on the cheap Formica-topped table. He almost turned to make himself breakfast when he spotted the blaring headline in the *Süddeutsche Zeitung*, Germany's most popular daily: SECOND AMERICAN CITY BOMBED. PANIC IN MIAMI. Forgetting all about his empty stomach, he continued reading. He absorbed every detail of the story. Authorities in Miami said the explosion was caused by a dirty bomb, very similar to the blast in Hawaii. As the radioactivity spread, panic had gripped all of southern Florida. People were fleeing not just the immediate area around the mall, but the whole city. The National Guard had been called in to restore order.

When Heiler finished reading the lengthy article, he pushed his wire-rim eyeglasses up the bridge of his nose.

Putting the newspaper aside, a feeling of accomplishment surged through him and a smile spread on his lips.

Chapter 23

Savannah, Georgia

Angel Stone drove the rented G.M.C. cargo van through the open entrance of the farmhouse barn. She stopped by the tall stacks of baled hay and turned off the engine. Climbing out, she went to the back of the van and opened the doors.

She could hear Frank Reynolds grunting, as the man pushed aside the bales of hay to get to the bombs.

"How's it going, Frank?" she called out.

"Could use some help," he replied, his voice winded.

She chuckled. "You're the doer, I'm the thinker."

"Fuck you," she heard him mutter, and she laughed again.

A few minutes later Frank came out from behind the stacks of hay, pulling a hand-jack with one of the bombs sitting on it. Beads of sweat covered his forehead.

"You look tired," she said with a smile.

He shrugged, said nothing. Pulling the hand-jack next to the rear of the van, he began to crank the jack until the bottom of the explosive device was even with the floor of the vehicle. Then he pushed the bomb into the van, the device's coasters creaking over the metal floor. He climbed in the vehicle, threw a tarp over the bulky, suitcase shaped object, then strapped it to the floor.

Climbing out, he said, "I'll go and restack the hay to cover up the other bombs."

"I'll help," Angel replied. He's a good man, she mused. No sense in pissing him off.

A pleased look crossed his face. "Really?"

"Yeah. I'm not a total bitch."

He smiled and turned back toward the stacks of hay. Angel closed the van's doors and followed.

***

An hour later Angel was on I-95, driving the Toyota Camry headed north. Just ahead of her was the black cargo van with Frank at the wheel.

Traffic was light on the interstate, a mixture of semis and passenger cars.

She turned on the car's radio, and began pressing the preset buttons. Hating the rock, country, and rap music stations that were set, she stabbed the scan button and finally found classical music. A piece by Bach was playing, one of her favorite composers, and she hummed along as she idly watched the traffic around her.

An hour later she spotted the *Welcome to South Carolina* sign flash by, and knew they were making good time.

Soon after she passed the first exit sign for Charleston, South Carolina, and the cargo van crossed from the middle lane to the right lane. She followed as Frank got off the interstate and took the local road east.

They entered a roadside strip mall and weaved their way through the parking lot until the van pulled into an empty slot in front of a Starbucks. Angel parked the Camry next to him.

Climbing out, she stretched her arms to ease the stiffness. They both walked into the store and got in line.

Buying a tea, she found a table at the mostly empty place, sat down and took a sip. She relished the hot, strong flavor.

Frank finished at the counter, grabbed a seat across from her, and began to happily devour an oversize pastry.

"Slow down, Frank," she said, "you don't want to choke to death."

He smiled and kept eating, washing it down with coffee.

Angel waited for him to finish, then said, "I changed my mind."

He took a sip of coffee. "About what?"

"We're not going to hit Charleston."

"We're not? Why?"

"Too close to Savannah. I've got a better idea."

"Where then?"

Pulling a map of the U.S. from her pocket, she spread it out on the table. She stabbed her finger on a city. "Here."

Chapter 24

Atlanta, Georgia

J.T Ryan knocked on Erin Welch's office door, saw her glance up and wave him in. Opening the glass door, he stepped inside.

She closed the lid on her laptop as he took a seat in front of her desk.

"Welcome back," she said, her voice tired. The attractive woman looked even more exhausted than last time he'd seen her. The bombings were taking a steep toll.

"Thanks," he replied. "Not much else I could do out in Chicago."

She nodded. "I heard all about your run-in with the ADIC out there when he found out about your talk with Rahim."

"I had to do it," Ryan said with a shrug. "Only way I could pry more info out of the imam."

She shook her head slowly. "But now you're banned from the FBI office in Chicago."

"It all worked out, though," he said with a grin. "Agent Cho didn't get in trouble, and better yet, I got what I was looking for."

"Tell me."

"I will. Got any coffee?"

She pointed to the coffee maker on the credenza. Standing, he went over, poured a cup and sat back down.

"On the flight back," Ryan said, "I had a lot of time to think. When I questioned Rahim, I had him detail his conversation with the mystery woman, Sarah. There's a reason we haven't been able to identify her."

She grimaced. "Besides the fact we don't have a last name, or an address, and only have a sketch of her face?"

"It's more than that, I think."

"Yeah?"

"What if she disguised her appearance?"

"Why would she do that?"

"Who knows, Erin. Maybe she's trying to set up the imam as the fall guy. Anyway, after questioning him, I believe he was telling the truth. He's not involved with the bombing."

"Going soft on me, J.T.?"

"No. Let's just say I was very persuasive in my interrogation."

She gave him a long look. "With your background, I'm not going to question your instincts. So – you think the woman wore a disguise?"

"Yes. Rahim told me she had a long scar on her face."

"That was in the original sketch."

"That's what's throwing us off, Erin – probably the reason the facial recognition programs aren't picking up her image. He described the scar as bright red and really stood out. I think the scar was a fake."

"Okay, J.T. I'll get an artist in here. We'll do a new sketch. Was there anything else he told you?"

"Yes. She had long, straight, black hair. She had bright green eyes. And she had a mole by her lip."

"Maybe some of that was part of the disguise. Thought of that?"

"Yes," he replied. "We'll have to do a couple of different versions, and run each of them through facial recognition programs."

"Okay." She picked up the handset on the desk phone and made a call. He drank coffee while she talked on the phone.

Erin replaced the receiver. "The artist will be here in a minute."

"Good." He studied the agent's tired face. "You look like hell, Erin. Getting any sleep?"

"No. Not since all this started. But you don't look that great yourself."

Ryan rubbed the stubble on his face, knowing he'd been neglecting sleep as well. "How are things in Miami?"

"Like shit," she groused. "The radiation is spreading. It's over a ten mile radius now. People are fleeing south Florida."

"Casualties?"

"Over 3,000 dead and 5,000 wounded. It's worse than Waikiki. That part of Miami is densely populated."

"Damn it," Ryan said, his hands forming into fists. "We've got to catch those bastards before it happens again."

She nodded, said nothing. Her expression was grim.

"Has the FBI heard from the terrorists?" he asked. "Since the Miami attack?"

"Nothing yet."

Erin's desk phone rang and she picked up the receiver. As she listened, a frown crossed her face and she rubbed her temple with her hand.

After a minute, she hung up the phone. "That was agent Cho. They've been monitoring Rahim's bank accounts since he was arrested. A large deposit was just made to the mosque's account."

"How much?" Ryan asked.

"$250,000."

Ryan let out a low whistle. "Who made the deposit?"

"No name on the account. Just an account number. The originating bank that made the wire transfer is located in Grand Cayman. The same account number and bank location as the one Al-Shirak wanted us to use for the ransom deposit."

"Damn it all."

Erin scowled and said, "You still think Rahim is innocent?"

Lee Gimenez

Chapter 25

Raleigh, North Carolina

Angel Stone was physically tired, but mentally wide awake. She stretched out on the motel's lumpy mattress, fully clothed, trying to find a comfortable position.

They had checked into the cheap motel an hour ago; Frank Reynolds was in the next room over, either asleep or drunk by now. But she was too wired to sleep, her thoughts racing about tomorrow. Fueled by too much caffeine and nervous energy, her brain was on overdrive.

Sitting up on the bed, she turned on the bedside lamp, its yellowish glow lighting up the cramped room. The place was full of scarred furniture, probably stuff the motel owner had picked up at Goodwill or Salvation Army. The room smelled of cigarette smoke, and other more rancid odors she couldn't, and didn't want to identify. But it was a cash-only motel, no questions asked, just the way she wanted.

Angel grabbed the maps resting on the bedside table and selected the city map of Raleigh she'd bought earlier.

Spreading the map out on the bed, she studied the main streets. She'd been to the capital of North Carolina several times before, years ago, and was familiar with its layout. Tracing a finger along a wide boulevard, she stopped at a specific spot and tapped it several times. "Perfect," she murmured to herself.

Folding the map, she stuffed it in her jeans' pocket, put on a jacket, and left the room.

It was after nine in the evening and the poorly-lit parking area in front of the motel rooms was in shadows and empty, save for the Camry and the cargo van.

She knocked on Frank's door and waited. There was no response and she knocked louder. Finally, a glassy-eyed Frank, reeking of booze, opened it and let her in. She immediately spotted a half-empty bottle of Smirnoff on the bedside table.

"Want a shot ... of vodka," Frank slurred. "I got ... plenty left."

Shaking her head, she strode over to the table, picked up the bottle and took it to the bathroom sink, where she poured out the contents.

"That was ... good stuff," he muttered, slouching down on the bed.

"You've had enough, Frank."

Angel searched the closet and looked under the bed. Finding no more liquor, she stood over the prone man, said, "I'm going out. I need to scout the area for tomorrow." She planted her hands on her hips. "No more booze tonight, Frank. And no whores either. I need you wide-awake and sharp in the morning."

He rubbed his face absently, then gave her a mock salute. "Aye, aye, sir ...," he said, chuckling. "Or ma'am ..."

Angel sighed, and without another word left the room.

***

She drove the Camry through the brightly-lit main streets of downtown, getting a feel for the area. Signs posted along the route advertised a music concert for tonight, which likely accounted for the heavy traffic. The city's streets were decked out with festive Christmas lights and the store-fronts were decorated with holiday wreaths and bunting.

Angel took a left and began cruising on Capital Boulevard. Spotting her target building, she drove past it and pulled into a nearby multi-story parking garage. Finding an empty slot, she zipped up her jacket and climbed out.

She exited the garage and walked toward the building, side-stepping the pedestrians who crowded the sidewalk.

Reaching it a moment later, she stood in front of the imposing facade. It's perfect, she thought.

Then she turned and headed back to the car.

***

By the time Angel got back to the motel it was almost midnight. She parked the Camry in front of the place and was about to go in her room when she heard shouting coming from Frank's room.

"What now," she hissed. She pounded on his door and it was immediately opened by a young woman in a skimpy halter top and short-shorts. The woman had garish blonde hair and a sour expression on her face.

"Who the hell are you?" the blonde demanded. "His wife?"

Angel pushed past her into the room, saw Frank sprawled on the bed, naked below the waist. He had a sheepish expression on his face. She grabbed the bedcover from the floor, threw it over him, then turned to face the woman.

"I want to get paid!" the blonde shouted. "I did him and now he says he doesn't have any cash." She crossed her arms across her ample chest. "I'm not leaving until I get my money."

"I don't want any trouble," Angel said, as she studied the young woman in front of her. The blonde had a pock-marked face, crooked teeth, and smelled of cheap perfume. The term 'skanky whore' crossed her mind.

"You'll get paid," Angel said, her adrenaline flowing as she assessed the situation. This was a complication they didn't need. Not now. "How much?"

The prostitute told her and Angel nodded. "I don't have that much cash on me. But I have it at our house."

"I don't care where it is, honey. I just want it. I don't work for free."

"Sure, I understand," Angel replied in a placating tone. "If you'll come with me, we can drive over there now."

The hooker's expression went from a scowl to a crooked grin. "Lead the way, sugar."

The two women left the room, got in the Camry and Angel began driving back towards downtown. She remembered passing a run-down area of Raleigh earlier in the day and she headed there.

Ten minutes later they were cruising down a narrow street lined on both sides by decrepit apartment buildings. The sound of loud rap music and barking dogs could be heard, even though the car's windows were closed.

"Can't believe you live in this dumpy area," the whore said. "Took you for more of an uptown bitch."

"Times are tough," Angel replied. She pulled the car into a darkened alley, stopped the car, and turned off the headlights. Glancing out the car windows, she saw no one around.

"Go get the money," the hooker said. "I'll wait here."

"Good idea," Angel said, as she reached under her jacket and pulled out the Sig Sauer automatic stuck in her waistband. She pointed the gun at the woman's face.

"What the fuck!" the hooker yelled.

Angel fired one shot, the woman's head snapped back and slammed against the window. As the blast echoed in the closed car, the whore's body slumped on the seat.

Angel put away the gun, then reached over and yanked open the passenger door. She pushed the body out of the car, careful not to get blood on her hands.

Grabbing the door handle, she closed the door and inspected the passenger seat. She'd have to clean up the bloody mess as soon she got back to the motel.

After another quick look around the dark alley, she put the Camry into drive and smashed the accelerator. With tires spinning, the car leapt forward toward the end of the alley.

"Too bad you saw our faces," Angel murmured.

Reaching the street, she took a right and sped off. A minute later she had forgotten all about the dead whore.

Chapter 26

The Oval Office
The White House
Washington, D.C.

FBI Director Michael Stuart sat across from President Layton and studied the man's face closely. The president had visibly aged in the last two weeks. His youthful good looks had been replaced by a worn-down, nervous appearance, accentuated by a twitch in his left eye. Never a strong person, Layton was having an extremely difficult time dealing with the dirty bomb crisis. He had been elected president because of his ability to pander to the ever-growing number of Americans who depended on government assistance programs. Now the panderer-in-chief was having trouble dealing with reality.

Stuart had always thought Layton was a political hack, someone not qualified to lead the nation. But as a career civil-service employee, the FBI director always kept his opinions to himself.

Layton leaned forward in his executive chair and nervously tapped a pen on Resolute, his ornate wooden desk. "What do you think we should do now, Mike?" he asked, his voice barely audible.

"As I said in the National Security meeting earlier," Stuart replied, "we're still trying to find the terrorists. It's the only option to resolve this crisis."

Layton stopped tapping his pen. "But we now have confirmation. The Honolulu and Miami bombings were almost identical. Surely they were done by the same people."

"Yes, Mr. President. That's correct."

A hopeful look crossed the president's face. "Maybe we should pay the ransom to Al-Shirak?"

Stuart shook his head. "I disagree, sir. Even if we pay the ransom, there's no guarantee they'll stop. And even if they stop after they get the money, what's to keep them from coming back a month, or a year from now, and doing it again? And there's another thing. As you know, besides Al-Shirak, other groups like Al-Quaida, and Hezbollah have also claimed responsibility for these bombings."

"But Al-Shirak contacted us is first, and gave us the specific warning. The other terrorist group threats have been vague."

"Yes, sir."

The president looked uncertain, and his left eye twitched again. The man swiveled his executive chair around and faced the three tall windows of the Oval Office, which overlooked the Rose Garden. It was a gray, overcast day in Washington. Light snow was falling.

Stuart said nothing as he stared at the back of the president's chair and the Rose Garden beyond. The majesty of the historic setting felt hollow under the current circumstances.

After a minute, Layton swiveled his chair again and faced the FBI director. His twitch was more pronounced now.

"Mike, what the hell am I going to do? It's two weeks before Christmas and the country's in panic. The stock market is cratering. The press is hounding me for answers."

The president stood up abruptly, took off his expensive suit jacket and loosened his red silk tie. "Damn it, it's hot in here."

The Oval Office was kept at an even 70 degrees, Stuart knew. The room felt fine to him. "Yes, Mr. President."

Layton slouched down on his chair again, pulled his tie looser. Beads of sweat appeared on his forehead. "How the hell am I going to get re-elected, with all this shit happening? Tell me that!"

"Calm down, sir."

"Easy for you to say, you bastard," Layton yelled, his voice cracking. "Where are you with the investigation?"

"We're still working the Chicago lead. There's an imam there ..."

"Fuck, Mike, you've told me about that before. I want answers now, damn it."

"As do I, Mr. President."

"Are your people incompetent?"

"Sir —"

"Don't sir me. Find me a fucking solution!" Layton pounded his desk with his fists, but his eyes showed raw fear. Stuart was worried the man was close to a nervous breakdown.

"Yes, Mr. President."

Just then Stuart's cell phone buzzed. He removed it from his jacket pocket and looked at the info screen. It said 'unknown caller'.

The FBI director's heart began to race. Instinctively, he knew who was calling. He took the call and began reading the text message:

DIRECTOR STUART:
YOU HAVE FAILED.
YOU WERE WARNED, BUT OUR DEMANDS WERE NOT MET.
HONOLULU.
MIAMI.
WHICH U.S. CITY WILL BE NEXT?
THE CLOCK IS TICKING.
DEPOSIT $500 MILLION INTO OUR BANK ACCOUNT WITHIN 24 HOURS OR A THIRD U.S. CITY WILL BE BOMBED.
WE WILL NOTIFY YOU OF THE NEW BANK CODES 23 HOURS FROM NOW.

FAIL TO MAKE THIS DEPOSIT AND YOU WILL HAVE MORE BLOOD ON
YOUR HANDS.
WE WILL NOT HESITATE TO CARRY OUT OUR THREAT.
AS THE PREVIOUS BOMBINGS OF HONOLULU AND MIAMI PROVE, WE ARE DEADLY SERIOUS.

ALLA HU AKBAR.

AL-SHIRAK

The color drained from Stuart' face. As his stomach churned, he re-read the text message again. Then he looked up at the president.

"What is it?" Layton said, his voice a whisper.

"It's a message from the terrorists," Stuart replied.

"What do they want?"

"The money."

Chapter 27

Atlanta, Georgia

J.T Ryan was at his gym, pounding on the speed bag, when his cell phone rang. Brushing the sweat from his face, he picked the phone off the floor and took the call.

"It's Erin," he heard her say. "We just got a big break on the case."

Ryan glanced at his watch. "Be there in twenty."

After a quick shower, he dressed, and drove to the FBI building.

Soon after he was sitting across from Erin Welch in her office. For the first time in weeks, the woman didn't have a strained expression on her face.

"As I told you on the phone," Erin said with a smile, "we finally caught a break."

Ryan leaned forward in the chair. "Tell me."

She slid several photographs across her desk toward him.

Picking one of them up, he scanned it quickly. It showed the face of an attractive woman with long black hair and green eyes. "Quite a looker. Who is she?"

"We think she's the mystery woman, Sarah. The facial recognition programs found her from the new sketch you gave us."

Ryan breathed a sigh of relief. Finally they were getting somewhere. "What's her name?"

"Angelica Stone," Erin replied. "Went by the nickname of Angel. She was a top CIA agent until seven years ago. Went rogue. Sold CIA secrets for money. Became a mercenary and later got into the illegal arms trade. She's a wanted fugitive with fourteen felony warrants for her arrest."

Ryan tapped on the photograph. "Where is she now?"

"That's our problem. She vanished. The CIA and FBI have been looking for her for years with no luck. We're sure she's assumed a new identity, probably several, and could be anywhere in the world."

"And that's where I come in," Ryan said.

"Exactly." She pushed a thick file folder across the desk and he picked it up and riffled through the contents. It was Stone's personnel file from Langley, along with reports about her activities after she left.

"Why did she go rogue?" Ryan asked.

"Hard to tell, exactly. But on her last field assignment, her partner was killed. She was found to be partially at fault and got demoted. Was assigned a desk job. From what I've read in her file, she became bitter after that. Not to mention, her pay at the Agency was slashed – another reason for the hostility." Erin paused, crossed her arms in front of her. "When you read the file, you'll find she's a woman who's used to the finer things in life. Has expensive tastes. So money was probably the main motivation for going rogue."

Ryan nodded. "That ties in with the terrorist's ransom demand of a billion dollars. It's all about the money. It also explains why the demand was made to the FBI and not in the media."

"That's my thought too, J.T."

"How does the imam in Chicago fit in to all this?"

"I don't know," she said. "I don't think he's a ringleader. But this Stone woman is smart. Really smart. The CIA records show that. My guess is she could be one of the top people in this terrorist cell."

"I agree. It's possible Imam Rahim was a diversion to throw us off."

Erin shrugged. "No way to know for sure. When you questioned him you thought he told you everything he knew."

"I was persuasive."

She held up her palms. "No details, please."

Ryan smiled, stayed quiet.

Just then Erin's laptop chirped loudly. Her face tensed and she lifted the lid on the computer and tapped a few keystrokes on the keyboard.

Grimacing as she read from her laptop, she looked up at Ryan after a moment.

"It's from Director Stuart," she said. "Al-Shirak sent another text message. The next American city will be attacked less than 24 hours from now."

Chapter 28

Savannah, Georgia

Angel Stone strode to the end of the dirt driveway in front of the old farmhouse, and began jogging on the gravel road that wound around for miles before reaching the state road.

Still wired from her trip to Raleigh, she needed the exercise to clear her head.

The gravel road was deserted, although it was mid-day. The nearest neighbors were miles away. In all the time she and Frank had been at the farmhouse, she had only seen two cars drive past.

The gravel surface was uneven, making a crunching sound as she ran over it. It was a sunny but cold December day and she zipped up her jacket, relishing the fresh, crisp air.

As she jogged, her thoughts drifted. Drifted to the beginning of the operation, six months ago. Now they were in the middle of it. With nothing to show for it. Doubt and fear crossed her mind. What if they don't pay? What then?

Following a bend in the road, she pushed those thoughts aside. *They'll pay*, she told herself silently. A grim smile lit up her face. *They'll pay the ransom, or with peoples lives.*

Feeling better from her new resolve, she continued running on the uneven surface.

After a while, she almost stopped to turn back toward the farmhouse, then changed her mind. Earlier today she had sent the text message to the FBI. Now she had time to kill. It would be tomorrow before she found out anything. Not wanting to join Frank as he watched daytime TV, she kept running. Picking up the pace, the irregular stones under her running shoes crunched more loudly.

Chapter 29

Atlanta, Georgia

Erin Welch was standing in her office, gazing out the windows that overlooked downtown Atlanta. In the distance, she could make out commercial jets as they circled Hartsfield-Jackson International, getting ready to land.

She was edgy as she waited for the director's call back.

Erin's desk phone buzzed with a distinctive tone and she turned, went to her desk and picked up the secure call.

"It's Stuart," she heard the man say as she sat down.

"Sir, did you receive the info I sent you on Angel Stone?"

"Got it. I've already assigned a team of agents to work on it."

"Director, Stone is the best lead I've come up with."

"Good work, Erin. Unfortunately, we don't have a hell of a lot of time on our hands. And there's no guarantee Stone is involved with the bombings. It's just your best guess."

"Yes, sir."

"Something else has me worried. No government agency has been able to locate Stone in years. She's gone deep underground."

"Yes, Director. I know that." She rubbed her forehead, trying to push away another migraine. "I've assigned several of my agents to try and find her." She paused, knowing what she was going to say next wouldn't be well received. "There's someone else I have working on it."

"Who's that, Erin?"

"J.T. Ryan."

"That's the contractor the Chicago office just banned, isn't it?"

"That's right, sir. But he was the main reason we were able to identify Stone."

"You sure about this Ryan guy? The Chicago ADIC was fuming mad about him."

"Sir, that ADIC is a prick, and you know it."

There was dead silence from the other end, then after a moment she heard Stuart laugh. "You're right, Erin. He is that. Tell me more about Ryan."

"The CIA and the FBI have never located Angel Stone, but I think Ryan has a better chance to find her." She paused a moment as she recollected. "He's a private investigator and speaks six languages. Spent ten years in Army Special Forces. He was a Ranger, and in Delta Force. Knows a lot about advanced weapons. And there's something else."

"What's that?"

"He doesn't play by any rules."

"I see. You're attaching him to one of your teams?"

"No, sir. He likes to work alone."

"Okay, go ahead. But we don't have a lot of time. Give him all the support he needs."

Erin felt a sense of relief. "Yes, Director."

"And something else."

"What's that?"

"This conversation never took place, Erin."

"Yes, sir."

Hearing a click from the other end, she realized the man had hung up.

Looking at the wall clock, she noted the time. Only twenty one hours until the next attack.

Chapter 30

Prison Complex
U.S. Naval Base
Guantanamo Bay, Cuba

J.T Ryan paced the interrogation room, as he waited for the prisoner to be brought in. The green-painted room smelled of mildew and urine. It was stifling hot, and his short-sleeve polo shirt was already soaked with sweat. December in Cuba, he mused, was no different than June in Cuba.

But it wasn't the heat that was bothering Ryan. It was the clock ticking on the wall. As he paced, he realized it was only fifteen hours until the next Al-Shirak bombing. The terrorists had been punctual in their attack on Miami, and he had no doubt they would be punctual now.

The only good thing that had happened in the last few hours was the FBI's about face. Erin had given him carte blanche on this assignment. She had provided a small FBI jet for him to fly here, a government-issued credit card, and a satellite cell phone. Best of all, she let him come alone.

Something had changed in Washington. Ryan surmised it had to do with the clock on the wall. Time was running out and panic had taken over at the highest levels in D.C.

Just then he heard a loud click and the metal door leading to the prisoner's wing swung open.

A bearded man with long hair was brought into the room by a pair of uniformed Marines. The prisoner wore a baggy orange jumpsuit and his hands and feet were shackled. The Marines guided the shuffling prisoner toward the table at the center of the room, pushed him onto a chair, and attached the manacles to the heavy metal loop on the table.

The soldiers saluted to Ryan and left the room.

The detective looked at the prisoner closely. His name was Tom Harris and he was one of the last people to have dealt with Angel Stone. He'd read the man's file and looked at his photos, but in real life Harris appeared much older than his forty-six years. Prison life had not been kind to him.

Ryan sat down across from Harris and slapped the file on the table. The detective said nothing, just stared at the man.

"Who the hell are you?" Harris asked.

Staying quiet, Ryan kept up the hard stare, knowing it was difficult for detainees to hold eye contact for too long, without speaking or looking away.

The prisoner shifted in the chair. "What do you want?"

Ryan opened the file in front of him, but still said nothing.

"Who sent you?" Harris demanded.

The detective pushed his chair back a bit away from the table. He grimaced and said, "You smell like shit, Harris."

A quizzical look crossed the prisoner's face. "What are you talking about?"

"You literally smell like shit."

Harris nodded. "Yeah. I guess I do. I've been here so long, everything smells the same to me."

Ryan looked down at the man's file and read from it out loud. "Tom L. Harris. Born Wichita, Kansas. Dishonorable discharge from the Army. Small-time drug dealer, four felony convictions. Armed robbery and other crimes. Graduated to selling black-market weapons. Caught in a conspiracy to sell Stinger missiles to Hezbollah. Charged under the Patriot Act for terrorist activities." He looked up at Harris. "Not a pretty picture, my friend."

"I came from a broken home," the prisoner said weakly. "My dad left us when I was seven."

Ryan held up a palm. "Save the sob story. I don't give a crap how you grew up. And, by the way, a lot of people grow up in single-parent homes and they don't end up at Guantanamo."

Harris shrugged.

"My name is J.T. Ryan," the detective said. "I work for the FBI. And I'm looking for information."

"Why should I tell you anything?" Harris replied with a smirk.

"How long have you been in this hell-hole?"

"Read the file. It's all there."

"Three years, two months and thirteen days," Ryan recalled from memory. "That's a long, long, time."

Harris leaned forward, his long, scraggly hair obscuring the sides of his face. His eyes burned with hate. "It damn well is!"

"How long you got left?"

In obvious frustration, the prisoner pounded the table with his manacled hands, the chains clanking loudly against the metal loop.

One of the Marines opened the door and looked in, but Ryan waved him away. The door closed and the detective turned back to Harris.

"How long you got left?" Ryan repeated.

"I don't know! I don't fucking know. They keep postponing my trial."

"That's the beauty of the Patriot Act, Harris. They could keep you here for the rest of your life."

Harris eyes burned bright and his body shook from the pent-up hatred. It was clear to Ryan that the man was fully aware he could die in this prison. "Do you want to spend the next thirty or forty years at Gitmo?"

"That's a fucking stupid question. Of course not. But what choice do I have?"

Ryan leaned forward in the chair, the prisoner's foul odor making him want to gag. "I can be your best friend, Harris."

"What do you mean?"

"You tell me what I need to know, and I can help you."

"Help me how?"

"I can get you out of this shit-hole."

Harris's eyes lit up. "You can get me out of prison?"

"I can get you out of *this* prison."

"Out of Gitmo?"

"Yes."

"And after that?"

"You'd serve your time in a regular Federal prison in the States. You'd have a clean cell, an exercise yard, cable TV. Three meals a day, and not the gruel they serve here. You'd get an attorney to represent you and a trial date."

Harris looked skeptical. "How do I know you're not bullshitting me?"

"I'm looking for important information. The FBI has already talked with a Federal District Attorney. If you cooperate, I'll give you my word it'll happen."

Harris still looked doubtful, but a moment later shrugged. "What the fuck. I'll trust you. I've got nothing to lose. I fucking hate this hell-hole. I'll never make it in here another five years, let alone thirty."

"Good."

"What do you want to know, Ryan?"

"Tell me everything about Angel Stone."

"I don't know who that is."

"Sure you do. You dealt with her four years ago."

"Refresh my memory."

Ryan pulled out an 8 x 10 photo from a second file and placed it in front of the man.

"Oh, yeah. I remember her. Great looking cunt. But cold as ice, that one. I bought all types of ordnance from her. M-16s, AKs, missile launchers. But her name wasn't Stone. When the FBI questioned me years ago, they said that was her name too. But she called herself Lila."

"What was Lila's last name? Lila what?"

Harris smiled. "Just Lila. She was one of those one-name people, like Madonna."

Ryan rolled his eyes. "Okay. Lila it is. Tell me everything about her."

Harris tapped the photo with his manacled hands. "The picture says it all. Long, luscious legs. Beautiful green eyes. And all the tits and ass a man could ever want. I get hard just thinking about her." A wistful look crossed the prisoner's face.

"Spare me the commentary. Just give me the facts."

Harris snapped out of his reverie and nodded. "Sure. Lila was beautiful, but she was a cold bitch. All business. I never got anywhere near her cunt."

"Tell me every detail you can remember about her. How she spoke, what accent she had, who she was with, what she said. What kind of food and drink did she like? What did she wear? Any mannerisms? Anything and everything you can think of."

Harris thought about this for a few moments, then spoke for the next twenty minutes, with Ryan peppering him with multiple questions. As the prisoner spoke, the detective took notes.

"That's all I can remember," Harris finally said.

"Where was the last place the two of you met?" Ryan asked.

"A cafe in Marseille, France."

Lee Gimenez

Chapter 31

Chicago, Illinois

Special Agent Tim Cho had just walked into the FBI building when he ran into Marge Smith, as the woman approached the first floor elevators.

"Just on my way to see you," Marge said. As usual, the tech was wearing a shapeless, white lab coat with her hair pulled back in a bun.

"What's up?" Cho replied. He loosened his tie – he'd just finished a ten-hour stakeout and was dead tired.

"Remember the Koran and the other items you had me run forensics on a while back?"

"Sure, Marge. How could I forget. You didn't find anything."

A self-satisfied smile spread on the woman's usually dour expression. "Well, you know me; I never give up. I kept working on it and I finally got a couple of hits."

Cho forgot about his exhaustion. "You did?" he said, excitement in his voice.

"I did."

The agent stabbed the elevator button. "Good. Let's go upstairs and you can tell me all about it."

The two stepped in the elevator and soon after were sitting in his cubicle on the third floor.

"Like I mentioned," Marge said, "I was able to pull trace from the Koran found at the Chicago bus station. I found a tiny particle of skin on one of the inside pages. Just enough to run a DNA test."

"Excellent. Whose is it?"

"I couldn't believe at first, so I double-checked the databases. But it turns out the DNA belongs to a former government employee. A woman who used to work for the CIA."

"Angel Stone?" Cho asked.

A puzzled look crossed her face. "How did you know?"

"Our Atlanta office has been working on a possible connection between the bombings and this Stone woman. This confirms it."

Marge nodded. "Okay. I've got something else for you."

"Shoot."

"Remember the control mechanism you found at Rahim's mosque?"

"Yes."

"Well, I've been working on that too."

"You traced that back to Stone?"

Marge shook her head. "No. The mechanism is manufactured in Germany and is distributed to supply houses throughout that country. And there's one other thing. Besides Rahim's fingerprints, which we already knew about, I was able to lift someone else's fingerprints from the device. It was a partial print, but enough."

"Whose print is it?" Cho asked.

"I don't know. I ran it through all of our databases and no hits. Whoever it is, their prints aren't on file that I could find."

Cho's initial excitement faded, but he didn't let it show. The lab tech was industrious and he didn't want to dampen her enthusiasm. "Good work, Marge. You'll stay on it?"

"Of course. You know me."

The woman got up and left the cubicle.

Cho settled back in his chair and processed the new information. After a few minutes he took out his cell phone and dialed a number he'd committed to memory.

He heard Erin Welch's voice a moment later.

"Erin," Cho said. "It's Tim Cho from the Chicago office."

"What do you have for me, Cho? Hope it's good news."

"It is. That lead you and Ryan were working on. Angel Stone."

"That's right."

"My lab just confirmed that Stone's DNA was on the Koran found at the bus station. The Koran with Al-Shirak's name on it."

"That is good news, Cho. At least now we know Stone is definitely involved with the terrorist plot."

"Got something else, but I don't know what it means."

"What is it?"

"My lab found a partial print on the control mechanism from the mosque. They haven't identified the print yet, but the device is made and distributed in Germany."

"Germany, huh? Okay, Cho, thanks for the info. I'll let Ryan know."

"Where is he now?"

"France."

"If I find out anything else, Erin, I'll call you."

"Thanks," he heard her say. Her voice sounded weary. "But we're running out of time, Cho. We only have eight hours before the next attack."

Chapter 32

Marseille, France

J.T Ryan paid the fare, got out of the cab, and walked into the cafe. Located on Canebiere Avenue, the city's main thoroughfare, Cafe Europa was a trendy, upscale place. Modern art hung on the walls and the wait staff wore all black. It was the restaurant where Harris had met Angel Stone several times.

Ryan sat down at a table by the windows, ordered a red wine and looked around at the clientele. They appeared to be mostly business people, which made sense. Marseille, France's second largest city, was also the country's busiest port. Probably the reason, Ryan thought, that Stone worked out of the city. Since she was in the arms trade, being close to a large shipping port would be ideal.

The waitress, a young brunette, came back with his drink. She set it down in front of him and asked in French, "Would you like anything else, *monsieur*?"

"Yes," Ryan replied in the same language. "I'm looking for someone, a woman. She was a customer here a few years back."

"I'm sorry. I've only worked here a month. I can get the owner, if you like?"

Ryan nodded, took a sip of wine and watched as the young woman went into the back of the cafe.

Moments later a tall, thin man, also wearing black, approached the table. "I'm the owner," the man said to Ryan. "How can I help you, *monsieur*?"

"I'm looking for a woman," the detective replied.

A sly grin crossed the owner's face. "We are all looking for a woman."

Ryan smiled back, then took a photo of Angel Stone from his jacket pocket. He handed it to the other man. "She was a customer here. Her name is Lila."

The owner scanned the picture closely. "Beautiful girl, *monsieur*. But, no, I don't know her. You said she came to my cafe?"

"It was four years ago."

"That is a long time," the owner said with a shrug. "And as you can see, I have a popular restaurant with many customers."

"Too bad. I need to find her and I'm willing to pay for the information."

The owner rubbed his chin. "I can put you in touch with someone who may know her. Not a pleasant man, but well-connected."

"What's his name?"

"You mentioned you would pay for the information, *monsieur*?"

"Of course. How much?"

The owner stated a large sum.

Ryan didn't have that much cash on him, then remembered the credit card Erin had given him. "Do you take American Express?"

Chapter 33

Atlanta, Georgia

Erin Welch was in the FBI's conference room meeting with her staff, when the door to the room opened and her assistant peered inside. "Excuse me, Miss Welch," he said. "But a priority e-mail just came in for you from the director."

"We'll finish this later," Erin said to the group as she stood.

Leaving the room quickly, she made her way back to her office and clicked open the e-mail on her computer.

The communication from Stuart was short and to the point. He'd just received the latest text message from Al-Shirak. The terrorists had given him the new bank codes for the ransom. This time, it was for a bank located in Hong Kong.

Erin closed the e-mail and looked up at the wall clock. They only had fifty-two minutes before the attack.

Chapter 34

Sachsenhausen Memorial Grounds
(site of the former Nazi concentration camp)
North of Berlin, Germany

Dr. H. Heiler stooped down and placed a bouquet of flowers at the foot of the memorial wall. The wall had been erected to commemorate the dead prisoners of Sachsenhausen – it depicted the scenes and names from long ago.

The camp was originally built by the Nazis during World War II as a forced labor camp. By the end of the war, it had been transformed into a death camp, complete with gas chambers. Those chambers were on the grounds nearby, not far from the memorial wall. But Heiler didn't need to be reminded of that.

His parents had died at the Nazi camp and he preferred to remember them as names on a wall, rather than by staring at the stark, grim reality of the gas chambers.

Heiler's knees and back ached as he stood back up.

If only the American forces had come sooner, he thought for the thousandth time. His parents, German Jews, had been imprisoned at the camp at the beginning of the war. They never left. If only the Americans had come sooner, they would have lived. For some irrational reason, one that he could not explain even to himself, Heiler blamed the Americans and not the Nazis for his parent's death in the chambers.

It was snowing today, and a bitter cold wind was blowing. As the snow swirled around him, he buttoned the buttons of his heavy coat and tied his scarf to ward off the chill.

Sachsenhausen usually attracted busloads of tourists to visit the museum and walk the grounds. But today there were only a handful of people.

The Americans will pay, he told himself silently. If not with money, then with blood.

Chapter 35

Madrid, Spain

Carlos Montoya nervously glanced at his watch, then scanned his computer screen.

Still nothing.

Montoya was in his study at home, monitoring the expected deposit to the Hong Kong bank. He heard a knock at the door, got up and opened it.

His wife Maria stood there.

"You've been locked up in here for hours, Carlos. What's going on?"

"Just business," he replied. "I'll be done soon."

With a resigned look on her face, she shook her head and walked away. The woman was used to his odd hours. The door closed and he turned back to the computer screen.

Still nothing.

A sinking feeling settled in the pit of his stomach. Could all their work be for nothing?

Suddenly his secure cell phone rang.

"It's Angel," he heard the woman say. After exchanging the pass code for the day, she said, "Anything yet?"

"No, Angel."

"It's an hour past the deadline."

"I know."

There was silence from the other end. After a moment she said, "Okay. I know what I have to do."

Chapter 36

Savannah, Georgia

Angel Stone turned off the cell phone. She stared at the device and squeezed it as hard as she could, her hand turning red from the effort.

She flung the phone into the front yard of the old farmhouse.

Frank Reynolds, who was standing next to her on the porch, said, "They make the deposit?"

"No!" she replied, her voice full of fury. "Fuck no."

"I need a drink."

"You're pathetic, Frank."

He grimaced. "Your great plan is turning to shit." The man stormed back in the farmhouse, slamming the door shut behind him.

Angel's hands formed into fists.

Taking a couple of deep breaths, she forced herself to calm down.

After a few moments, she walked down to the front yard to retrieve the phone. She had another call to make.

Lee Gimenez

Chapter 37

Marseille, France

The taxi slowed and stopped in front of the gray, multi-story building. The structure was located in a gritty warehouse district, close to the commercial port. The street in front of the building was choked with truck traffic.

J.T. Ryan paid the fare, stepped on the sidewalk and glanced around. Rows of loading bays lined the right-hand side of the building, with tractor-trailer rigs occupying all of the bays. A large crew of men using forklifts was in the process of loading the 40 foot container rigs. The strong odor of diesel fuel hung in the air.

Busy place, Ryan thought.

He approached the metal-reinforced front door and rang the buzzer, noting that the only sign on the building was the street number.

A small slot on the door slid open.

"What do you want?" a male voice asked in French.

"The owner of the Cafe Europa sent me," Ryan replied in the same language. "My name is Ryan. I'm here to see Nico."

"Wait there." The slot closed abruptly.

Moments later the detective heard bolts unlocking and the door swung open. A large man toting an Uzi submachine gun stood there.

"Come in," Uzi said. "But we have to search you."

Ryan stepped inside and a second man, this one carrying an AK-47 assault rifle, approached him. The man slung the AK and proceeded to pat him down. Finding Ryan's S&W pistol, he pocketed it. "He's clean now," the man said.

"Follow me," Uzi told Ryan.

The two burly guards led him down several corridors until they came to a wide door. Uzi opened the door and they stepped inside.

The large room was obviously used as an office, but its bare concrete walls indicated that it was just a partitioned-off part of the warehouse.

Sitting behind a scarred metal desk was a heavy-set, bald man with no neck. His face was fleshy and scrunched-up, giving him the appearance of a bulldog.

"I'm Nico," the man said in guttural French. "What do you want?"

"My name is J.T. Ryan. I'm looking for information."

Nico stared at him for a long moment. "Your French is good. But your accent sounds American."

"Yes. I'm from the U.S."

The man nodded. "What kind of information?"

"The owner of the cafe told me you're well-connected. I'm looking for a woman. Also an American. Goes by the name of Lila. Her real name is Angel Stone." Ryan pulled out the photo of Stone and placed it on the desk.

Nico scanned the photo, and Ryan sensed a flash of recognition in the man's eyes.

The man pushed the photo aside. "I don't know her."

"Are you sure, Nico? She used this port to make shipments. Many shipments, from what I know."

"What kind of shipments?"

"Arms, weapons, that kind of thing."

The heavy-set man shook his head. "Sounds illegal. I wouldn't know anything about that."

Ryan glanced at the two guards who had brought him into the room. "Your men are well-armed," he said. "Looks like you're prepared for a war."

Nico shrugged. "Theft is a big problem is Marseille. I have to protect my business."

"What kind of business is it?"

The man glared. "Import-export. But that's not your concern."

"You're right, it's not. I just need to find this woman."

"Why are you looking for her?"

Ryan pondered this. It was clear Nico was involved in illegal activities. Mentioning the FBI was a bad idea. "I'm looking to purchase a large quantity of rocket-propelled grenades," he lied. "I hear Lila might be able to accommodate me."

Nico looked skeptical. "You've come to the wrong place. As I said before, I don't know her. And I don't know anything about black market weapons."

"I'm willing to pay for the information."

The heavy-set man went silent. Eventually he said, "How much?"

"Name your price."

Nico barked out a harsh laugh. "I don't believe your story, my friend. In fact there's something about you that seems wrong. You don't look like an arms smuggler." He paused. "You look more like a cop. And I hate cops."

Nico waved a hand and in the split-second it took Ryan to turn toward the guards, he saw the wood stock of the AK-47 race toward his head.

He felt a blinding pain as the stock smashed his face.

Then everything went black.

Lee Gimenez

Chapter 38

Atlanta, Georgia

Erin Welch was at her office computer when out of the corner of her eye she saw the words *Breaking News* scroll across the TV screen.

Getting up, she crossed the office and stood in front of the set. She took the sound off mute and watched the live CNN broadcast.

"In a scene eerily similar to Honolulu and Miami," the male reporter said, "a third U.S. city has been bombed. This time the target is Raleigh, the capital city of North Carolina. The explosion just took place in downtown." He paused and touched his earpiece as if straining to hear something. "The exact location of the bombing has not been determined, but it appears the main television station in Raleigh was the probable target. The building that houses the station, along with several surrounding buildings, have been demolished. The number of dead and wounded is not known, but our sources on the scene estimate it will be in the thousands."

The reporter looked off-screen a moment, then turned back to face the camera. "We don't know if this was a terrorist attack, but the parallels to the other two bombings are inescapable. We now bring you a live shot of the scene from our news helicopter."

The image switched from the reporter to an overhead visual of a large metropolitan area.

Erin watched intently, her mind racing. As she looked on, she rubbed her forehead, trying to massage away another migraine.

There was a knock at her door and her assistant opened it. "The news," the man said, his face ashen. Then he must have noticed that her TV was on because he simply nodded and left the room.

Erin turned back to the CNN broadcast. Columns of smoke rose from the downtown core, while scores of fire trucks and police cars surrounded the area.

She watched for another five minutes, and her headache intensified as more gruesome details poured in. Sickened by the images, she muted the TV and went back to her desk.

Opening a drawer, she took out a bottle of Excedrin, shook out four tablets and swallowed. Washing them down with a sip of Coke, she drummed her fingers on the desk. A feeling of utter helplessness filled her.

Turning off the TV set with the remote, she took out her cell phone and punched in Ryan's number. Maybe, she hoped, he'd been able to track down a lead in France.

His phone rang for a long time but there was no answer.

Chapter 39

Savannah, Georgia

"Turn that shit off," Angel Stone demanded when she came into the living room of the farmhouse. "I'm tired of it."

Frank Reynolds was sprawled on the sagging couch that fronted the old black & white TV set. He'd been watching the news coverage of the Raleigh explosion for hours.

Nodding, he got up and turned off the TV. He poured himself another vodka from the bottle on the side table, and settled back down on the couch.

"So what now?" Frank asked her.

Angel sat down on the opposite sofa. Like everything else in the house, the sofa was ancient and its worn springs creaked. "I don't know, Frank," she replied in a tired voice. "I thought they would have paid the ransom by now."

Frank took a long swallow from his drink. "Maybe we should pack it in. Cut our losses and go home."

Angel crossed her arms in front of her. "When have you known me to quit anything?"

"Never."

She went quiet, her mind filled with self-doubt. Although she was keeping a brave front for his benefit, she was having serious reservations about her plan's chance of success.

Frank finished his drink and poured himself another.

Instead of scolding him as she usually did when he drank, this time she stayed silent. Maybe he's right, she pondered. Maybe we should terminate the operation and get the hell out. All they had lost so far was time and some money. But with every new bombing, the odds of getting arrested or killed increased dramatically.

Her mind did a quick calculation. If they quit now, she'd still have enough money to live comfortably for a long time. She wouldn't be super-rich like she craved. But she'd still be able to afford her Paris apartment, and dinners out at 5-star restaurants. Was that so bad?

"Want a drink?" Frank asked, snapping her out of her reverie.

"What?"

"Do you want a drink, Angel? I got plenty for both of us."

For the first time in years, she actually considered it. She hated losing control, but today the thought of it was oddly appealing.

"Sure," she said. "A small one."

Frank's face lit up. "Hot damn. That's more like it. This bottle's shot but I've got another stashed away."

"I figured."

He went into the kitchen and a moment later was back with a full bottle of Smirnoff and a tall tumbler for her. Filling the glass, he handed it to her.

She took it, lifted it high in the air. "To better times, Frank."

"Amen to that," he toasted back. He refilled his own drink and sat back down.

Angel sipped the vodka slowly, relishing the burn. It had been so long, she'd almost forgotten the taste. Stretching out on the lumpy sofa, she continued to sip from the glass.

Her sour mood lifted and she got sleepy. Setting the empty glass on the plank floor, she closed her eyes and was asleep in minutes.

***

Angel awoke sometime later to the sound of Frank's snoring. Glancing over at him, she saw he was sound asleep on the opposite couch.

Still light-headed from the vodka, she got up from the sofa and poured herself another drink from the now almost empty bottle of Smirnoff. She took a long gulp, then went over to Frank's couch and sat next to him.

As the jolt of vodka coursed through her system, a feeling of relaxation and even tenderness settled over her. She reached out with one hand and gently caressed the sleeping man's face. If only they could have made their relationship work, she thought. Could it still? Could she and Frank be a normal couple? She smiled sadly. No. There's nothing normal about our lives. We're both wanted felons.

He awoke suddenly, startled by her touch.

"What's going on?" he mumbled.

"I was just thinking."

"About what?"

"About us."

His face registered surprise. "Are you okay?"

"Yeah."

"You know I love you, Angel. I always have."

"I know you do."

"Did you ever love me?"

"A long time ago, Frank." A sly grin crossed her face. "When was the last time we fucked?"

"It's been so long, I don't remember."

"Maybe it's time," she said, her hand sliding down his face and caressing his chest.

"Is that the booze talking, Angel?"

"Does it matter?"

"Hell, no."

She smiled. "Let's go upstairs."

***

Much later they lay in bed nude in one of the second-floor bedrooms. Frank was asleep, obviously satiated from alcohol and the many hours of love-making.

But Angel was wide awake, her mind racing. By now the liquor had worn off, and her thoughts turned to the future. She felt re-energized from the sex.

Turning toward him, she traced her fingers along his bare chest, then lower down his abdomen. It felt good to touch him. As her fingers explored him, her mind replayed their recent love-making, savoring the satisfaction it had brought her. She held him in her hand and became sexually aroused once again.

Pushing those thoughts aside, she took her hand away. "Wake up, Frank."

"What?" he mumbled with a yawn.

"Time to wake up."

He rubbed his face, then grinned. "You want to fuck some more?"

"No. We need to get up."

"Why?"

Angel got up from the bed, looked down at the man. "Time to get going."

"Where?"

"We have to load the van with another bomb. We have a long drive ahead of us."

"Shit," he said in an irritated tone. "I thought we were done with all that."

"No, Frank. We're not." She stooped to the floor, picked up his shirt and pants and threw them at him. "Now get dressed."

He shook his head slowly, but after a moment shrugged. "Okay."

Chapter 40

Marseille, France

J.T. Ryan opened his eyes and was blinded by the bright light of a naked bulb hanging from the ceiling. He was laying flat on his back with his hands tied behind him. The side of his face hurt like hell.

Disoriented, Ryan tried to make sense of where he was. Then his memory flooded back. Nico. The warehouse in Marseille. The AK-47.

Blinking, he let his eyes adjust to the harsh light from overhead. Turning his head, he realized he was in a small, bare room, probably in Nico's warehouse. The place was cold and dank. A basement maybe?

His face throbbed, the pain so intense he felt a wave of nausea. Glancing down at himself, he saw he was still dressed in his own shirt and pants. But his jacket, belt, and shoes were gone, and his shirt was stained with dried blood. His own, he was sure.

No telling how long he'd been knocked out. It could have been hours or days, he couldn't be sure.

Ryan tried to sit up, but the pain came back with a vengeance so he eased back down on the cold concrete floor and closed his eyes.

Sometime later he heard the sound of creaking metal and the door to the room opened. Three men strode in – Nico, and the two burly guards from before, the ones toting the Uzi and the AK-47.

Nico stood over Ryan, his bald head glistening from the bright light.

"So, you are awake," Nico growled, his fleshy hands planted on his hips.

Ryan stared up at him, said nothing.

"You lied to me," the heavy-set Nico continued. "I've been checking. You're no arms smuggler. Far from it." He kicked Ryan in the ribs with his boot, a fresh wave of pain shooting through the detective. "I have good sources. As I suspected, you're a cop. A private investigator from Atlanta." The man barked out a harsh laugh. "You've done work for the FBI in the past." He kicked Ryan again, and the detective groaned. "Are you working for the FBI now?"

"I told you," the detective responded. "I'm just looking for a woman."

Nico laughed. "Lila. Yes, I know Lila. I've known that bitch for a long time. I've made good money dealing with her."

"Tell me about her," Ryan said, "and I'll pay you."

Nico kicked him a third time and Ryan gasped.

"Don't worry about that," Nico said with a chuckle. "We've already used your credit card to pay ourselves."

Nico turned to go, then looked back toward Ryan. "Consider yourself lucky," he said. "I would have killed you already, but my boss wants to question you himself."

The man left the room followed by his guards and the door slammed shut.

Lying there, Ryan's mind raced. Knowing he probably had little time, he forced himself to sit up, ignoring the pain from his face and ribs.

Awkwardly, he stood up and scanned the barren room. The place was completely empty. There was nothing to cut whatever was binding his hands behind his back. With his fingers he felt the binding material – it was a rope of some kind.

Approaching the closed door, he backed up against and turned the knob. As he suspected, it was locked. Think, he told himself. *Think!*

After a few moments, an idea emerged. It was long shot, but the only one he had. What if he could use the room's concrete wall to cut the rope?

With his back to the wall, he side-stepped around the room, his fingers feeling for a sharp edge in the concrete, anything that could serve as a crude saw.

Three of the walls were smooth, but on the last side he found a sharp outcropping of cement on one of the concrete blocks. With a sigh of relief, he began rubbing the rope binding against the sharp edge.

Ten minutes later the rope gave way.

Now free of the bindings, he realized the hard part was ahead. He needed to get out of the locked room.

Going to the door again, he felt around the metal frame and pushed against the metal door. He had hoped it was made of wood, now knew it was constructed of solid metal. No way he could kick it in.

Ryan's mind churned, knowing his options were limited. Recalling his training in Special Forces, he tried to formulate a plan. It finally came to him – if he could utilize the element of surprise, he might just make it out of there alive.

He stared at the light bulb hanging from the ceiling. It was too high for him to reach, but could he break it somehow?

All he had was the frayed length of rope. Tying it into a tight knot, he flung the rope hard at the bulb. He missed twice, but on the third attempt the rope made contact. The incandescent bulb shattered, making a loud popping noise. As the shards of glass fell to the floor, the room was suddenly pitched into darkness.

Now unable to see, Ryan felt his way to the door. Standing to one side of it, he waited.

Someone outside must have heard the noise because the door bolts clicked and the door swung open.

Ryan saw light from the corridor, then a large shadow as someone stepped inside. The detective tensed his body and threw himself full-force against the other man, toppling him to the floor. The guard's AK-47 clattered to the ground.

The prone man struggled to get up, but Ryan was on him in an instant, straddling him and punching him with several vicious blows to the face.

But the beefy guard was incredibly strong and instead of crumpling as the detective expected, the man reached out with his thick hands and grabbed Ryan's throat. He began to squeeze with a vice-like grip as Ryan gasped for breath.

Ryan punched him with a massive uppercut, breaking the man's nose, blood spurting everywhere. The guard groaned, but his grip on the detective's throat held firm, literally squeezing the life out of him. Ryan felt light-headed from the lack of oxygen.

Desperate, Ryan stopped punching and instead grabbed the back of the man's head with one hand and his jaw with the other. Then he jerked his hands violently, twisting the guard's head. Ryan heard a sharp cracking sound and felt the guard's body slump beneath him. He rolled off the inert man and gulped in air.

Still gasping, he reached out and felt the guard's neck for a pulse. There was none.

Knowing he had no time to waste, the detective staggered to his feet, grabbed the AK-47 from the floor and leaned against the wall. Still struggling for breath, he checked the load on the weapon. Realizing he was barefoot, he placed the assault rifle on the floor, removed the dead man's boots and put them on. They fit tight but would have to do.

Ryan felt like hell; the pain was intense in his face, ribs, and now his neck. Then he recalled a mental trick he'd used when he'd been wounded in Iraq years ago. Put the pain in a box, he told himself, and close the lid. He still felt the throb, but now it was contained in a small space in his mind.

Holding the AK at the ready, he approached the open door of the room and peered outside. The well-lit corridor was empty. At the end of it he spotted a staircase leading up. As he had suspected, they had kept him in a basement.

Stepping into the hallway, he reached the stone staircase. Looking up, he saw a door at the landing. He climbed the steps and slowly turned the knob. The door was locked.

Suppressing the urge to blast it open like he'd seen in countless Hollywood movies, instead he retraced his steps down the staircase back to the room where the dead guard lay. Searching the man's pockets, he found a ring of keys. Grabbing the keys, he made his way back to the staircase landing. Rambo was cool, he mused, but in real life when you're out-numbered it was best to keep the element of surprise as long as possible.

On the third try, one of the keys unlocked the door. He quietly turned the knob and partially opened the door. With a finger on the trigger of the assault rifle, he looked out to the large open space in front of him. The high-ceiling room was probably the main part of the warehouse. Scores of filled pallets lined the walls, stacked on heavy-metal racks that almost reached the ceiling. Rows of other pallets fronted the racks. On the pallets were wooden crates; filled with weapons, he guessed. At the opposite side of the room were the loading bays. Workmen using forklifts were loading and unloading trucks. Clanking metal and grinding gear noises filled the room.

Ryan saw at least six heavily-armed guards patrolling the loading bay area and realized that escaping was going to be complicated. But escape was the furthest thing from his mind at the moment. First he had to find Nico. Find him and get him to talk. Nico knew Angel Stone and this was the only lead Ryan had.

The detective crouched, and using the stacked pallets for cover, slowly made his way along the side wall of the warehouse, the wall furthest away from the loading bays. Several times men on forklifts drove close by and he ducked behind the wooden crates.

He eased his way along the wall until he reached the front end of the warehouse, which had a wide corridor at the end.

Peering from behind a pallet, he observed the hallway. Standing outside a closed door was the guard from before, the one with the Uzi. The man was leaning casually against the wall, toting the pistol-like submachine gun loosely. He wasn't expecting trouble, Ryan thought.

Guessing Nico was in that office, Ryan's mind churned. How to get past the guard without alerting the rest of the armed men in the warehouse? Shooting him was out of the question.

Ryan spotted a water spigot on the wall leading to the corridor. Maybe, just maybe, it might work. Hugging the side wall, he made his way to the spigot and turned it on.

Water spurted out as he turned the valve fully open. A puddle collected under the spigot and as it grew, the water pooled on the warehouse floor and into the corridor.

Peering around the corner, he looked toward the guard, who was still leaning casually against the wall. The collection of water grew and eventually reached his area.

Ryan observed the guard as the man looked down at his now wet shoes.

"What the fuck?" the guard exclaimed and glanced around bewilderedly.

The detective quickly ducked and got himself ready. He heard footsteps splashing on the corridor floor and an instant later spotted the Uzi guy emerge from the hallway.

Holding the AK by the barrel, Ryan swung the weapon like a club and struck the guard in the head with the wooden stock butt. The guard grunted and the whites of his eyes rolled up. His legs buckled and he collapsed to the floor.

Wasting no time, Ryan put down the AK, grabbed the man by his shoulders and dragged the inert body behind a row of crates.

Scanning the area to make sure he hadn't been spotted, Ryan then went through the guard's pockets. He found a cell phone, a wallet, and a large switchblade. Pocketing all of these, he checked the man's pulse. He was alive, just knocked out.

Ryan hated what he had to do next, but realized he had no choice. The guard could recover at any moment.

He took out the switchblade and flicked it open. Then he shoved the long, sharp blade into the man's gut. Removing the blade, he wiped the blood on the man's pants and put it away.

Next he picked up the guard's Uzi and stuck it in his waistband. After picking up the AK, he turned off the water spigot, and made his way down the corridor to the office door.

Holding the assault rifle with one hand, he turned the door knob with his other. The door opened and he stepped inside.

Nico was sitting behind his desk, an amazed look on his face. "What the fuck ...!" he shouted, standing up.

Ryan raced across the room and punched the heavy-set man in the stomach. Nico gasped and folded, his body sagging further into the chair.

Turning, Ryan went back, closed and locked the door, then returned and stood over the man. Nico was groaning and holding his wide abdomen. Rummaging through the office cabinets, the detective found a roll of duck tape, and with it bound Nico's feet and hands to the chair. Lastly he slapped a piece of the tape over the man's mouth.

By this time Nico had recovered from the punch and struggled to free himself. But it was no use, the layers of duct tape held firm. His eyes were wide with fear.

"So, Nico," Ryan said as he stood over the man. "How does it feel to be the captive? Not so good, I'm guessing."

The man once again tried to free his hands, but gave up a moment later.

Ryan felt the side of his own face, which was still throbbing. In a rage of fury he closed his fists and hit Nico with a right crosscut, and followed it with a left uppercut. Nico's head snapped one way, then the other, and blood dribbled from his lip and nose. The man's head lolled on his chest.

"That was payback," Ryan said to Nico, who was grunting.

"Now that we have that out of the way," Ryan continued, "I need to conclude our business. You tell me what I want to know and I won't kill you. I think that's a fair deal. Don't you?"

Nico grunted some more, the tape over his mouth distorting whatever he was trying to say.

"Nico, I just need to find Angel Stone. Or Lila, as you know her. You tell me how to find her and I'll let you go. Okay?"

The man nodded his head and Ryan said, "That's good. Now we're getting somewhere. But just to show you I'm serious, I want you to see something first." Pulling the switchblade from his pocket, he flicked it open. He held the long blade close to the other man's face.

Nico's eyes went wide once again and suddenly the foul odor of excrement filled the air. The man must have lost control of his bowels.

"You tell me what I want to know," Ryan hissed, his voice full of menace. "or I'll use this."

Nico nodded furiously.

"Okay. Now I'm going to take the tape off your mouth. You talk and you live. Understood?"

Nico nodded again.

Ryan ripped the duct tape off but still held the blade close to the man's face. "Tell me about Lila," the detective demanded. "Where does she live in Marseille?"

Nico shook his head. "She ... she doesn't live here."

"Don't lie to me, Nico. I already killed one of your men with this knife. I won't hesitate to use it on you."

"It's true! It's true. You've got to believe me," the man said, his voice breaking. "Lila doesn't live here ... she only comes here to do business ..."

"Where does she live then?"

"Paris."

"Where in Paris? Give me the address!"

"I don't know."

"You're lying!"

"No –"

Ryan held the knife to the man's throat, the sharp blade cutting the skin slightly. "Tell me or you die." A trickle of blood oozed from the cut.

"Please ... Ryan ... I don't know."

By the terrified look in the man's eyes, the detective figured he was telling the truth.

"I need more, damn it! Tell me whatever else you know about her, Nico."

"Please ... don't kill me ..." Nico whimpered, and Ryan pulled the blade a fraction of an inch away from his throat.

"She had an accomplice," Nico said, "someone she worked with. An American, like her."

"Who?"

"She called him Carter. A tall, muscular guy with blond hair."

"Okay. That's helpful. What else can you tell me?"

Just then there was a knock at the door. "Damn," Ryan muttered. But before he could react, Nico shouted for help.

The pounding on the door grew louder and Ryan dropped the knife, grabbed the AK-47 from the floor and swung it at Nico, hitting him and sending him, still strapped to the chair, toppling to the floor.

The detective whirled around and faced the door. He knew the element of surprise was gone. The only thing that mattered now was escape.

Pointing the assault rifle at the closed door, he fired off a five-round burst, the sound of the shots deafening in the room.

The rounds shredded large holes in the wooden door, sending splinters flying. Hearing yells of pain from outside the room, Ryan pulled the door open and found a crumpled man lying in a pool of blood.

Looking out toward the warehouse area, he saw two of the armed guards racing his way, their weapons trained on him.

Ryan fired off another burst from the AK and the guards scattered. His mind raced as he tried to figure out what to do. Go toward the warehouse? Or toward the building entrance? Hoping to avoid more guards, he chose the latter, and sped down the hallway to what he thought was the entrance area. Furiously trying to remember the layout of the building, he took a right at the end of the corridor, and then a left, and found another interior door.

Holding the assault rifle at the ready, he opened the door and to his relief saw the front entrance was just ahead at the end of the hallway. Seeing no one around, he sprinted toward it.

Suddenly he heard shouts from behind him, turned and saw two guards leveling their weapons at him.

Pointing the AK-47 at them, he pulled the trigger. He heard a metallic click, but the rifle didn't fire. With a sick felling he knew the weapon had jammed.

The two guards opened fire, just as Ryan dropped to the floor of the corridor. As a hail of bullets whizzed over him, Ryan let go of the AK and pulled the Uzi from his waistband.

Firing wildly toward the guards at the far end of the corridor, Ryan rolled left and crouched by the wall. He pulled the trigger again, this time with precision, the ejected brass cartridges clattering to the floor.

One of the guards fell, but the other kept blasting away, his heavy rounds drilling holes in the wall above Ryan, sending pieces of concrete raining down. One of the shots zinged the detective's ear and he flinched from the pain. Firing again, Ryan hit the remaining guard, the bullets shredding the man's leg. The guard cried out and toppled over.

Ryan heard the thudding of boots and knew more of them were coming from the warehouse. Turning, he hustled down the corridor toward the front entrance, knowing he had only seconds before they arrived.

Reaching the metal door, he tried opening it, but it was locked. Aiming the Uzi at the lock, he blasted away, the shells at first ricocheting, but finally cracking the heavy lock. As he pulled the door open, he heard the crack of shots behind him.

Rushing out of the building and to the sidewalk, he quickly spun around and dropped to one knee.

Two guards emerged from the doorway and he fired the submachine gun at close range, the weapon making a high-pitched clatter. One of the guards crumpled to the ground, while the other retreated inside.

Ryan tried firing again and realized the weapon was empty. Dropping the Uzi, he turned and raced out into the crowded street, which was jammed with trucks and semis. With brakes squealing and horns blasting all around him, he weaved his way around the slow-moving trucks.

Crossing to the other side of the street, he ran along the opposite sidewalk for several blocks. Spotting a flat-bed truck with tarps covering the back, he hoisted himself onto the bed and pulled one of the tarps over him.

It was dark and cramped under the tarp and everything stank of diesel fuel. But Ryan was exhausted and oblivious to all that.

The truck rumbled forward slowly, but after a while traffic must have thinned because it began to speed up. The truck's engine roared to life just as Ryan drifted off to sleep.

Chapter 41

New Orleans, Louisiana

Angel Stone sat at the small, wrought-iron table in Cafe Du Monde and sipped strong coffee. Located across from Jackson Square, the open-air cafe was packed with tourists and locals. It was noon, and since it was so close to Christmas, there were more people than usual at the popular French Quarter eatery.

Taking a bite of her beignet, her thoughts drifted.

It had been a huge mistake, Angel realized now. She shouldn't have slept with Frank. The man had misconstrued the sex as something more than what it was. To her it had been a simple fuck. But in his mind, it had rekindled his simmering love for her. After the sex, she had shut him down, and the man had sulked during the whole long drive here.

Angel took another sip of coffee, knowing she had to repair the damage. She needed his help to complete the operation – no way could she pull it off by herself.

Just then she spotted Frank stride past on the sidewalk, craning his neck, obviously looking for her. She raised her hand and he must have seen her because he pushed his way through the throng on the sidewalk, and weaved his way through the crowded place to her table.

Frank sat down across from her, a glum look on his face.

"You park the van?" she asked.

He nodded, but stayed quiet.

Angel slid her plate of beignets towards him. "Have some," she said, "they're good."

"I'm not hungry."

"You're always hungry, Frank."

A grimace was his only response.

"I'm sorry," she said, her voice low. "I really am. We should have never ..."

"You're fucking right!" he hissed.

She reached over with her palm and rubbed his hand, which was flat on the table. "I'm sorry. Can you forgive me?"

She studied his eyes, saw the anger there.

"I screwed up, Frank. It was my fault. I led you on. Please forgive me."

The anger in his eyes finally gave way and he gave her a sad smile. "Okay," he said with a sigh. "You know I can't stay mad at you very long."

Angel smiled back. "Thank you."

He reached over, took one of the beignets from the plate and began munching on it.

She signaled a waiter and when the man came over she ordered another plate of the pastries and a coffee for Frank.

When the waiter moved away, Frank asked, "What's next?"

She leaned forward in the uncomfortable, wrought-iron chair. "I want you to take the Camry and check us into the motel I told you about earlier." She paused a moment, then added, "Get two rooms."

He shrugged. "I figured that. What are you going to do?"

"I want to scout the area."

"You got a target in mind?" he whispered.

"Yes. But I need to get a feel for the place to make sure."

The waiter came back and set down a heaping platter of the pastries on the table. The beignets were freshly made, steam rising from them.

Frank grabbed one and happily wolfed it down. Two minutes later the plate was empty.

"Guess you liked them," she said.

"You know me."

"I do."

He drained his coffee cup. "Want me to pick you up after you've had a chance to look around?"

Angel shook her head. "I'll catch a cab."

Frank stood. "In that case I'll get going."

"Okay. See you later."

The man left and she paid the bill.

Slinging her tote bag over one shoulder, she made her way to the busy sidewalk and began walking south on Decatur Street. A long while later she reached Riverwalk Marketplace, the city's largest shopping mall. Pulling her baseball cap lower over her eyes, she strode in and went to the second floor, which overlooked the Mississippi River on one side.

The mall was packed with shoppers, all of them laden with bags. It was only a week before Christmas and the stores were full. Holiday decorations adorned the wide aisles and storefronts, while festive Christmas songs played over the loudspeakers.

Perfect, she thought, as she strolled along.

But then she noticed something else.

There was a large police presence at the shopping center. Mall cops and N.O. P.D. officers were everywhere. It was clear the bombings in Miami, Raleigh and Honolulu had spooked the authorities – the New Orleans police were on high alert. She should have anticipated the cops would focus their resources on a place like this, where huge numbers of people congregated. The nearby parking lots would be inspected carefully, and often.

Making a snap decision, she exited the mall and walked north, past Harrah's Casino and the waterfront aquarium, finally ending up where she had started, Jackson Square.

Standing in front of Cafe Du Monde, she looked across the Square. On the far side of the large grassy area, past the statue of Andrew Jackson, was St. Louis Cathedral, one of the city's most notable landmarks. It's imposing white facade dominated the skyline, its three tall spires reaching high into a cloudless sky. Although not nearly as crowded as the mall she'd just visited, it had potential.

Angel crossed Decatur Street and strode toward the large church. Standing in front of it soon after, she admired the handsome appearance of the historic building. Completed in 1794, the structure's architecture was a mix of Renaissance and Spanish Colonial.

A church service must have just concluded, because people were streaming from the exits. Pulling her cap even lower over her eyes, she stepped inside.

Going past the entrance foyer, she watched as the place emptied. The cathedral had the familiar and comforting scent of incense and burnt candle wax.

She took a seat in one of the now-empty pews and crossed herself. A silly habit, she realized. But old habits were hard to break. Raised Roman Catholic by her very devout parents, Angel had strayed far from her religion during her checkered life.

It was massive cathedral, with a high, vaulted ceiling. At the far end of the sanctuary stood the imposing, ornate altar. Tall, stained-glass windows lined both sides of the church, depicting images of Jesus, Mary, and the various saints. Gazing at them, she thought about her own soul. She was sure she would be damned to hell. If she even had a soul anymore. But the afterlife didn't concern her; her only interest was the here and now.

Just then someone must have turned off the cathedral's interior lights, because the vast room was pitched into semi-darkness, the only light coming through the stained-glass windows.

Sitting quietly in the empty church, she thought through the upcoming operation.

Yes, she mused. The cathedral would do. Quite nicely, actually. She just needed to work out the logistics. They needed to park the van nearby, at a place that wouldn't arouse suspicion.

"Are you okay?" she heard someone say from behind her.

Angel froze. She thought she was alone in the empty church.

Staying seated in the pew, she turned her head. A white-haired man in a black suit and a clerical collar was standing there.

"Are you okay?" the elderly priest repeated.

She almost reached under her jacket for the Sig Sauer, then decided against it. "Yes, Father, I'm fine," she replied.

"I saw you sitting in the darkness and figured something was wrong," the priest said in a heavy Irish brogue. "By the way, I'm Father O'Malley. You don't look familiar. Are you a parishioner here?"

Angel stood. "No. I'm not a member of this church."

"That's fine. Everyone is welcome here."

She smiled at the kindly old man, trying to figure out an angle. And then it came to her. Sorting through her previous aliases, she said, "My name is ... Donna ... and ... I didn't tell you the truth before. Actually, I'm not okay at all."

"What's the problem, Donna? Maybe I can help."

She slumped back down in the pew, covered her face with her hands and forced herself to cry as best she could. The muffled, fake sobs sounded artificial to her, but she hoped they were good enough to fool the old man.

She heard steps, and felt a hand touch her shoulder. Pulling her hands away from her face, she saw the priest sitting next to her.

"Tell me what's wrong," he said in a kindly voice.

"I ... it's embarrassing," she began. "I lost my job. My savings are gone. I got kicked out of my apartment because I couldn't make the rent. Now I'm homeless."

"There, there," he said, patting her shoulder again. "Life is difficult. But God is always there to help."

"That's why I came here, Father. To pray. I don't know what else to do ..."

"Do you have any family, Donna?"

"No. I grew up in an orphanage," she lied. "And my husband died two years ago."

"I see."

"I don't know what to do," she said, her voice breaking. "I'm living out of my van. But I don't have any money... not even for food."

"I may be able to help."

"Really?"

"Yes. Our church runs a shelter. It's staffed by our nuns. We take in people who are homeless."

"You do?"

"That's right. You sound like a good candidate, Donna."

"Where is this shelter?"

"In a building right behind the church."

Angel's eyes lit up. "That's wonderful, Father."

"There is one thing, though."

"What?"

"It's only temporary. We ask that you stay at the shelter for no more than a month."

"That's not a problem, Father. I'm sure I'll find something permanent by then."

The priest smiled and stood. "Good. You can move in anytime today. I'll let Sister Madeline know you'll be coming."

"Thank you. You don't know how much this means to me. By the way, is there a place I can park my van?"

"Yes, of course. We have a parking lot next to the shelter."

"Perfect, Father. And God bless you."

***

Angel found a cab on Decatur Street and took it to the cheap motel on the outskirts of the city. Finding Frank's room, she knocked on the door and he let her in.

The TV in the room was blaring and he turned it off. "So, you find a target?" he asked as he sat on the bed.

"Yeah. It wasn't my first choice, but it'll do fine."

"What is it?"

"St. Louis Cathedral on Jackson Square."

"Why there? Figured you'd want to hit Riverwalk or the casino."

Shaking her head, she said, "Those places were crawling with cops."

He nodded. "You figure out a place to stash the van?"

"Oh, yeah," she replied with a smile. "I got the perfect place for it." She told him about the priest and the church shelter. "I'll have to put up with the nuns for a couple of days to make it look good, then we can head back to Savannah and leave the van at the shelter."

Frank laughed. "You amaze me sometimes. I guess your Catholic upbringing came in handy, huh?"

"Imagine that," she replied with a chuckle.

Chapter 42

Atlanta, Georgia

Erin Welch was in her Lexus driving home when her cell phone rang. She unclipped the phone from her belt and took the call.

"This is Welch," she said, her eyes focused on the heavy traffic all around her. There was road construction on this part of Interstate 285 and her commute was always difficult.

"It's Ryan," she heard the man respond.

A pick-up truck tried to cut in front of her and she leaned on the horn. "J.T. Where the hell have you been? I've been calling you for days."

"I was following a lead and things went sideways on me."

"Are you okay?"

"Yeah. I got knocked around a bit, but I'll be fine."

"Where are you now, J.T.?"

"Outside of Marseille. I found a doctor here – he patched me up. I'll be good as new in a day or so."

The tail lights of the semi just ahead of her lit up and she tapped on the brakes. "Glad to hear it. What'd you find out about Stone?"

"She's definitely involved in black-market weapons. I met one of her dealers. A low-life by the name of Nico."

Erin thought about that a moment. "Marseille is a port city – my guess is Stone ships arms from there?"

"That's right."

"At least you're getting closer to finding her," she said. "You've made more progress than the CIA did in years of looking for her." She slammed on her brakes and cursed under her breath at the slow-moving traffic, which had almost ground to a halt.

"I saw the news about Raleigh," he said. "How bad is it?"

"Bad. Just like the other two bombings. Casualties about the same. Downtown Raleigh is contaminated with radiation. The whole thing is a fucking mess."

"I hear you."

"We've got to find Stone, J.T., before she does it again."

"Believe me, I know. Did the terrorists leave any clues?"

"Not a damn one. We're fucked right now. It's a week before Christmas and we think the terrorists have a specific timetable in mind. We think they're building toward one of the holidays – Christmas or New Year's to maximize the panic."

"Jesus. Have they made any new demands?"

"Not yet," she replied. "The last time we heard from them they wanted 500 million. Since we didn't pay it, I'm sure now they'll want 750 million or they'll attack another city."

"And if we don't pay after that?"

She massaged her temple, trying to push away another painful migraine. "Then they'll bomb Washington D.C., unless they get the total amount they wanted – one billion dollars."

"What are the chances the U.S. will pay the ransom?"

"Three weeks ago I would have said zero chance. But now ... D.C. is in total panic mode. I've heard rumors the president isn't well..."

"Okay, Erin. I'm doing everything I can to find Stone. But I need a few things."

"Like I told you before, whatever you need."

"When I got beat up, they took my passport, credit card and everything else on me."

"I'll call the American consulate in Marseille, J.T. Go see them. They'll set you up with anything you need."

"Good. Thanks."

Erin took the exit-ramp, relieved to be off the slow-moving interstate. "I hate to be a bitch," she said, "But we're getting kind of desperate here. I need you to find Angel Stone ASAP. And I mean ASAP."

"I got a good lead from Nico. Stone works out of Marseille, but doesn't live here. Right after I visit the consulate, I'll head there."

"Where's that, J.T.?"

"Paris."

Chapter 43

The Oval Office
The White House
Washington, D.C.

FBI Director Michael Stuart was shown into the Oval Office and took and seat across from President Layton.

Layton looked bad, Stuart thought. Sitting behind the imposing desk, the president appeared shrunken, his expensive suit looking two sizes too big. His face was sallow and he had dark circles under his eyes. His left eye was a mess, with an almost constant twitch.

"What have you got, Mike?" Layton asked, nervously tapping his pen on the desk.

"Mr. President," Stuart replied, "I just received a new text message from Al-Shirak."

He saw the president's face tense. "What now?" Layton said, his voice no more than a whisper.

"Sir, they want $750 million or the next U.S. city gets hit."

The president's left eye began twitching uncontrollably and the man rubbed it with his hand. "God almighty. Mike, what the hell am I going to do?"

Standing abruptly, Layton took off his suit jacket and pulled down his red silk tie. He began pacing the office, crossing back and forth in front of the three tall windows that overlooked the Rose Garden. A heavy, wet snow was falling over Washington and the beautiful garden was serene.

"This shit has to stop," Layton muttered as he paced. "The country is falling apart and everyone is looking to me for answers. God, why did this have to happen on my watch?"

"Mr. President, we've notified the P.D.'s across the country. Everyone is on the highest alert."

Layton stopped pacing, stabbed his index finger in the air toward the director. "You did that *before*, damn it, and nothing happened! Did you *catch* the terrorists?"

Stuart swallowed hard. "No, sir."

"Fucking right, you didn't. You're no closer to finding Al-Shirak than you were two weeks ago."

The director was about to protest, but knew the man was right.

Layton crossed back to his desk, sank into his executive chair, and covered his face with his hands.

Stuart had served three presidents as FBI Director and had been in countless meetings in the Oval Office. He thought he had seen everything before. But what he was hearing now shocked him. Although muffled by his hands, the president was sobbing.

The director realized the man was on the edge of a nervous breakdown. Stuart stayed quiet, not wanting to make the situation worse.

After a time, the crying stopped and the president pulled out a handkerchief and wiped his eyes. The man's face was red and his eye was twitching rapidly.

Leaning forward in the chair, Layton said, "What do I do?"

"Sir ... maybe you should talk to your doctor."

The president waved a hand in the air. "He's already got me on tranquilizers. If he gives me any more I'll turn into a zombie."

"Yes, sir."

Layton rubbed his twitching eye. "The only solution I see is to pay the ransom."

"Sir, even if they get the money, there's no guarantee they'll stop."

"I know that, damn it!"

"Mr. President, we've got every Federal agency in the country, not to mention the state and local cops looking for the bombers. Al-Shirak is bound to make a mistake."

"So you keep saying. But it hasn't happened yet."

"Yes, you're right," Stuart grudgingly admitted. "If you were to pay the ransom, which I don't recommend, how would you do it? We'd have to pay them in secret, otherwise every other terrorist group in the world would demand ransom for planned attacks in the future."

"Yes, yes, I know that. Coming up with a billion dollars without getting Congress involved is going to be difficult. Extremely difficult. Some of those congressional bastards would fight me on this and before I know it, news of the ransom would be leaked to the press."

Stuart nodded, knowing he was right.

"This is a nightmare, Mike. A fucking nightmare. Did you see the poll Gallup released yesterday? My approval ratings are in the tank."

The director said nothing, more worried about the next bombing than getting the president re-elected.

A beep sounded from the intercom on the president's desk and Layton tapped on the device. "Yes, Margaret?"

"Mr. President," she responded, "you have the Cabinet meeting scheduled in five minutes."

"Cancel the meeting. I can't deal with that now."

"Yes, sir."

Layton's brow was beaded with sweat. He bolted out of his chair and began pacing the room again. "God, it's hot in here," he mumbled.

After a moment he stopped and stared at the director. "How much time do we have?"

Stuart glanced at his watch. "Twenty-three hours, Mr. President."

Chapter 44

Savannah, Georgia

Twenty-five hours later Angel Stone was in the front yard of the farmhouse, in the area away from the trees. Pulling out her secure cell phone, she quickly punched in a number.

Carlos Montoya answered on the first ring.

"It's Angel," she barked. "You got it?"

"The code word is Red Grass," Carlos said. "What's the response?"

"Fuck that. Did they deposit the money?"

There was a long pause from the other end. "I'm afraid not, Angel. There was no wire transfer into our account in Buenos Aires."

"You're sure? How about to any of the others? Hong Kong, or Grand Cayman?"

"Nothing."

Angel ground her teeth. The bastards were screwing her again. She was *certain* they would have caved by now.

"Are you still there?" Carlos asked.

"Yes, I'm still on." She stared at her watch. It was an hour past the deadline.

"What are you going to do, Angel?"

Her mind raced as she thought about the van in the church shelter's parking lot. Three days ago, she wouldn't have given a second thought about what to do. But that was before she'd met the dozens of homeless mothers and their children who were staying at the shelter. It had been easier before, when the victims were people she didn't know – nameless, faceless people she read about in the newspaper or saw on the news.

"I don't know what I'm going to do," she answered.

Abruptly, she turned off the call.

Chapter 45

The White House
Washington, D.C.

FBI Director Stuart stood with his arms outstretched away from his body and allowed himself to be frisked by the Secret Service agents posted in the corridor.

After the Honolulu bombing, White House security had been beefed-up, to the point where even top-level people were searched before seeing the president.

The scans done, Stuart was admitted into the Oval Office.

President Layton was on the phone so the director sat on one of the visitor's chairs fronting his desk. Trying to ignore the mental image of a ticking clock, Stuart instead focused on the historic paintings hanging on the sky-blue walls. His favorite painting was on his right. It depicted General George Washington crossing the Delaware. A copy, he knew; the original was in the Metropolitan Museum of Art in New York City.

After a moment, Layton hung up the phone and turned towards him, his eyes showing raw fear. "You have news?"

"Yes, Mr. President."

"Good, I hope."

"Good and bad."

"Give me the good first. God knows I need it."

"Yes, sir. We finally caught a break. A big break. Remember I told you we were working several leads –"

"Get on with it, Mike."

"Of course. Our intel led us to a rogue CIA agent by the name of Angelica Stone. She's been dealing black-market weapons for years ..."

"Just give me the Cliff Notes version will you?"

"Yes, sir. Anyway, we suspected Stone was involved with the Al-Shirak group. Our FBI office in New Orleans just identified her from a surveillance image taken by a security camera. The picture was taken in a mall in New Orleans called Riverfront Marketplace. We think that's the next target. The N.O.P.D. has evacuated the mall and they're searching all of the vehicles parked in the adjacent lots."

The president leaned back in his executive chair and let out a long breath. "Thank God." Then he leaned forward again. "But what's the bad news?"

"Sir, it's an hour past the deadline and we didn't pay the ransom."

Chapter 46

Savannah, Georgia

"You've got to be kidding," Frank Reynolds uttered, shocked by what she'd just said.

"Maybe we should hold off hitting New Orleans," Angel Stone repeated.

They were in the farmhouse's kitchen, he drinking coffee while she sipped tea. Frank put his cup down on the chipped Formica dining table. "Why the hell would we want to do that?"

"I don't know, Frank. I have a bad feeling."

"Ever since you got back from that shelter, you've been acting weird. I swear to God, I think those nuns brainwashed you."

"It's not that ... it's just ..."

Frank stared at the beautiful woman. Rarely was she unsure of herself. In fact, she was the most determined and confident woman he knew, part of the reason he loved her.

He pushed aside his half-finished cup of coffee. "I don't have to remind you that the U.S. hasn't paid us a cent. All we have to show for all our work is a big fat nothing."

"I'm well aware of that, Frank."

He shook his head. "I know you're the boss and that you're smarter than me. But my opinion counts too. I've risked my life to make this operation a success. And now is not the time to quit, damn it. I want that money. I need that money!"

Pausing, he stared into her green eyes. But the only thing he saw there was uncertainty.

Chapter 47

Paris, France

J.T Ryan drove the rented Peugeot coupe along the nearly deserted Champs-Elysees. It was four in the morning and the only other vehicles on the famous avenue were an occasional taxi and the street-cleaning trucks that lumbered along, their gears grinding loudly. Lit up by ornate street lamps and Christmas lights, this part of Paris glistened. In the distance, at the end of the avenue, he could make out the Arc de Triomphe, back lit in grand splendor.

Having been to the city several times before as an operative, he'd also spent time in the outer suburbs, the high-crime areas populated by destitute Arab immigrants from Algeria and Morocco. Most people didn't know that the population of France was over ten percent Arabic.

After visiting the U.S. consulate in Marseille and getting the necessary gear, he'd driven straight here. Tired from the long drive, he needed to crash for a few hours before setting out in the morning to find Stone.

Approaching the Arc de Triomphe, he slowed the Peugeot, looking for the right cross-street to the hotel. The consulate people had picked out the hotel, telling him it was a clean and non-descript place where he would blend-in easily. Spotting Rue La Boetie, he turned off the avenue and made his way around the curving, cobble-stone street.

Minutes later he found the small hotel, parked, and checked in. Ten minutes later he was in his cramped room, sprawled on the narrow bed, fast asleep.

***

Waking two hours later, Ryan showered, dressed, and walked back to the Champs-Elysees. Finding an open-air cafe that fronted the avenue, he grabbed a table and ordered breakfast. The place must have been popular, because it was packed with Parisians and early-morning tourists.

Unlike a few hours earlier, the avenue was already choked with traffic, mostly Citroens, Renaults and motor-scooters. Horns blared and brakes squealed, drowning out the conversations of the cafe's other patrons.

As he munched on a croissant and drank ink-like coffee, he thought about the coming day. Nico and Tom Harris had given him some leads, and with the picture of Angel Stone, he hoped to make progress finding her. But Paris was a large city, he knew, and very old – full of small side streets and warrens of apartment buildings. It would not be easy.

Quickly finishing the breakfast, he paid, and began walking on the crowded sidewalk along the avenue. It was a cold, overcast day and he zipped up his jacket.

Passing a newsstand, he spotted a glaring newspaper headline, went over and bought a copy of *Le Monde*. In bold, very large type, the headline said, *Dirty-bomb explodes in New Orleans.*

His heart sank as he read the article and stared at the accompanying photos. Authorities in New Orleans had confirmed that a large explosive had been detonated in the French Quarter, destroying the historic St. Louis Cathedral and parts of the nearby areas in Jackson Square. Radioactivity had been detected, and the whole area had been cordoned off. Panic had set in as nearby residents fled; the National Guard had been ordered in. Official estimates of casualties were not given, but some sources said it had to be in the thousands. The pictures in the newspaper showed bloody scenes of the badly wounded, being treated on the scene or rushed into ambulances.

Ryan clenched his teeth and stopped reading, unable to absorb any more of the gruesome details. Sickened by the attack, he threw the newspaper away in a nearby trashcan.

Finding a quiet alcove by a retail shop, he pulled out his new satellite cell phone. He dialed Erin Welch's number, and despite the fact it was one a.m. in Atlanta, she answered immediately.

"It's Ryan," he said.

"J.T.," she responded. "You heard about New Orleans?"

"Just read about it. The paper said it was a dirty bomb ... is that right?"

"Yeah. Same as the other cities. It was Al-Shirak, no question about it."

"Casualties?"

"Bad. Too soon to know for sure, but Homeland Security says it'll be similar to Miami and Raleigh."

Ryan gripped the phone tightly. "I'm sorry, Erin."

"Sorry for what?"

"That I didn't find Stone in time."

"It's not your fault, J.T. She's not in France, anyway. Surveillance cameras picked up her image at a mall in New Orleans, before the explosion. We're certain she's still here, in the U.S."

He thought about that a moment. "Maybe I should head back to the States."

"If I were you, I'd keep following your leads there. The FBI is conducting a massive search for her in New Orleans, and the rest of Louisiana. Director Stuart has sent in hundreds of agents. If she's there, we'll find her."

"Okay," he replied. "Have you heard from the terrorists?"

"Nothing yet. But it's only three days before Christmas. We're thinking they're locking in on that date."

"Washington D.C. is the next target?"

"Yes, J.T. We're pretty sure we'll get a text message in the next day or so."

"Since we know D.C. is the next target that should help us."

"You're right," she said. "Washington is on lockdown right now. Security is the highest it's been since 9/11."

"It's going to be hard for Al-Shirak to bring in a bomb now, isn't it?"

"These people are pros," she said. "They may have planted the explosive months ago."

His stomach began to churn. "Let's hope not ... otherwise ..."

"Yeah. I hear you. Listen, I've got to go, J.T. The director has a video conference call with all the field offices in two minutes. Let me know if anything breaks on your end."

He heard a click as she disconnected the call. Putting away the phone, he mulled over the conversation. Erin was right to have him stay in Paris. He wouldn't be much help in New Orleans, now that the FBI was conducting a large manhunt there.

Pushing aside the visual image of the carnage in New Orleans, he continued walking on the crowded sidewalk.

***

The American Embassy in Paris was located on Avenue Gabriel, not far from the Champs-Elysees. An imposing white stone building with columns, the embassy was set well back from the avenue, and surrounded by high walls and a gated entrance.

Ryan was there now, talking to the U.S. Marines at the entrance. After showing his ID, being searched, and surrendering his Glock, he was admitted in and shown to the office of Terrance Fox, a Foreign Service officer.

After shaking hands, Ryan took a seat across from the man's desk.

"The Marseille consulate told you I'd be stopping by?" Ryan asked.

"Yes," replied Fox. A middle-aged black man in a gray suit and tie, the embassy officer had the look of former military. "They called me yesterday. Said you were working on the Al-Shirak case."

"That's right."

"You're an FBI contractor?" Fox asked in a skeptical tone. "I would have thought the bureau would have sent one of their agents."

"I do special assignments for them," Ryan said. It was clear Fox would rather deal with government employees. Trying to put the man at ease, Ryan said, "Which branch of the service were you in?"

"How'd you know I used to be military?"

"The close-cropped hair, a certain bearing. I can always tell."

Fox nodded. "Marines. Twenty years. I was a major when I got out. You?"

"Army captain. Delta Force."

The embassy man let out a low whistle. "A snake-eater, huh?"

Ryan knew what he was referring to. Special Forces soldiers, in particular Green Berets and Delta, were often referred to as snake-eaters. It had to do with their ability to conduct missions in jungles and deserts without supplies if need be. "Yeah. I've been called worse."

Fox grinned. It was clear the ice was broken. He leaned forward in his chair. "I'll be glad to help you. Anyway I can."

Ryan smiled back. He unzipped his jacket and pulled out a 5 x 7 photo from his pocket. Placing it on the desk, he said, "You know who this is?"

The embassy man scanned the photo. "Of course. Angelica Stone. All the U.S. embassies around the world have recently been briefed on her. Possible ties to the bombers."

"That's right. The FBI is pretty sure she's in the States right now, but I've been working several leads. I believe she lives here in Paris."

"Why do you think that?"

"She's an arms dealer, ships out of Marseille. I met one of her contacts there." Ryan then gave Fox a detailed account of his run-in with Nico.

Fox pointed to the bandages on the detective's face. "So that's how you got those."

Ryan nodded, gingerly touched his cheek. It still hurt like hell. "You run security at the embassy?"

"Yes," Fox said. "I'm in charge of the Marines here, and the undercover people we have on staff. I also liaison with the FBI in the States, the French police, and Interpol."

"Good. The FBI is already working with Interpol, but I need you to show this picture to all of your confidential informants. Maybe they'll come up with something."

"No problem, Ryan. I'll get on it right away. What else can I do?"

"Nothing right now."

"What are you going to do?"

Ryan thought about that moment. "There's a lead I need to run down."

"Need help? I can assign one of my men to help you."

"I appreciate it, Terrance, but I like to work alone."

Fox nodded, then said. "A word of caution. The French police are not keen on foreigners carrying firearms. If you get stopped by the *gendarmerie*, they'll take your Glock."

"Okay. I'll keep that in mind. Give me your cell phone number in case things go south on me."

The men exchanged numbers and Ryan stood. "I'll get going, then."

***

One of the things Tom Harris had told Ryan when he questioned the man at Guantanamo was that Angel Stone liked iconic art. So he thought he'd start his search by scouting the Louvre. It was a long shot, but he'd been a detective a long time and sometimes one thing led to another. And since the Musee du Louvre was not far from the embassy, it wasn't like he was wasting much time.

As he stood in line to pay the admission fee to the museum, he admired the huge, glass pyramid that served as the entrance. According to the sign by the door, the ultra-modern pyramid had been designed by I.M. Pei and built in 1989. But its sleek design clashed with the classical architecture of the historic museum, originally built in 1793. The tradition-bound French mostly hated the glass pyramid, Ryan knew, although around the world the pyramid had become the calling card for the Louvre.

To avoid problems with security, Ryan had left the Glock in the parked Peugeot. Paying the entrance fee, he made his way through the grandly marbled and tiled hallways of the museum. Throngs of tourists crowded the corridors and exhibit rooms, and a large group of camera-toting Japanese surrounded the Venus de Milo statue.

Going past the Egyptian and Roman antiquities exhibits, he strode by the room where the Mona Lisa hung, and took the elevator to the underground Visitor's complex. Ryan had been to the museum many times, and figured that if he was going to find anything, he'd have better luck skipping the art exhibits and visiting the upscale bar in the complex. A popular watering hole, the bar was favored by high-end art dealers, rich party-types, and assorted hangers-on.

Although it was only eleven a.m., the smoke-filled bistro was full of customers, mostly drinking wine.

He grabbed a table, ordered a Kronenbourg, and scanned the place. He needed to find a veteran waiter or waitress, someone who'd been around a long time and knew most of the patrons. The young guy who had taken his drink order looked like he was just out of school.

When the waiter brought him the beer moments later, Ryan paid for the drink and included a large tip. "I'm looking for someone on your staff who's worked here a long while," Ryan said in French. Although some people spoke English in Paris, it was usually best to converse in the local language. "I need to talk to them."

"Of course, *monsieur*," the young man replied. "That would be Louise. She's worked here forever." He craned his neck to look around. "I'll go find her for you."

As the waiter moved away from the table, Ryan took a sip of the beer.

A tall, thin woman with graying hair walked up a minute later. Past middle-age, the woman still had an elegant, if faded, appearance. "I'm Louise," she said. "How can I help you, *monsieur*?"

Ryan smiled. "I'm looking for someone. I believe she was a frequent customer here."

Louise looked suspicious. "Are you police?"

Ryan held up his palms. "No, nothing like that. She was my girlfriend years ago, and I'm trying to find her."

The waitress still seemed skeptical.

The detective took several large bills from his pocket and placed them on her serving tray. Glancing at the money, her expression softened.

"I may be able to help you, *monsieur*."

Ryan took a photo from his jacket and handed it to her. "Her name is Angel, but she also goes by Lila."

The waitress took the photo and studied it closely. "She looks familiar – but different somehow. The woman in this picture has black hair, but the customer I remember is a redhead."

He thought about this. Stone had altered her appearance before – maybe she had done it here also. "My girlfriend may have dyed her hair. Please, take a closer look. Do you think it's her?"

Louise scanned the picture again. "Yes. I remember. My customer had green eyes also. Except for the hair color, this is the same woman."

"Good. Do you know where she lives? Or what name she goes by?"

"I am sorry, *monsieur*, I do not. We get a lot of customers here."

Disappointed, Ryan pressed on. "Is there anything else you can tell me about her?"

Louise pondered this. "She was here several times with a man, a muscular blond man."

This fit what Nico had told him. One of Stone's accomplices was a blond man. "Was he American?" he asked.

"Yes, that's right. I heard them speak in English."

"Okay. Now we're getting somewhere. Do you know who the man is?"

Louise shook her head. "No, *monsieur*. But I know who does."

"Who?"

She pocketed the bills Ryan had placed on her serving tray. "Information is not free."

Ryan chuckled. "No, I guess not." He took out more money and gave it to her.

She began jotting on a pad. "This American man frequented a friend of mine, Chantelle. I'll give you her address."

Ryan took the note and read it. The address was in a somewhat seedy part of town. "What does Chantelle do?"

"She's a working girl, *monsieur*."

***

Ryan found the place an hour later. Located in one of Paris's less-affluent Districts, the worn, five-story apartment building had none of the charm of the Louvre or the Champs-Elysees. The small lobby was shabby, with worn carpet and faded paint. The elevator was broken so he took the stairs to the fourth floor and knocked.

He heard several locks unbolt and the door was opened by a statuesque woman with long, platinum-blonde hair. She was probably thirty, but looked older, with too much makeup and tired-looking eyes. Wearing a tight-fitting, low-cut dress, she was good-looking in a cheap sort of way.

"I'm J.T. Ryan," he said.

"I'm Chantelle," she replied, waving him in with a suggestive smile. "Louise called me, said you were coming. Told me you pay well." She was using a heavy, musk-like perfume that pervaded the room.

Ryan stepped into the small apartment. Like the rest of the building, the place had a run-down appearance, with worn furniture and a threadbare carpet.

"Have a seat," Chantelle said. "Would you like some wine?"

"No thanks." He took a seat on the flower-print sofa and she pulled up a chair and sat across from him. Chantelle leaned over, so that her much of her ample cleavage was exposed.

"I'm looking for information," he said, pulling cash from his pocket and giving it to her.

She counted it and with a smile, said, "Louise told me you were interested in the blond American. His name is Carter. He's a client of mine. But that's *so* boring. Let's talk about you instead. It's not everyday I get a looker like you." She reached over with one hand and placed it on his knee. "I bet I can relieve all your ... stress ... in no time."

Ryan tried not to stare at her almost fully-exposed breasts.

"You like what you see?" she asked playfully, sliding her hand up his pants leg.

He became aroused at the woman's touch. It was clear she was very good at her job.

A mental image of Lauren, Ryan's longtime girlfriend came to mind. She and Ryan had been together for years, and he didn't want to betray her trust.

"I appreciate the offer, Chantelle, but all I need is information."

Undeterred, the prostitute's hand reached his crotch, and over his pants, massaged him deftly.

It took every ounce of determination for him to push her hand away.

Chantelle looked disappointed. "You don't like me?"

"Sure, I like you. But I have someone at home."

She unbuttoned the buttons of her low-cut dress, allowing him to see all of her pendulous breasts. "That's just a taste, sugar. Let's go in the bedroom. Bet I can show you things you've never done before. You like S&M? Bondage? I do it all."

"No thanks."

Chantelle shook her head slowly, a sour look on her face. "Your loss." Quickly, she re-buttoned her dress.

Ryan nodded. "Now. About Carter."

"I need a drink first." Chantelle stood, walked to the kitchen and moments later came back holding two glasses. She handed him one and sat back down. After taking a sip from her glass, she said, "I need more money for the information."

Ryan drank some of the wine – it tasted slightly bitter, and was probably cheap jug wine. "I already gave you plenty."

"You pissed me off, Ryan. I wanted you. But you blew me off. Now it'll really cost you."

"How much more?"

"Four hundred."

The detective pulled a wad of bills from his pocket and counted out the money.

She took it and tucked it in the cleavage of her dress. Then she leaned back on the chair and sipped more wine.

"Okay," he said. "Let's hear it."

"Finish your drink, honey. If you're not going to fuck me, at least drink my wine."

Ryan drank, becoming impatient with the whore. Putting his empty glass on a side table, he said, "Talk. Now."

She gave him an enigmatic smile just as a sudden dizziness overtook him. He felt lightheaded and sleepy, much more than he should have been from one glass of wine.

Closing his eyes, he slumped on the sofa, out cold.

***

When Ryan awoke sometime later, he realized he was in trouble. Big trouble.

He was flat on his back with his arms tied behind him, in what felt like the back seat of a small car. A thick, wool blanket covered him, so he saw nothing. The blanket smelled of mildew and onions. The car jostled on squeaky, tired springs, so the vehicle was probably moving at high speed.

Ryan kept quiet and didn't move, as he listened to the loud voices from the front seat. Two people were arguing. One he recognized as Chantelle, the other was a man's voice.

"Why the hell did you have to do it?" the man growled. "You should have taken his money and told him what he wanted to know."

"Fuck you, Andre," Chantelle snarled. "I told you why. He didn't want me."

"Too late to play the scorned woman. You forget you're just a whore, Chantelle."

Ryan heard a slapping noise, and Chantelle said, "You may be my pimp, you asshole, but show me some respect. It's because of me that you have any money at all."

The man didn't reply at first. "All right," Andre finally said, his voice low. "Did you at least get all his money?"

"Yeah. He had plenty. Got his credit cards and gun too."

"Who is he, anyway?"

"According to his ID, he's an American private investigator."

"Great," he said sarcastically. "Now we'll have the *gendarmerie* on our ass."

"Not if we do this right."

"Where do you want me to go, Chantelle?"

"Shut up and let me think."

The two went quiet and all Ryan could hear was the traffic noises and the squeaky springs.

"Get off at the next exit and go north along the river," Chantelle said. "We're pretty far out of town and I remember there's an abandoned warehouse not far from here. We'll shoot him, strip him, and dump his body in the river."

"Jesus, Chantelle. Do we have to kill him? Let's just rough him up, dump him in the river and forget the whole thing."

"He knows who I am and where I live. I'm not taking the chance."

"Okay," Andre said.

Ryan's mind raced, trying to come up with a plan of action. He stayed very still and quiet, not wanting to let on he was awake.

He felt the car veer right, then slow down, make a turn and begin moving again, this time at a slower pace. A few minutes later the vehicle stopped.

"This is the place," Chantelle said. "Drive to the back of the warehouse, right by the river."

The car moved again and stopped a moment later. Ryan heard the front doors open, and slam shut. He closed his eyes and relaxed his muscles, letting his body slump in the back seat.

The back door creaked open and Ryan felt the blanket being pulled off his body.

"He's still unconscious," Andre said.

"Don't worry," the woman replied. "I gave him enough sedative to knock out a horse."

Large hands grabbed Ryan's ankles and he felt himself being pulled out of the car, feet first. He heard Andre grunt with the effort.

Ryan, his eyes still shut, was dropped to the muddy ground on his back.

"Give me the gun," Andre said.

"Fuck no," Chantelle argued. "I want to do it."

Ryan realized he only had seconds to react.

Quickly opening his eyes, he saw Chantelle standing only a few feet away, facing Andre. The woman was holding the Glock.

The detective rapidly rolled over on his stomach, pulled his knees to his chest and stood up. Although his hands were still tied behind his back, he threw himself against Chantelle, who by now had leveled the Glock at him.

Hitting her full-force, he knocked her over, toppling to the ground beside her. The gun flew off, splashing into the river.

"What the hell?" Andre roared as he reached down to grab Ryan by the shoulder.

But Ryan slipped away and once again stood up to face the other man.

Andre was huge, Ryan realized. Although the detective was well over six feet, the other man towered over him. And the Frenchman was broad too, with enormous muscles.

Andre rushed him, his arms wide open, obviously trying to bear-hug Ryan and tackle him to the ground.

Ryan side-stepped on the soggy ground, and as the other man went past him, he delivered a karate kick to his kidney.

Andre groaned, but quickly recovered and turned to face him. But the Frenchman's eyes were wary now and instead of rushing Ryan again, began to circle him.

The detective knew he had little time. Chantelle would recover in another moment and join the fight. And she probably had other weapons in the car.

Feigning left, then quickly right, Ryan turned his body sideways and delivered another fierce side-kick, this time to the large man's crotch.

Caught by surprise, Andre grunted, gasped for breath and fell to his knees, while clutching his crotch with both hands.

Ryan hit him again, this time with a front-kick to the face, sending Andre's head snapping back. With a wet thud, the big man dropped to the muddy ground.

The detective turned, saw Chantelle getting up and running to the car, an old, dented Renault. He sprinted toward her and as she reached the car, he slammed into her, pinning her back against the vehicle.

The whore's eyes were wide as he brought his knee up and struck her in the abdomen. She grunted, he kneed her again, and this time she fell to the mud.

By now Ryan was exhausted, but knew there was no time to rest. He had to find a way to free his hands, which were bound with plastic cuffs.

Squatting on the ground, he brought his tied hands under his feet and up so at least he had them in front of him. He raced to the front of the Renault and began to rub the plastic cuffs on the edge of the old-style metal bumper. Moments later the plastic gave way and he looked over at Andre.

The huge man was still on the ground, not moving.

But Chantelle was on her feet, opening the car door. Running over, he grabbed her and punched her in the mouth. She staggered, her lip bleeding.

Holding a closed fist in front of her face, he said, "Now, bitch, tell me what I want to know or I'll fucking kill you."

Her scared eyes darted to the inert Andre, then back at Ryan. "Don't hurt me. I'll talk."

"Do it now."

She wiped the blood from her lip with one hand. "The man you're looking for, his name is Jim Carter. Like I told you before, he's one of my customers."

"Where does he live?"

She rattled off an address in Paris's 10th District.

"If you're lying to me, bitch," he growled, "I'll come back and kill you. Understand?"

Chantelle nodded furiously, and by the way the woman was shaking, he knew she was telling the truth.

"Where's all the stuff you took from me?" he yelled.

"In my purse, in the car."

"You could have saved yourself a lot of trouble, Chantelle, if you'd told me all this before."

She nodded, her eyes wide.

He punched her again, this time in the gut, and she folded and dropped to the muddy ground.

Walking to the Renault, Ryan got in, started it up, and sped away.

Chapter 48

FBI Building
Washington, D.C.

FBI Director Michael Stuart stood at the back of the vast amphitheatre, located two floors below street level. On the massive wall at the front of the room were thirty large TV screens, each showing a different part of Washington, D.C.

Rows and rows of workstations faced the screens, each occupied by agents monitoring their respective sectors. Named the Tactical Command Center (TCC), the amphitheatre was the control hub of information for the Bureau. Satellite images, traffic camera feeds, and police patrols all fed information to the Center.

And for the last several weeks, the primary focus of the room had been the nation's capital. The city was in lockdown mode. Anything out of the ordinary, anything suspicious, would be picked up.

Although it was after 11 p.m. on December 23, the room was a hive of activity. As Stuart watched, agents scurried across the room while images on the screens flashed by at a rapid rate. The director had been here an hour, trying to gather any new information. He could just as easily monitor the situation from his own office, but he had too much nervous energy. Maybe by coming to the Center personally, he had thought, he might find out something sooner.

The problem was, there was nothing. No suspicious activity had taken place for weeks. All the technology, the satellite images, computers, informants, and patrols, had failed to pick up any sign of the terrorists.

Stuart's stomach churned as he glanced at his watch. 11:22 p.m. It was now 24 hours until Christmas Eve. Although Al-Shirak had not contacted him since the New Orleans bombing, he was certain they were targeting Christmas Day for the climactic attack. The signs were all there, he was sure. Attack Washington D.C., the center of American government, on the Christian holiday of Christmas. It all fit. Islamic terrorists, bent on destroying America and its Christian heritage. What better day than December 25th?

But if he was right, they would be sending him a text very soon.

Stuart stared at his watch again. 11:47 p.m. Beads of perspiration formed on his forehead.

Weary from the tension and pent-up fear, he found an empty workstation at the rear of the room and sat behind the console.

Looking up at the screens, he saw the night-time images of the city. The Capitol Building, the White House, the Pentagon, the other iconic buildings. All was quiet. A light snow was falling, giving the city a calm, even serene appearance. Traffic was light on the streets. The only vehicles that were out were police cruisers and Army National Guard trucks. The president had activated the Guard in anticipation of any trouble.

Just then Stuart's cell phone vibrated in his pocket. He glanced at his watch. 12:00 a.m.

With a sick feeling, he took out the phone and stared at the screen. As he anticipated, it was a text message from Al-Shirak. He began reading.

> DIRECTOR STUART:
> THE END-GAME IS HERE.
> YOU HAVE NO MORE TIME.
> WE WILL DETONATE A DIRTY-BOMB IN WASHINTON, D.C. IN 24 HOURS, UNLESS YOU DEPOSIT ONE BILLION U.S. DOLLARS INTO OUR BANK ACCOUNT.
> WE WILL NOTIFY YOU OF THE NEW BANK CODES 23 HOURS FROM NOW.
> FAIL TO MAKE THIS WIRE TRANSFER AND YOU WILL BE RESPONSIBLE FOR THE DEATH OF THOUSANDS OF AMERICANS.
> AS WE HAVE PROVEN WITH HONOLULU, MIAMI, RALEIGH, AND
> NEW ORLEANS, WE ARE DEADLY SERIOUS.
> THE PEOPLE OF PALESTINE WILL BE AVENGED, ONE WAY OR THE OTHER.
>
> ALLA HU AKBAR.
>
> AL-SHIRAK

Stuart put the cell phone away. Looking around the Center, he spotted his assistant conferring with another agent and motioned him over.

"Yes, sir?" his assistant said as he approached.

"Go get my car," the director said, urgency in his voice.

"Where are we going, sir?"

"The White House."

Chapter 49

Savannah, Georgia

Angel Stone turned off the cell phone and rested it on the kitchen table of the farmhouse.

Now that she'd sent the text to the FBI Director, she felt a sense of relief. It was out of her hands now. The success or failure of the operation depended solely on the reaction of the U.S. government.

Getting up from the table, she poured herself a cup of tea and went to the kitchen window and looked out. It was just past midnight and there was a full moon out, casting a bluish haze over the wooded, overgrown yard.

Would Stuart and the American government cave, she wondered? It was impossible to tell. Certainly their actions so far said no. But it was too late to second guess herself now. She simply had to wait and see.

Taking a sip of tea, the horrific images of the New Orleans attack crossed her mind. That bombing she did regret. She should have never stayed at the shelter. Years from now, she knew, the faces of the dead mothers and their babies would still haunt her. But Frank had been right. They were in too deep to quit. Maybe, over time, the faces would fade from her dreams.

Hearing a noise from behind her, she turned and saw Frank came into the room.

"You make the call?" Frank asked in a quiet voice.

"Yeah," she replied.

Frank looked dejected. "They've screwed us every time before. I don't have much hope they'll pay."

"Hopefully this will be different," she said without much enthusiasm, "since D.C. is the target."

Frank shrugged and glanced at his watch. "It's 12:30 a.m. on December 24th. With everything going on, I almost forgot. Today's the day before Christmas." He looked back at her. "We should celebrate. I could go outside and cut down a tree. We can decorate it for Christmas."

"That's a stupid idea, Frank."

He shrugged again. "You're probably right."

"Why don't you get some rest?"

"Okay. How about you, Angel?"

"I'm too wired to sleep. Think I'll stay up a while longer."

"Suit yourself." He turned and left the room.

Angel finished her cup of tea, refilled it and went back to the window.

The nighttime scene outside had changed. Clouds must have formed, because the moonlight was gone and the wooded area looked dark and foreboding.

Tree branches were swaying, and she heard thunder in the distance. A storm must be coming.

Chapter 50

Atlanta, Georgia

Erin Welch was in her FBI office when her desk phone rang. Picking up the receiver, she said, "Welch here."

"It's agent Cho from Chicago," she heard the man say.

"Cho, haven't heard from you in a while. What's up?"

"Thought you should know. Another large deposit was just made to Imam Rahim's bank account."

"How much?"

"$250,000," Cho replied.

"Who made the deposit?"

"Same as last time. The originating bank that made the wire transfer is in Grand Cayman. The same account number and bank location as the one Al-Shirak wanted the original ransom sent to."

"Damn," she said. "No way that's a coincidence. You're still questioning Rahim?"

"Of course. But we're getting nothing out of him. Ever since he lawyered-up, we've gotten zero."

"Sometimes, Cho, I fucking hate our legal system."

"I hear you. If anything else breaks, I'll call you."

"Thanks." She hung up the phone and looked up at the wall clock. It was 1:02 a.m.

Her laptop chirped loudly and she turned toward the computer screen, knowing it was a code one alert from the director.

Opening the high-priority e-mail, she quickly read Stuart's communication, which included the one billion dollar ransom demand from Al-Shirak.

Although she had been expecting the news, she was still shocked to see it in writing.

Closing the e-mail, she leaned back in her chair. She was mentally and physically drained, having been at the FBI offices for the last 72 hours straight. But it wasn't the lack of sleep that upset her. It was the feeling of utter helplessness.

Chapter 51

The White House
Washington, D.C.

FBI Director Michael Stuart had just been searched by Secret Service agents and was on his way into the Oval Office when he saw Margaret, the president's assistant coming out of the room.

"How's he doing?" Stuart whispered to her.

Margaret had a grim look on her face. "Don't ask."

The director stepped into the Oval Office and took a seat across from the president's desk.

President Layton was slouching in his executive chair, nervously drumming his fingers on the desk. Layton looked terrible. He wore no jacket or tie, and his white dress shirt was wrinkled and stained. His eyes were sunken in the sockets, and it appeared he hadn't shaved in days. The man had gone from thin to emaciated, and his compexion was pasty white.

"Mr. President," Stuart said, "as I told you on the phone, we've received the latest ransom demand from the terrorists."

Layton's left eye began twitching. "How much time do we have?"

"It's 1:10 a.m. now. We have less than 24 hours to make the payment."

The president continued drumming his fingers on the desk, while his left eye twitched uncontrollably. "And if we don't, we'll be bombed on Christmas Day." He stopped drumming. "You've got hundreds of agents scouring Washington. Plus police and National Guard patrolling the area. Any sign of the bomb?"

"No, sir."

The president's face turned red and his hands closed into fists. "I should fire you now, you incompetent son-of-a-bitch!"

Stuart held his anger in check. "Yes, Mr. President."

Layton opened a desk drawer, took out a prescription pill bottle and removed three tablets. Swallowing the pills, he leaned back in the chair and closed his eyes.

"Sir, I have more news."

Opening his eyes, Layton said sarcastically, "Go ahead, Mike. The country is collapsing under my watch. How can things get worse?"

"Sir, I received a call from my ADIC in Chicago. A $250,000 bank deposit was just made to the imam we have under arrest there. The link between him and Al-Shirak is strong."

"Pretty compelling reason, Mike, that the attack would come on Christmas, considering the Islamic terrorist connection." Layton waved a hand in the air. "But how does this help us find the explosive device?"

"It doesn't, sir."

Layton shook his head slowly. "We've known each other a long time. You've given me valuable information that's helped me stay in this job, even forestalled the impeachment charges my enemies in Congress were demanding last year. So I've trusted your advice until now. But I need the bottom line here. Will you find the bomb in the next 23 hours?"

Stuart thought about this carefully before answering. The lives of thousands of Americans could depend on his answer. "I don't know, Mr. President."

Layton's eye twitched again and he massaged it with one hand.

Reaching over, the president took three more tablets from the pill bottle and swallowed them. He went quiet, as if waiting for the pills to take effect.

As Stuart waited for the president to continue, he looked over to his left. Behind one of the armchairs stood a tall, proud Christmas tree, decked out with elaborate decorations and lights. With the on-going crisis, the festive look of the tree seemed incongruous. In fact, it did nothing to improve the director's morose mood.

"In that case," Layton continued, this time in a calmer voice, "I have no choice."

The president pressed a button on the intercom on his desk. "Margaret, call the Secretaries of Treasury and Defense. I want them in my office."

"When, sir?" the woman asked.

"Now."

Chapter 52

The Oval Office
The White House
Washington, D.C.

President Layton nervously drummed his fingers on his desk and stared at the two men sitting across from him. Although the president had already taken a massive amount of his powerful prescription medicine, he was still edgy.

The terrorist crisis felt like a crushing weight on his shoulders. The pills helped him cope, but he realized they also made him confused and lethargic. He had to pull it together, at least for the next critical several days.

He took a deep breath and let it out as he focused on the two men. To his left sat Josh Hamilton, the Treasury Secretary, and to his right was the Secretary of Defense, Samuel Brody. The two men were quite different. Hamilton was gregarious and flamboyant, while Brody, a former Marine 4-star general, was bland and laconic.

"Gentlemen," Layton began, "as you're well aware, we're facing a serious national crisis." He paused, took another deep breath to compose himself. "A short while ago the FBI Director received the latest ransom demand from Al-Shirak. As we expected, they want one billion dollars or they will set off a dirty bomb in D.C."

Although Hamilton and Brody knew of the previous threats, their faces still registered shock.

"How much time do we have, Mr. President?" Hamilton asked.

Layton felt his eye twitch and he massaged it with one hand. "Less than 23 hours."

Hamilton leaned forward in his chair. "What do you plan to do?"

"I've given this a lot of thought," Layton said. "Director Stuart is not sure he'll find the bomb. And I agree. We've made very little progress in finding the terrorists. I don't think I have a choice. I can't stand by while the nation's capital is attacked, especially during an election year. And there's one other thing. We're dealing with a dirty bomb. The radioactivity will last for years." He took another deep breath. "We have to pay the ransom."

"But, sir," Hamilton protested. "The U.S. government has never bargained with terrorists!"

Layton closed a fist and slammed it down on the desk. "I'm well aware of that. But we have no choice."

Hamilton glanced over at the Secretary of Defense as if looking for assistance, but Brody said nothing. The Treasury Secretary turned back to Layton. "One billion dollars is a lot of money, Mr. President. Congress will have to authorize it. Since we're in the holiday recess, both the House and Senate are not in session. And we only have 23 hours. It would be extremely difficult to get everybody back here in time to vote on an appropriations bill."

Layton nodded. "I agree, Josh. There's no time for that. Plus, a lot of people in Congress hate my guts. Chances are, they wouldn't go along." He paused, took another long breath. He felt queasy and lightheaded from the medicine, but pushed on. "That's why I called both of you in here."

Hamilton and Brody looked quizzically at each other, and then back at the president.

While nervously drumming his fingers on the desk, Layton said, "We have to come up with another way to get the money."

Hamilton's jaw dropped. "You want us to find that much money out of thin air?"

The president's eye began to twitch again and he slammed his fist on the desk again. "Fucking yes!"

"But sir," the Treasury Secretary protested. "We can't just create the money. That would be illegal. There's at least five statutes we'd be violating. Only Congress can authorize Federal funds."

Layton opened a drawer in his desk and took out two manila folders. He handed each man one of the files.

"Over the last several years," the president said, "I've had the FBI keep close tabs on all of my Cabinet members. The Bureau gives me regular reports, which I read and put away. Most of what they come up with is incredibly boring." He smiled. "But every once in a while, they find something interesting. For instance, what they found out about you, Josh. I know you're a married man with three great kids. But I also know about the seventeen-year-old girlfriend you secretly have on the side."

Hamilton opened the file he'd been handed and began reading. His face turned white.

Layton turned toward the Secretary of Defense. "You on the other hand, have been playing games with your tax returns for years. If the IRS ever started to dig into it ... well, let's not dwell on that."

Brody didn't even open his file, but rather dropped it on the desk as if it were a scalding hot pan.

The president's eye twitched again, and he tried to ignore it. "But don't worry, guys. All this will remain our little secret. As long as you play ball."

It was clear both secretaries were rattled. They said nothing, simply nodded their heads.

"I need one billion dollars," Layton stated in a low voice. "And I need it now."

The Secretary of Defense, who had remained quiet the whole meeting, finally spoke up. "Sir, there may be a way."

"I'm listening."

"The Pentagon has a large budget," Brody began, "and almost all of it is closely scrutinized by the Government Accounting Office and Congressional subcommittees. But there's one area that's largely unsupervised."

"I like the sound of that."

"Sir, it's our military black-ops budget. It funds covert operations around the world. Not many people even know it exists."

Layton leaned forward in his chair. "Is there enough money there ... to solve our current problem?"

"Yes, Mr. President. We'd have to curtail several ongoing operations –"

Layton slammed his hand on the desk. "I don't care about that. Can you get the money out on short notice?"

Brody turned toward the Treasury Secretary. "It would be difficult, but with Josh's help, we can do it."

"Is that right, Josh?" Layton asked.

Hamilton nodded. "Yes, sir."

"Okay, gentlemen," the president said. "You have your marching orders. Make it happen. We don't have much time."

The secretaries stood and filed out of the room.

Layton felt like an immense weight had been lifted from his shoulders. Reaching into his desk drawer, he removed the prescription bottle and took out the four remaining tablets. After swallowing them, he turned his executive chair and stared out the tall windows.

Even though it was the middle of the night, the Rose Garden was well lit from numerous flood lights. It was snowing heavier now. The bushes and trees were covered in white, and they shimmered peacefully.

Closing his eyes, he leaned back in the chair and let his mind drift. The powerful sedatives kicked in and he fell into a deep, but disturbing sleep.

Chapter 53

FBI Building
Washington, D.C.

FBI Director Michael Stuart was exhausted. He'd spent the last six hours at the Tactical Command Center, trying to uncover any new information on the terrorists. But the Bureau, along with the NSA and Homeland Security, had been unsuccessful in locating the bomb.

Now back in his office, Stuart was feeling the affects of multiple days without sleep. Even the gallons of energy drinks he'd consumed hadn't helped. He had trouble keeping his eyes open.

Sitting at his desk, Stuart looked out his office window. It was morning now, on December 24th. It was still snowing heavily, making visibility difficult. The gray skies cast an ominous shadow over the city.

The red phone on his desk rang and he picked up the receiver.

"It's Margaret," he heard the president's assistant say. "The president needs to speak with you."

"Should I drive over, Margaret?"

"No. He'll do it over the phone."

Stuart heard a click and then Layton's voice. "Find anything, Mike?"

"Not yet, Mr. President."

"What are the odds you'll locate the bomb in the next eleven hours?"

"Not good."

"I agree, Mike. But I have good news."

"Sir?"

"I've been able to come up with the money."

"How did you that, Mr. President?"

"It's better if you don't know. As soon as we get the bank codes from Al-Shirak, we'll make the wire transfer. But I can't stress this enough. Under no circumstances can the media find out about the ransom payment. I want it kept secret. Are we clear on this?"

"Yes, sir."

"One more thing, Mike. I'm leaving the White house this morning. I'm taking Air Force One to an undisclosed location. No sense in pushing my luck. If for some reason the terrorists set off the bomb after we've paid them, I don't want to be anywhere near Washington on Christmas Day."

"Yes, sir."

"Mike, I've just signed an Executive Order, directing the evacuation of D.C., starting at noon today. After I hang up with you, I'm calling the Pentagon, staffers on the Hill, and the National Guard. The news media will be notified also. The official line is that we're evacuating the city as a precautionary measure. By the way, I suggest you and your people at the Bureau move to another location outside the city as well."

"Yes, sir."

Stuart heard a click and realized the president had hung up. He replaced the receiver and stared out the window again.

It was snowing harder now.

Chapter 54

Paris, France

As J.T. Ryan drove through the light traffic of central Paris, his thoughts turned to Lauren. It was four a.m. on Christmas Day and he longed to be home, spending time with her. To his regret, he'd missed the holiday season once again. It was something that had happened frequently during the last five years. But his work as an operative, with its numerous overseas assignments, never had a set schedule. Pushing those thoughts aside, he focused on the traffic. He figured it would take him another hour to reach the apartment of Stone's accomplice.

Making his way to the city's 10th District, Ryan eventually located the right street. Parking along the narrow, cobblestone road, he walked up to the three-story brownstone. The building where Jim Carter lived was nondescript, but a big step-up from the prostitute's run-down place.

He took the elevator to the third floor and found the right apartment. There were several delivery packages piled in front of the door, as if the occupant hadn't been there in some time.

Placing one hand on the butt of the pistol tucked in his jacket, he knocked on the door. There was no answer so he knocked again. After another minute, he took out a lock-pick set and fiddled with the lock.

The mechanism clicked open.

Drawing the Taurus semi-automatic he'd found in the French whore's car, he stepped inside. The apartment was dark and musty. Flicking on a light, he scanned the room.

It was a typical bachelor pad. Simple furniture, no art or pictures on the walls. A large, flat-screen TV fronted a leather couch. Sports and car magazines were stacked haphazardly on a coffee table.

Holding the Taurus in front of him, he searched the small kitchen, the bathroom, and the only bedroom. He found no one. And from the dead plant in the bedroom, he deduced Carter hadn't been there in weeks.

A printer and scanner were on a small desk by the bed, but no computer, something he'd hoped to find. On the desk were several framed photos. The pictures were of a muscular blond man, Carter he was sure, and a variety of smiling women. One photo showed Carter and Angel Stone standing on a sailboat.

Disassembling the frames, he took out the pictures and snapped photos of them with his cell phone. Then he put the pictures back in the frames and set them on the desk where he'd found them.

Next he rifled through the desk drawers. He found receipts, copies of bills, and other innocuous paperwork, all under the name of Jim Carter.

Taped underneath the bottom drawer he found a small address booklet. Leafing though the book, he tried to read the hand-written entries. But the words were in some type of code, unintelligible at first glance. After taking photos of the book's pages, he re-taped it underneath the drawer, and continued the search.

In the bedroom closet he found several weapons: a Smith & Wesson .44 caliber handgun, a Mossberg shotgun, and a Sig Sauer automatic pistol. Boxes of ammunition were stored under a shelf of shoes. Leaving the weapons as is, he went back to the living room to finish the search.

Ten minutes later he was done. Looking around one last time to make sure he'd put everything back in its proper place, Ryan left the apartment.

***

Back in his cramped hotel room an hour later, Ryan looked at the photos he'd taken at Carter's apartment. Sitting on the narrow bed, he studied them on his cell phone while drinking a Kronenbourg.

He focused on the addresses in the book, trying to make some sense of the code Carter had used. Ryan tried reversing the letters front to back, but the words still made no sense. The last page of the booklet had only one line faintly written on it, a long combination of numbers and letters. Finally, after flipping back and forth between the entries for several hours, Ryan figured it out. Carter had assigned different numbers to the letters of the alphabet. Instead of 'A' being one as you would expect, it was now 13. That solved, he finished the beer, and opened another bottle.

Then he set to work, decoding the booklet's entries, in which only first names were listed. Several he recognized immediately. One of those was Chantelle, the French prostitute, with her address. Another one was for Nico, the arms dealer in Marseille. There were also five other women listed, with various addresses in Paris. There was also an entry for a 'Doctor H.' in Berlin, Germany.

Then he found what he'd been looking for all along. A Paris address after the entry 'Angel'. Memorizing that address, he turned off the cell phone.

He was drained from the lack of sleep, but instead of stretching out on the bed, he got up and put on his jacket. After checking the load on the Taurus pistol, he left the hotel room.

Lee Gimenez

Chapter 55

Madrid, Spain

Carlos Montoya stared at his computer screen in utter disbelief. He was in his office at home, dressed in pajamas and a bathrobe.

It was seven a.m. local time on December 25th and he'd been up all night, checking the Thailand bank account balance. He was bleary-eyed from the hours of constantly scanning the screen. There had been no change in the bank balance until five seconds ago.

Just to make sure, he read the amount out loud, then let out a low whistle.

With a burst of excitement, he realized the Americans had deposited the billion dollars into the account. All the planning and work had finally paid off!

Wasting no time, he punched a six-digit code into the computer. The code instantly launched a complex software program that would route the billion dollars through a dozen bank cut-outs from around the world, finally ending up in an unnamed, numbered account in Switzerland.

A second later the Thailand bank's balance dropped by a billion dollars. Closing that screen, Carlos opened a screen showing the Swiss account.

Beads of perspiration formed on his forehead as the seconds ticked by and no deposit appeared. Did the computer program fail? He'd tested it numerous times before with no problems.

Just as he was beginning to panic, the wire transfer to the Swiss account appeared on the screen. With a sigh of relief, he closed the screen.

He heard a knock on the closed office door.

"As estado en tu oficina toda la noche!" he heard his wife say. *"Es le dia de Christmas. Cuando vas a salir, Carlos?"* Her tone was angry. *You've been in your office all night! It's Christmas Day. When are you coming out, Carlos?*

"Pronto," he replied. *Soon.*

She cursed, then he heard her move away from the door. Carlos smiled, knowing she'd forget all about the lousy day once she began spending their new found wealth.

Picking up the secure cell phone from the desk, he dialed a number he'd committed to memory.

"It's Carlos," he said as soon as the woman picked up on the other end. "The code word is Half Track. What's the response, Angel?"

"Full Throttle," Angel replied. "Did we get the money?"

"Si! We got it, Angel. We finally got it!"

"How much?" she asked, her voice full of anticipation.

"All of it. One billion U.S. dollars."

Angel yelled out Frank's name, as if the man were in another room. Then she said, "Great news, Carlos. Where's the money now?"

"In the Swiss account."

"Good. Per my previous instructions, go ahead and distribute the money to me, you, Frank, Heiler, and the silent partner. At the numbered accounts in the banks we had set up."

"Si, Angel. As soon as I hang up, I'll do that immediately. The wire transfers will show up at the final destinations in the next minute."

"Excellent work, Carlos."

"Actually, you had a lot more to do with it than I did."

She laughed. "That's why my share of the money's a lot bigger."

"I'm not worried. I'll have plenty to last me several lifetimes."

Angel laughed again. "Me too. When I see you again, we'll celebrate."

"*Si.*"

The line was disconnected and he rested the phone on the desk. Then, with a wide smile on his face, he opened another screen on his computer and began to distribute the money.

Chapter 56

Savannah, Georgia

At the farmhouse, Angel Stone placed the cell phone on the kitchen table, and turned to her laptop in front of her. Opening her online bank account, she watched as her share of the money was posted. She could barely contain her excitement.

Angel closed the program and yelled out Frank's name again. As before, she heard nothing in reply.

Leaving the kitchen, she bounded up the stairs, eager to find the man and share the great news. It was past midnight and he was probably asleep in his bedroom.

She found Frank Reynolds in the darkened room a moment later, sprawled on the four-poster bed, snoring. A sheet partially covered him, but it was clear he was nude underneath. Turning on a light, she spotted the empty bottle of Smirnoff on the bedside table. But she couldn't blame him, not this time. He, like her, had fully expected the U.S. not to pay.

Sitting next to him on the bed, she slapped him lightly on the face. "Wake up, Frank."

He mumbled something, blinked his eyes rapidly, and sat up on the bed. "What? What's up?"

"We got it, Frank. All of it!"

His face registered a range of emotions – confusion, then surprise. "You're kidding."

"I wouldn't kid about something like that."

"Jesus H. Christ!" he shouted. "We did it!"

She held up a palm for a high-five and he slapped it hard. It stung, but it didn't matter, she was so ecstatic.

"We fucking did it," she screamed.

Frank let out a long, bellowing laugh. When he finally stopped moments later, he said, "It's ironic, isn't it?"

"What's that?"

"That the only time we didn't plant a bomb, they pay."

She nodded, knowing he was absolutely right. It *was* incredibly ironic. "Yeah. You're right. But with all the security in D.C., there's no way we could have gotten that bomb in there."

Frank laughed again and she joined him, the months of pent-up tension easing out of her.

"Where's the money now?" he asked.

"Carlos has already deposited our individual shares. I just checked my bank account."

"God damn! I still can't believe it."

"Believe it, Frank. We did good, you and I."

"Yeah, we did. We should celebrate. It's Christmas Day, after all. You want me to get another bottle of vodka? I've got several left."

Angel thought about this a moment. The idea of booze didn't sound appealing. But the thought of all that money excited her. Like caressing the bomb, the idea of all that cash gave her a sexual thrill.

Tugging the sheet off Frank, she gave him a sly grin. "No booze. Let's fuck instead."

He laughed as he pulled her towards him.

***

Angel lay nude on her back an hour later, satiated from the intense lovemaking. Frank, lying on his side next to her on the wide bed, was once again snoring loudly.

But instead of being relaxed she'd expected, her thoughts turned toward the future. Her mind raced, still elated from the success of her operation.

Turning toward him, she slapped his naked ass. "Wake up, Frank."

He muttered something, then rolled over and faced her with a grin. "Want to fuck again?"

"No. I'm done with that." Her voice was all business now. "We need to talk about something else."

"Can it wait? You wore me out."

"No, it can't wait."

He shrugged. "Okay. What?"

"I want you to buy this farmhouse."

"Why?"

"Because I changed my mind."

"About what, Angel?"

"Instead of destroying the leftover dirty bombs, I want to bury them. Right here, on this property."

Frank looked perplexed. "Why? We got all the money we demanded."

"Yeah, I know. But the plan worked so well, why give up on it now?"

"I don't understand."

"It's simple, Frank. We buy this property and bury the bombs. Then, in five years, or ten, if we need more money, we'll do it again."

The man appeared surprised by the idea. "That's not playing fair, is it?"

"Fuck that," she hissed. "Nothing's fucking fair in life. You should know that."

He went quiet a moment, and then nodded. "You're the boss."

Chapter 57

Paris, France

J.T. Ryan was driving through the city's upscale riverside area, looking for the cross street to Angel Stone's apartment. Known as the Latin Quarter, this district was one of the most exclusive. To his right flowed the Seine River, while to his left rose the beautiful spire of St-Severin, the historic Gothic church. Rows of tony apartment buildings overlooked the riverfront and he knew her place would be nearby.

Ryan spotted boulevard St. Michel a moment later, turned left and drove down the wide avenue. It was late afternoon on Christmas day, and traffic was light. Passing Stone's building, he found a spot on the street and parked the Peugeot. Zipping up his jacket, he exited the car and began walking back.

He noticed several things quickly as he approached the impressive six-story apartment structure. Although the architecture was 18th century French classical style, the security was high-tech. Several surveillance cameras pointed down from the arched entrance to the building, while a uniformed doorman and a security guard were stationed by the door. Ryan was sure it was one of those buildings where you had to be buzzed in by the resident. He'd have to find another way to gain access.

Walking past the building, he stopped at the end of the street and looked up toward the woman's apartment. Located on the sixth story, the top-floor penthouse overlooked the river. He suspected the mansard roof of the building had a flat area at the top. Studying the adjacent buildings, he came up with a plan. But it was still light out and there were too many people out walking. He'd have to come back later, at night. He debated going back to his hotel and decided against it. He'd find a nearby cafe, have dinner, and wait.

***

It was past midnight when Ryan entered the lobby of the building next to Stone's. Unlike hers, this one was not as secure. Although it had a security camera at the entrance, there were no doormen or guards. Walking into the lobby, he noticed the lobby desk was staffed by an elderly man poring over a *Le Monde* newspaper.

Ryan gave the old man a wide smile and strode past him purposefully, as if he owned the place. Stepping into the elevator, the detective took it to the top floor. Getting out, he walked down the corridor and looked out the window.

Luckily, Stone's penthouse was just across the alleyway that separated the two buildings. Less lucky was that the alley was approximately fifteen feet wide. He'd have to jump across the span, grab the roofline and haul himself up. But first he'd have to get on the roof of this building. Access to the roof in these historic structures was usually through a door somewhere on the hallway of the top floor.

Striding past the various apartment entrances on the corridor, he found an unmarked door at the very end. Pulling out his lock-pick set, he fiddled with the lock and heard a click a moment later. Opening the door, he took the stairs upward and soon was on the roof.

It was dark and cold outside, but from this vantage point the view of Paris was breathtaking, lit-up for the holidays, living up to its name as the city of eternal light.

Walking on the narrow, flat part of the mansard roof, he approached the edge. Looking down, a mostly dark alleyway stared back at him. He gauged the distance across. If he got a running start, the chances were pretty good he'd make it to the other side.

Removing the Taurus pistol from his waistband, he tucked the weapon in his pant's pocket. Then he walked back to the far side of the roof and took a big breath.

He began racing at full speed and right before he reached the edge, leapt across. Ryan didn't reach the flat part of the other building's roof, but rather landed flat against the angled mansard part. Gripping the stone tiles furiously, he managed to hold on. He peered over his shoulder at the ominous dark alley below.

Pulling himself carefully along the tiles, he inched his way to the area of the roof that overlooked the open terrace of the woman's apartment. Then he loosened his grip on the tiles and let himself drop to the floor of the balcony.

Crouching quietly while he caught his breath, he looked into the dark apartment through the tall French doors. Nothing moved inside and the only things he heard were the wind and muted traffic sounds in the distance.

Standing, he approached the glass doors, stared at the door lock, and at the security system's contact point. He pulled a specialized magnet from his pocket and placed it next to the contact point. Specially designed magnets were ideal for disabling security alarms. Once again using his lock-pick set, he played with the door lock. This lock was much more sophisticated than the one in the adjacent building, and it took him several minutes to pick it. When it clicked open, he pulled the Taurus, stepped inside and closed the door behind him.

It was like a vault in the large room – he heard no sounds; even the traffic noises were totally absent. The apartment's walls and thick glass doors must be sound-proof, he realized. After closing the windows's heavy drapes, he turned on a lamp.

The place was magnificent, he thought. Intricately carved furniture sat on gleaming wood floors. Expensive paintings in ornate, gilt frames hung on the walls. He spotted at least one Monet. Just as he'd been told, Stone had extravagant tastes. Unlike Carter's apartment, which smelled musty, this place had the aroma of wood polish, as if Stone had the place professionally cleaned.

The lavish living room was unoccupied. After a search of this room, he moved to the large kitchen, and then the opulent bedroom. A massive 17th century style four-poster bed dominated the room. On the opposite wall was a huge cabinet with a large, flat-screen TV and a variety of high-end stereo equipment.

Going into the huge walk-in closet, he searched for filing cabinets or computers, but found none. But what he did find was interesting. There was a dressing table with a mirror in the closet. Resting on the table were four women's wigs, all of different colors and length. Going through the drawers, he found an actor's makeup kit. Now he realized why it had been so difficult to find Stone – the woman was a master of disguise.

The bottom drawer was locked but he got it open. In it was a box of jewelry and cash. Ignoring this, he kept looking. Finding nothing else of interest in the closet, he went back to the bedroom to continue the search.

Chapter 58

Flying at 35,000 feet
Over the Atlantic Ocean

"God, you're good," Frank Reynolds uttered with a grin, as he lay on his back, nude on the jet's bed.

Angel Stone, also naked, was sitting astride him, rocking back on forth, her hands on his chest. Deep in the throes of lovemaking, her only response was a low moan. She was close now, almost there, and she gritted her teeth from the pleasure as she picked up the pace.

They were in the Gulfstream G500's small bedroom at the rear of the jet. The only sounds were the low-pitched whistle of the plane's twin engines and the rustling of the sheets. The room smelled of sex and booze. An empty bottle of Chivas rested on the night table next to the bed.

Frank reached out, cupping her breast with one hand while grabbing her hip with the other, urging her to grind faster. He grunted, and from the look on his face, it was clear he was about to climax. It felt exhilarating to have his hands on her and to have him deep inside her.

Her cell phone, which was on the night table, vibrated and she cursed. Without breaking her stride, she reached over and picked up the phone. Looking at the info screen, she cursed again.

She stopped rocking and read the short text message.

Underneath her, Frank groaned. "Damn it, Angel. You can't stop now! Don't do this to me."

All her sexual excitement and desire now gone, she rolled off of him and got up from the bed. Throwing on a robe, she went to the small desk at the rear of the room and powered up her laptop.

"What the hell's going on?" Frank groused.

"We got problems," she replied, as she tapped on the computer's keyboard.

"What is it?"

"Somebody broke into my apartment in Paris."

"How do you know?"

"I programmed my security system to send me a phone text in case there was a breach."

Frank sighed. "Come back to bed. It's probably your cleaning lady. She must have accidentally tripped the alarm."

"No. That's not it. She's been with me for years. She knows the system password. And she's forbidden to go into my study. I've got a motion detector there. That's what triggered the alarm."

"You worry too much, Angel. Now get your ass back in bed so we can finish this."

She looked over at him and gave him an icy stare. "Take a cold shower, Frank. I've got to deal with this."

He grunted and threw a pillow at her. "Bitch!"

She ducked as the pillow flew over her head. "Bastard," she replied. Then she went back to studying her computer screen.

With a few more clicks of the keyboard, she pulled up the program that controlled the apartment's security system. Small boxes opened on the screen, giving her live feeds from the cameras inside. The living room, bedroom, and kitchen were all unoccupied, but there was a man in her study. After closing all the images except the one from the study, she enlarged that one full screen.

She observed as the stranger walked around the study. He was tall, rugged, and good-looking.

By this time Frank had gotten up from the bed and was standing behind her, looking over her shoulder at the computer screen.

"Do you know who that is?" Frank asked.

"Never seen him before," she said.

"Probably a burglar."

"Don't think so, Frank. Look at the way he's going through my books in the bookcases. He's leafing the pages, skimming them – what burglar does that? They'd take my jewelry, electronics, the paintings, and be gone by now. No, this guy's looking for something else."

"You may be right."

"There's one other thing. This guy's a pro. He got past the building's security people and disabled my perimeter alarm system. The only reason I picked him up was because of the motion detector in the study."

"Okay. There's still a lot of hours before we land in Paris. We'll never get there in time to catch him before he leaves. And you can't call the cops. Accept it, Angel. He's going to rob you. You lose some of your rare book collection, your paintings, whatever else. There's nothing you can do about it."

"I can't let him get into my safe room. I've got a lot of my computer files in there. All my info and contacts in the arms business."

Frank placed a hand on her shoulder. "He'll never get in there. It's too secure. And anyway, we've got all the money we'll ever need now. Forget about all that crap in your apartment."

Frank was right, in one way. They did have all that money. But he was wrong too, she knew. All her information was in that safe room. Sure, it was encrypted. But a smart tech guy at the NSA or FBI could decipher it, given enough time. And all that data would give them clues as to her whereabouts, no matter where she hid in the world. No, there was no way she could let anyone get a hold of that information.

Angel watched closely as the man walked around the apartment's study, picking up items and methodically inspecting them. The guy had the look of law enforcement, not a burglar.

Frank squeezed her shoulder. "Turn off the computer. It'll just aggravate you. Let's go back to bed."

Not taking her eyes off the screen, she pushed his hand off her shoulder. "Fuck off, Frank. There's something I *can* do. I don't *want* to, but I may not have a choice."

"What's that?"

Angel went quiet as she thought about all the years of work she'd put into her beautiful Paris apartment. The remodeling, the furniture, the paintings. She loved the place more than anything. Then she thought about the explosive device she'd planted in her safe room, years ago, just in case something like this happened. Her fingers hovered over the keyboard as she recalled the seven digit code that would activate the bomb. If the intruder somehow got in the safe room, she'd have no choice.

"I could blow it up," she whispered, sadness in her voice.

Chapter 59

Paris, France

J.T. Ryan was in Stone's study, going through her extensive collection of rare books. The books filled the floor-to-ceiling bookcases that covered every wall. So far he'd found nothing out of the ordinary, nothing suspicious. Just historic texts, in their original weathered leather bindings. Many were in the original languages – Latin, Greek, old English, French, Arabic. Quite a collection, he realized, and very expensive.

That done, he tackled the ornately carved wood desk at the center of the room. He could tell it was only for decorative purposes, since there was nothing on the desk, save a few cut-glass figurines. Also on the desk was a small, framed photo of Angel and Carter, standing on a sailboat. It was a copy of the photo he'd seen at Carter's place.

In the desk drawers he only found blank, linen-paper stationary. Preprinted at the top of the expensive stationary was the name 'Lila Norris'.

It was clear the woman kept her files some other place. So far, he'd failed to find what he was looking for – a computer, flash drives, a hard drive, or a filing cabinet.

Next he turned his attention to the other pieces of furniture in the room. Turning over the armchairs and side tables, he inspected them carefully, but found nothing.

Since he'd already searched every inch of the apartment, he was worried. What if Stone kept nothing incriminating here? If that were so, he'd be at a dead end. All they could do then would be to put surveillance on the apartment and wait for her to return.

But what if she never did? What if she had several homes and decided not to return to Paris? Pushing that thought aside, he decided to do a more through inspection of the study and its contents.

He started to methodically inspect each of the bookcases. Previously he had pulled out only a few books in each, but this time he removed and examined each of the volumes. It was time-consuming, but he saw no alternative. He found nothing out of the ordinary in the books on three of the walls, but found something intriguing in the bookcase that covered the left wall. Hidden behind a historic Bible was a recessed tab. He pressed the tab and to his surprise a section of the bookcase popped out from the wall. Grabbing that section of the bookcase, he slid it aside.

On the wall where the bookcase had been was a closed metal door, and a retinal-scanner panel next to it.

Excited by his find, he studied the door for a long moment. It had no lock on it, only a pull bar. He couldn't use the lock-pick this time. The only way to gain access was with the retinal scanner. He gave the high-tech mechanism a closer look. It was sophisticated – and tailored for one person, he was sure. Angel Stone.

Standing back from the door a few feet, he stared at the door frame, especially the spots where the lock would fit into the jamb and where the hinges would be. The door, along with the casing around it, were constructed of heavy-gauge metal. Prying the casing out of the concrete wall would take a long time. He couldn't take the chance of being discovered in all that time. And although he didn't want to damage the contents behind the door, he didn't have many options. He'd have to use his gun.

Drawing the Taurus, he fired a single round into the door by where he estimated the lock mechanism to be. The blast echoed throughout the room.

The slug pierced the door, but only partway, making an oval dent. It was going to take several more to break through. Pulling the clip out of the pistol, he counted the remaining bullets. Seven. Reinserting the clip, he aimed the weapon again.

Ryan fired off two more rounds and inspected the damage. He was still a long way from breaking the lock. Aiming again, he squeezed off four more.

Still not enough. He had one round left.

Taking aim, he fired the last shot. By now the door had a deep, ragged puncture where the lock would be. With his ears ringing, he inspected the door, realizing a swift kick could finish the job.

After pocketing the empty pistol, he delivered a powerful front-kick to the door once, then a second and third time, until he heard a metal scraping sound and a loud click.

Grabbing the pull bar, he swung the door open. The interior was dim. But what he could see put a grin on his face.

He spotted a console computer, two laptops, some other electronic gear, and filing cabinets.

But as he was about to step into the small room, he saw a blinding flash and heard a thunderous roar. The explosion blew him off his feet and threw him toward the opposite wall of the study, where he crashed into one of the floor-to-ceiling bookcases.

Dazed from the enormous blast, he slid to the floor.

Ryan felt intense pain all over his body, and then everything went black.

Chapter 60

Flying at 35,000 feet
Over the Atlantic Ocean

Angel Stone turned off her laptop and closed the lid.

She felt sick as she thought about her treasured possessions in the Paris apartment. The Louis XV furniture, the Monet paintings, the 14th century Bible. Some of them destroyed, the others probably damaged. And if not damaged, they were all gone anyway. Gone because she could never go back there.

The explosion would bring in the French police by the hordes. No, she could never go back.

Angel sat quietly at the small desk for a long time. Behind her on the jet's bed lay Frank, sleeping. They had been flying so many hours that the faint drone of the plane's twin-engines was white noise.

Pushing aside the morose thoughts, she instead focused on all the money. Her cut of the billion dollars would buy many more possessions. And better yet, if she ever ran low on cash, which was unlikely, she still had the buried dirty bombs in Savannah. She smiled at the thought. The future was bright. Very bright.

Standing, she walked over to the bed. Frank looked so peaceful as he slept. He was a good man. Not perfect. But who is?

Deciding not to wake him, she headed out of the jet's bedroom. She needed to talk to the pilot. They wouldn't be landing in Paris. They were going to a different destination.

Chapter 61

Atlanta, Georgia

Erin Welch was at her desk in her office, massaging her temples. Her migraine, compounded by the lack of sleep, had been constant for hours.

Her desk phone rang with a distinctive tone, alerting to her to a call from Director Stuart. Picking up the receiver, she said, "Welch here."

"Erin, it's Stuart."

"Yes, sir."

"I'm calling all of the ADICs personally. Since its been four days since Christmas and D.C. was not attacked, we're pretty sure the crisis is over."

"I see. Was the ransom paid, sir?"

"I can't say, one way or the other. But the president feels we're out of the woods."

"Was the bomb ever located, Director?"

"No. DHS is still looking, but no luck so far."

"What's next?"

"The president has signed a new Executive Order. The evacuation of Washington is being lifted. People will be returning to the city."

"What about the investigation?"

"The president and I both feel that Al-Shirak is an Islamic terrorist group. Most likely based in the Middle East. We'll be focusing our efforts on Afghanistan and Yemen."

"Sir, I still have one operative following a lead in France. Although I haven't heard from him in days."

"Okay, Erin. Continue with that. But most of our resources will be deployed to the Middle East."

"Yes, sir."

"There's one other reason I'm calling."

"Sir?"

"All of us – me, you, our FBI staffs across the country, have been working around-the-clock for almost a month on this crisis. I want you to get some rest. Go home tonight and get some sleep. Okay?"

"Thank you."

Erin heard the man disconnect and she replaced the receiver.

She was looking forward to getting some much needed sleep. But in the back of her mind, she wondered if the crisis was really over.

Chapter 62

Paris, France

J.T. Ryan blinked his eyes open. Still disoriented, he felt sore all over, with a dull pain in his back, legs and face.

He was reclining on what looked like a hospital bed, with IV tubes attached to his bruised arm. Loud beeping emanated from the medical equipment in the small, white room. An antiseptic smell filled the air.

Sitting on a chair next to the bed was a black man dressed in a gray suit and tie.

"Where the hell am I," Ryan asked.

"Pitie-Salpetriere Hospital," the man replied.

"Where's that?"

"Paris."

Ryan went to scratch his face, felt the bandages there. "Who are you?"

"I'm Terrance Fox. You don't remember me?"

The detective shook his head.

"I'm with the U.S. Embassy in Paris," the man said.

After a moment, Ryan's memories flooded back. The explosion in Stone's apartment. "I remember you now. The jarhead."

Fox smiled. "Welcome back, snake-eater."

Ryan tried to laugh, but it hurt too much. "How long have I been here?"

"Five days. You're lucky to be alive. The apartment you were in is in bad shape."

"Did you find the computers?"

"No," Fox replied. "They were all blown to bits. The French cops called us when they found you."

Ryan's hopes sank. "What about the files? Were you able to recover anything?"

"The room you were in, the one filled with books, and the small room with all the tech gear, were damaged pretty badly. The *gendarmerie* weren't able to save any of that. However, they did find several priceless paintings in another room."

Ryan shook his head. "Damn. You've got the place under surveillance now?"

"Of course. You think Stone will come back?"

"Maybe. That Monet I saw was probably worth a small fortune."

Fox nodded. "Don't worry. We've got teams watching her place day and night. If she returns, we'll catch her."

"Thanks, Terrance." A grim thought popped in his mind. "What about Washington? Was it bombed? We're way past the deadline."

"Good news on that front. The dirty bomb wasn't set off. The rumor is, but no one is confirming it, that we paid the ransom money."

Ryan grimaced. He was glad D.C. was safe, but angry the terrorist plan had worked.

"I know what you're thinking," Fox said. "But don't worry. We're not going to quit until we find the bastards. FBI Director Stuart has sent teams to Yemen, Libya, and a few other countries."

Ryan gingerly rubbed his bandaged face. "How soon before I can get out of this place?"

"I talked to the doctor before I came in. At least two more days. You'll be going back to the States, right?"

"No," Ryan said. "I'm going someplace else. But I'll need a few things."

"Sure. Like I told you last time we met. Anything you need."

Ryan told him, already formulating a plan in his mind.

Chapter 63

Berlin, Germany

The Lufthansa A300 Airbus touched down with a thump and rolled on the runway, its jet engines powering down. From his window seat, J.T. Ryan gazed at the concourses of Shonefeld Airport and at the gray sky overhead. Although he had been to Germany many times before, this was only his second visit to the capital city.

The Airbus taxied to the gate and stopped. Within minutes, the passengers began disembarking. Ryan grabbed his bag, exited the plane, and made his way into the airport. After showing the Interpol badge he'd obtained from Terrance Fox, he cleared customs.

He found an internet cafe on the airport's main concourse and rented time at one of their computers. From Carter's encrypted book he'd obtained the name 'Dr. H.', with a Berlin address. That, and the fact Ryan had found a German control device at Rahim's mosque, is what brought him to this city.

Now he hoped to find out more about this 'Dr. H.'. Logging on to Google, he input the name and address, but found no listing in the city. He tried several other search engines, and even widened his search to a larger geographical area, but was unable to turn up anything. Odd, he thought, in an age where usually everything was online.

Turning off the computer, he had lunch at an airport restaurant, bought a detailed street map of Berlin, and rented a car.

Getting into the Audi sedan, he opened and studied the map. At first, he didn't find the doctor's street, but eventually located it. The road was in the eastern part of the city, past the Brandenburg Gate.

Using the A100 Autobahn, he drove the Audi into Berlin. It was January 2nd and traffic was light. It looked like most Germans were still not back to work following the New Year's holiday.

Using the Fernsehturm, the television mast that towers over the city as a reference point, he found Strasse Des 17 Juni Avenue minutes later. Taking the wide avenue past the Brandenburg Gate, he crossed into what used to be East Germany. The areas just east of the Berlin Wall had been revitalized. To Ryan it no longer looked like an impoverished communist country, but rather a cosmopolitan metro area with plenty of upscale shops and restaurants.

But as he drove further east the modern facades faded and a gray, monotonous area of the city appeared. Here the buildings were constructed of unadorned block concrete, with graffiti everywhere. The cars on the road were mostly old, dented Trabants.

Finding the correct side street, he parked the Audi and got out. It was a bitter cold day, making him wish for a heavier coat. Zipping his jacket to his neck, he began walking along the narrow street, looking for the right building number. The squat apartment edifices all looked the same – gray and uniform. The only differences were the colors and designs of the graffiti.

At the end of the block he found the address. The stubby building was only two stories, with broken concrete steps leading to a door with peeling paint.

As he walked up the steps, Ryan rehearsed what he would say. Although he was not totally fluent in the language, his German was passable.

Pressing the ringer on the door, he pulled out the Interpol badge and waited. There was no answer so he rang again.

Finally he heard footfalls from behind the door and it opened part way. A thin, elderly man stood there wearing a bathrobe and sleepwear. He had cold eyes, round wire-frame eyeglasses, and a pock-marked face. He had the look of a retired college professor or a scientist.

"*Ja?*" the old man said. *Yes?*

The detective held up his badge, and responded in German. "I'm agent Ryan, with Interpol. I'm conducting an investigation and I need to speak with you."

The elderly man took the badge and inspected it carefully. It wasn't authentic, but Ryan hoped the man wouldn't know the difference.

Returning the badge, the old man said, "What do you want with me?"

"You're Dr. H., aren't you?" Ryan replied.

The man looked suspicious. "*Ja.* I am Doctor Heiler. What does Interpol want from me?"

Trying to put the man at ease, Ryan said, "You're not being investigated. We're hoping you can help us find someone you may know. Can I come in?"

Heiler still seemed wary, but he opened the door fully and stepped aside. "All right. But I am very busy. I do not have much time."

"Of course." Ryan walked into the dimly-lit living room. The furniture was old, worn, and industrial looking. The smell of cabbage hung in the air.

"Have a seat," the doctor said. "I have to turn off my stove. I was cooking when you rang the bell." Turning, the man shuffled into the nearby kitchen.

While the man was gone, Ryan put the badge away. Reaching inside his jacket, he felt the grip of the Glock pistol he'd gotten from Fox. It was reassuring to have the gun.

The doctor shuffled back a moment later and the two men sat across from each other.

"What do you want to know?" Heiler asked, an edge to his voice.

"I'm looking for two people. One, a woman named Angel Stone. And a man, Jim Carter."

Ryan thought he saw the man's jaw clench. "Do you know them, Doctor?"

Heiler shook his head, but said nothing.

"They're Americans," Ryan continued. "And they go by a variety of names. The woman is also known as Lila Norris."

"No, I do not know these people."

Ryan leaned forward in the lumpy armchair. "Are you sure? I found your name and address in Carter's address book."

The old man seemed taken aback. "There must be some mistake. I told you I do not know them."

"Maybe you'll recognize them from a photo." Ryan reached into his pocket and took out his cell phone. Scrolling through the stored images, he stopped at the picture of Stone and Carter standing on a sailboat. He handed the phone to the other man. "Take a look."

Heiler stared at the photo and the detective saw a flash of fear cross the man's face. Quickly handing back the phone, the doctor said, "I am sorry. But I have never seen them."

Ryan was sure the man was lying. But he had to be certain, before doing anything drastic. "Could I trouble you for a glass of water, Doctor?"

The man looked relieved by the question. "Of course." Standing, he walked slowly to the kitchen.

Ryan reached in his pocket and took out a small device with a digital readout. It was a radiation detector he'd obtained from Fox. Turning it on, the device emitted a low crackling sound. As he waved the detector around the room, the sound became louder and the numbers on the readout increased.

Heiler came back into the room a minute later holding a glass. When he saw the detector his face turned white and the glass dropped to the concrete floor, shattering on impact.

Ryan drew the Glock and aimed it at the man's chest. "Sit down, Doctor. We have a lot to talk about."

Stepping over the wet, broken glass, the old man sat down in the shabby armchair. "Who are you?" he asked, his voice shaky.

"I told you, my name is Ryan. I'm looking for Angel Stone and her accomplice Jim Carter. And since you have radioactive materials in this house, my bet is you're working with them also."

"No. That is not true."

"How do you explain the radiation?"

"I am a scientist. I do work with radioactive materials. But for medical purposes only. I have a lab downstairs. I do contract work for hospitals in Berlin."

Ryan wasn't buying it. "Bullshit. Start telling the truth or you'll regret it."

Heiler held his palms up in front of him. "I am not lying. I will show you my lab, the records, my equipment, everything. You will see."

He still didn't believe the old man, but his interest was piqued. The lab might have clues on how the dirty bombs were made. "Okay." He motioned with the gun. "Lead the way – I'll be right behind you. But one false move and you're dead."

Heiler stood, turned, and shuffled slowly past the kitchen and into a hallway. Opening a door, he began descending a staircase. He flicked on a switch and the area below was flooded with light.

Ryan followed him down. When the detective reached the foot of the steps, he glanced around the large but crowded basement. Lit by harsh fluorescent overhead lights, the room was packed with equipment. He saw several bulky desktop computers, metal-working equipment, and other unfamiliar apparatus.

Heiler went to one of the computers and turned it on. Then he opened a computer file and pointed at the screen. "See? This is one of the projects I am working on for Universitatsmedizin Hospital."

Still aiming the gun at the man, Ryan approached the computer and read the screen. Just like Heiler said, the file contained detailed instructions from a medical center in Berlin. Not convinced, Ryan said, "Show me more."

The doctor proceeded to open three more computer files from a variety of German hospitals. After looking through these, Ryan said, "Step aside. And don't try anything – I've got a twitchy trigger finger." While still training the pistol at the man, Ryan scrolled through a long list of documents on the computer.

He saw nothing suspicious at first, but toward the end of the list he spotted a file titled "USA project." Opening this, he read through it quickly. It appeared to be notes Heiler had taken from phone conversations. The transcripts referred several times to 'Angel' and someone named 'Carlos'. There were also references to bombs and large amounts of money.

Satisfied Heiler was part of the conspiracy, Ryan turned toward the doctor. "Just as I thought," he said, a hard edge to his voice. "You're involved. No sense in denying it."

A flash of panic spread across Heiler's face.

Chapter 64

Berlin, Germany

Dr. Heiler stared down the muzzle of the Glock semiautomatic pistol pointed at his face. Heiler's mind raced as he tried to figure a way out of this. His options were limited. He was unarmed and the man holding the gun was much younger, bigger, and stronger. And worse yet, agent Ryan was with Interpol.

The doctor realized he only had one way out. Stall for time.

"That file proves it," Ryan spat out. "You're part of the bombing terrorism conspiracy. Start talking or you're dead."

"Please," Heiler pleaded. "Do not shoot."

"Start talking, old man."

"I am not involved. It is true I know Angel Stone, and we discussed a project that would take place two years from now. But I have nothing to do with her current plan," Heiler lied. "I asked for too much money up front and she said no. She went to someone else to build the bombs."

"I don't believe you. You're responsible for the deaths of thousands of Americans. I swear to God I'll kill you if you don't start talking."

"I am telling the truth!"

"Bullshit!"

Ryan slapped Heiler across the face, hard, and the doctor staggered back, the pain from the blow blinding him momentarily.

"Talk, Doctor!"

Still reeling from the pain, Heiler said, "Please do not hurt me. I cannot tell you anything if I do not know anything!"

"We'll see about that. Now move. We're going back upstairs."

Ryan motioned with his gun and Heiler shuffled up the steps, with the other man close behind.

When they reached the first floor hallway, Ryan asked, "Where's the bathroom?"

"Over there," Heiler responded, perplexed as to why the man was asking.

"Lead the way, Doctor."

Heiler opened the bathroom door and stepped inside.

The Interpol man came in behind him and while still pointing the pistol at him, went to the cast-iron tub, closed the drain and turned on the cold-water faucet.

Confused, Heiler asked, "What are you doing?"

"You'll see."

The two men stared at each other during the minutes it took for the tub to fill. Once it was full, Ryan motioned with the gun. "Get in, Doctor."

"Why?"

"Shut up and get in the tub!"

Heiler glanced at his watch, saw only minutes had passed since he'd looked last. Still too soon. Realizing he had no choice but to comply, he approached the bathtub and carefully sat on the edge. Then he maneuvered one foot and then the other inside the tub. The water was icy cold, making him shiver.

"Hurry up, old man. I don't have all day."

Using the edges of the tub for support, Heiler slowly lowered himself into the frigid water, his now sopping-wet sleepwear weighing him down. With only his head and hands above the water line, he stared up at the other man. A stab of fear settled in the pit of his stomach.

"Ready to talk now, Doctor?"

"I told you before, I do not know anything."

Suddenly Ryan pushed down on his head and Heiler felt himself go under the water.

Fighting back panic from the fear of drowning, Heiler struggled to raise his head. But Ryan was too strong.

The doctor's eyes were wide open, but all he could see was a blurry image of the man above him. Holding his breath, Heiler's lungs felt like they were going to burst. Seconds passed. Then a full minute. Knowing he would drown in a matter of seconds, he began to nod his head furiously.

Ryan let go and the doctor jerked his head out of the icy water. Gasping, he took in huge mouthfuls of air.

"Ready to talk now?" Ryan said, menace in his voice.

"*Ja! Ja!*" Heiler sputtered in reply.

"Good. Now talk."

"I know Angel Stone ..." Heiler said, still breathing heavy. "And I know the other man in the picture. The man you called Carter. His real name is Frank Reynolds."

"What's your involvement with them?"

"I manufactured the dirty bombs."

"Where?"

"In my lab downstairs."

"She paid you?"

"*Ja.* She paid me money up front. Then a cut of the ransom."

"Okay, Heiler. Now we're getting somewhere. How does this Al-Shirak group figure into all this? Where are they based?"

"I do not know."

"What's the Islamic connection?"

"I do not know. I only dealt with Angel. It was her plan."

"Who else is involved?"

"Frank Reynolds."

"Angel and Frank live in France, right?"

"Yes, that is correct. Paris. We communicated by computer and phone."

"I saw in the file on your computer someone named Carlos. Who is he?"

"Carlos Montoya."

"What does he do, Heiler?"

"He handles the money transfers. The banking side of the operation."

"Where is he?"

"Spain."

"Where in Spain?"

"Madrid."

"Tell me about the bombs, Doctor."

Heiler took another gulp of air. "As I said, I built them here. And shipped them through dummy company cut-outs, to the U.S."

"How many did you build?"

"Eight in total."

Ryan looked confused. "You're sure it was eight?"

"Of course."

"But only four were detonated. Where are the rest?"

"I do not know. I shipped the first bomb to Hawaii, and the seven others to the port of Savannah, in Georgia. I shipped them and I got my money."

Ryan was quiet for a moment.

"Can I get out of the tub?" Heiler pleaded. "I am freezing in here."

"Shut up and let me think."

Heiler glanced at his watch. They should have been here by now. But not taking any chances, he said, "If you let me go, I will give you part of the money. I will give you ten million dollars."

"Shut up."

"Twenty million dollars. Please! I cannot go to prison. I am too old to go to prison!"

"Forget it."

"Fifty million. That is half of what I received. I'm begging you."

"Shut up. There's no way I'm letting you go. You're a mass murderer. And you're going to pay for that."

Just then Heiler heard a cracking noise from another part of the house.

With a sigh of relief, he knew they were here.

Chapter 65

Berlin, Germany

J.T. Ryan froze as soon as he heard the noise.

He heard it again, a scraping noise from outside the bathroom. He aimed the Glock at Heiler, who was still inside the filled tub. "What's that noise?" Ryan whispered.

The doctor said nothing, but a smile spread on his face.

"You bastard," Ryan said, figuring it out. "You set off a silent alarm when we were on the computer downstairs."

The fear was gone from Heiler's face. "It is your turn now, Ryan."

"Who is it?"

"My men."

"How many?"

The doctor laughed. "That is for you to find out. But they are former *stasi*, so you are in deep trouble."

Ryan knew *stasi* were the secret police of the former East Germany. After reunification, many of them became criminals. Mob enforcers and killers for hire. Just then he heard a man's voice from outside the room.

"*Dr. Heiler, es Josef. Geht's dir gut?*" the man said. *It's Josef. Are you okay, Dr. Heiler?*

Before Ryan could stop him, the doctor screamed out, "The intruder is in here! He has a gun!"

Ryan slashed the Glock across the doctor's face, knocking him unconscious. The man's head came to rest on the edge of the tub and a trickle of blood oozed from his nostrils. The tub water began to turn pink.

Turning toward the bathroom's closed door, the detective trained the weapon in front of him and listened closely at the approaching footfalls.

Taking a guess where the *stasi* man would be, Ryan fired two shots, one high and one low. The rounds penetrated the wooden door, sending splinters across the room. He heard the roar of the gun and a cry for help.

But there was no return fire – it was clear Heiler's men didn't want to shoot back just yet, probably afraid they would hit their boss by mistake. Ryan also knew he couldn't stay in the bathroom forever. There was no window in the room and the only way out was right in front of him.

Crouching down, he approached the door, slowly turned the knob, and eased it open.

A large man with a crew cut was slumped along the opposite wall of the corridor, his leg bleeding. He was holding a large revolver with both hands.

Ryan fired off two more rounds, the ejected spent shells clattering on the concrete floor. The large man dropped the revolver and clutched his chest.

Hearing two more voices down the hall, the detective strained to hear them, as he continued to crouch inside the bathroom by the door. The two men were not in his line of sight, but it was clear they were arguing about what to do next.

"Dr. Heiler," one of the voices called out, "it's Josef. Are you hurt?"

Still crouching, Ryan quickly rolled himself out of the room and across the hallway. Using the large man's corpse as a shield, he fired four more shots in the direction of the men.

"*Sheibe! Ich bin treffen!*" one of them yelled. *Fuck! I'm hit!*

This time there was a volley of return fire, the multiple rounds striking the wall above Ryan, chunks of plaster spraying down on him. Other shots thumped into the dead body.

Ryan flattened himself even more, so that all he could see was the corpse in front of him. Aiming wildly, he squeezed off three more shots.

He heard another man shout out in pain, and then heard a shuffling noise. Moments later there was the sound of a door opening and slamming shut.

Cautiously, he peeked over the dead body. At the end of the hall he saw a bleeding man slumped on the floor. Getting up, he trained the gun in front of him and crept down the corridor. The man was unmoving so he checked for a pulse. He was dead.

Doing a quick search of the living room and kitchen, Ryan found no one else. The third *stasi* guy must have fled.

Going back to the bathroom, he looked inside. Heiler's limp body was still in the filled tub, but his head had slipped off the ledge and was now underwater.

Rushing over, he dragged the doctor's inert body out of the tub, the sodden sleepwear splashing water on the floor. Once again he checked for a pulse and realized the man had drowned.

"Damn it!" he cursed. "I wasn't done with you!"

Knowing he'd get no more information from Heiler, Ryan left the room and headed to the basement. He'd find a flash drive and copy the doctor's computer records. But before he descended the stairs, he heard the high-low wail of police sirens nearby.

Racing back to the living room, he peered out the window. He saw flashing blue lights and three German police cars in front of the building.

Not good, he knew. Not good at all. He was in a foreign country, with fake ID, and three dead bodies in the house. Sprinting to the back door, he glanced out its small window. There was another police car in the alley, with two cops climbing out.

Their weapons drawn, the cops approached the door.

Ryan placed the Glock on the floor, opened the door slowly, and raised his hands over his head.

Chapter 66

Atlanta, Georgia

Erin Welch was asleep in her Buckhead townhome when her cell phone on the nightstand rang, waking her up.

Groggily, she picked up the phone and looked at the info screen. It read Berlin Correctional Facility. Sitting up on the bed, she took the call. "Who is this?"

"It's me, Ryan."

"J.T.? What are you doing in Berlin? Last time we spoke you were in Paris."

"It's a long story. Listen, Erin, I've been arrested and I need your help."

"Arrested? For what?"

"Manslaughter."

"What the hell? J.T., what have you gotten yourself into?"

"I was involved in a shootout. Three people are dead. One of them was a Dr. Heiler, one of the conspirators in the American bombing plot."

Wide awake now, Erin turned on the bedside lamp. "How was this Heiler involved?"

"He manufactured the bombs."

"Jesus. He worked with Angel Stone?"

"Yeah. Looks like she's the ringleader."

"Good detective work, J.T. What about the Islamic connection? Did you find where Al-Shirak is located?"

"I'm afraid not. Heiler didn't know about that part of it."

"Okay. We've got a dozen FBI teams combing the Middle East. We'll find them soon enough."

"Erin, any news on Stone's whereabouts?"

"No, not yet."

"I got one good lead from Heiler. But I need to get out of jail to follow up on it. You've got to call the State Department and help me get out of here. You've got to convince the Berlin District Attorney to drop the charges."

"As soon as we hang up, I'll start to work on it."

"Thanks, Erin. When the cops came to Heiler's place, they sealed the area as a crime scene. In the basement are the doctor's computer files. There's info there that will help get me released and help us catch Stone."

"Okay, I got it."

"There's one more piece of information I got from the doctor. And it's very bad news."

Erin gripped the phone tighter, steeling herself for what the man was going to say. "Go ahead."

"Heiler built and shipped eight dirty bombs." He paused. "Only four were detonated. So there's still four out there, somewhere."

Erin got a sick feeling in the pit of her stomach. The crisis wasn't over. Not by a long shot.

"Okay, J.T. I hear you. I'll get this information to the Director. And I'll start to work right now to get you out of jail. Hang in there."

She turned off the call and glanced at the glowing digits of the clock on her nightstand. It was 4:32 a.m.

Standing, she padded to the bathroom for a quick shower. Afterwards she dressed, grabbed her briefcase, and headed out.

***

An hour later Erin was in her FBI office, talking on the phone with Director Stuart.

That done, she began looking up her contacts at the U.S. State Department. In her years at the FBI, and at the Secret Service before that, she'd worked with several people at State, some of them high-level. Picking up the receiver, she began dialing.

Lee Gimenez

Chapter 67

Annotto Bay, Jamaica

"What do you think of it?" Frank Reynolds asked, turning to face Angel Stone.

Angel glanced out from the second story balcony of the oceanfront estate. Just below was an immense, carefully manicured lawn leading to a wide, very private beach. A light surf was lapping the white sand beach, providing a soothing, almost hypnotic sound. The scent of gardenias filled the air. To Angel, the scenic property seemed ideal.

It was a crystal-clear day, the Caribbean sun shining brightly. Although it was mid-January, the temperature was a perfect 72 degrees.

The estate consisted of a luxurious main house, where they were now, and a modest guest house, both sitting on ten acres in a remote area of Jamaica. The place featured a large swimming pool and tennis courts. The estate also had its own dock. Tethered to the dock was their dinghy, and anchored just beyond in the sheltered cove was Angel's sailboat.

"I like it, Frank," she replied with a smile.

"The whole ten acres," Frank said, "is bordered by an 8 foot wall. The previous owner had extensive security. Surveillance cameras, motion sensors, you name it. And the nearest neighbor is miles away."

"What's the property going for?"

"Six million. But that's the best part. The realtor told me it's in foreclosure. He said we can get it for a lot less."

"You used an alias when dealing with the realtor?" she asked.

"Of course. To him we're Mr. and Mrs. Tobias."

Angel scanned the extensive, secluded property again. "I see there's a guest house over there. If we buy it, you'll live there?"

Frank looked disappointed. "I was hoping we could both live here in the main house."

She gave him a hard stare. "Forget it, Frank. You can visit anytime, friends with benefits and all that. But I need my privacy. Those are the ground rules. Take it or leave it."

Grudgingly, he nodded. "Okay."

A soft breeze blew, rustling the fronds of the nearby palm trees. She inhaled, took in the invigorating scent of the crisp sea air. They'd scouted a lot of homes in Jamaica, but only this place felt perfect.

"Call the realtor, Frank. Buy it."

Chapter 68

Madrid, Spain

The Iberia Airlines flight from Berlin to Madrid had been uneventful, something J.T. Ryan appreciated. After spending five days in the German jail, he was glad to be a free man, enjoying the simple pleasure of an uninterrupted nap.

Ryan's flight had just landed at Barajas International Airport, and after collecting his bag, he rented a SEAT coupe and stowed his gear in the trunk of the car.

It was a cold, rainy day and once in the car he cranked up the heater.

Pulling out his cell phone, he dialed Erin Welch's number. The woman answered on the second ring.

"It's Ryan," he said. "I wanted to thank you again for getting me out of jail. That Berlin District Attorney was a bastard."

He heard Erin chuckle. "Glad I could help. Where are you now?"

"Just landed. Listen, were you able to find anything on Carlos Montoya?"

"Yeah, J.T. But I found too much information. That's a pretty common name there. I found twenty-three Carlos Montoyas in Madrid."

"Great," he replied sarcastically.

"I'll text you the addresses."

"Thanks, Erin. By the way, any progress on finding Stone?"

"Maybe. One of our informants said he spotted her in Libya. But that hasn't been confirmed. In any case, Director Stuart is sending more teams to the Middle East. All the D.C. people are convinced she's there somewhere."

"Okay. I got the money you wired me, but I need a couple of other things."

"Like what?"

"A weapon."

"No can do, J.T. I pulled a lot of strings to get you out of that Berlin jail. I can't have you shooting up half of Madrid too."

The inside of the car had warmed up and he turned down the heater. "All right. I'll figure it out."

"I'm sure you will. You're a resourceful guy."

Ryan heard her disconnect and he put the phone away. Then he input the address of the hotel Erin had booked for him in the car's Nav system, and studied the map on the screen. He had been to Madrid many times and estimated he'd be there in an hour.

***

The small, quaint hotel was located on Calle de Segovia, not far from the Plaza Mayor in the center of Old Madrid. After checking in, Ryan feasted on seafood *paella* in the hotel's restaurant.

Exhausted from the fitful sleep he'd gotten in jail, he went to his room, stretched out on the bed, and slept for the next twelve hours.

When he awoke the next morning, he showered, shaved, and changed into clean clothes. Then he read through the text message from Erin, with its long list of Montoyas. Doing internet searches on each, he ruled out some by age and profession and narrowed the list to five good possibilities.

Putting on a jacket, he headed out of the hotel room. He needed to take care of a couple of things before paying the five men a visit.

An hour later he parked the SEAT in front of a seedy-looking pawn shop, climbed out, and locked the car. The pawn shop was located in Vallecas, one of the city's poorest neighborhoods. Although it was only ten a.m., hookers were already on the streets, along with furtive, shabbily-dressed men, probably dealing dope. Cigarette butts and empty bottles littered the sidewalk, and the area stank of stale beer and urine.

Ignoring the come-on from a one of the painted ladies sporting short-shorts, fishnet stockings, and a see-through blouse, he pressed the buzzer at the door of the shop. The place had burglar bars on the windows and door and had probably seen its share of robberies. A security camera was located by the door.

Ryan heard the barred door click open, and he stepped inside.

The pawn shop was large and packed with goods. Floor-to-ceiling racks by the walls were stuffed with all types of household items. Stacked on plywood shelves in the center of the place were worn TVs, radios, stereos, and computers. At the back of the store was a glass case displaying jewelry on the left and handguns on the right. Standing behind the counter was a tall, thin man. He had slicked-back hair and wore a hip holster with a semi-automatic. It was clear the man was used to trouble.

Ryan approached the counter and perused the weapons displayed in the case.

"Puedo ayudarte?" the thin man asked in Castilian Spanish. *Can I help you?*

"Si, necesito una pistola," Ryan replied. *Yes, I need a pistol.*

"Do you have a weapons permit?" the thin man asked.

"No, I don't."

The man frowned. "Sorry. There's a city ordinance. I can't sell it to you without a permit."

Ryan pulled out his wallet and took out a large denomination bill. He placed it on the counter. "How much does a permit cost?"

The frown didn't leave the man's face. "More than that."

The detective pulled another bill and laid it on top of the other.

"That should do it," the thin man said with a crooked smile. "My name's Jorge, by the way. What kind of gun were you looking for?"

"One that works."

Ryan stared at the pistols on display. It was a wide assortment of Glocks, Rugers, Sig Sauers and Heckler & Kochs, most of them worn-looking. Knowing semi-automatics were prone to jam unless well-kept, he pointed to a Smith & Wesson revolver. "That one doesn't look bad."

Jorge unlocked the glass cabinet, took out the S & W and handed it to Ryan.

Ryan inspected the .38 caliber closely. It had a two-inch barrel and a chrome finish. He opened the empty cylinder and twirled it around. He closed the cylinder and dry-fired the pistol several times. "How much?"

Jorge mentioned a large sum.

Ryan shook his head. "Too much."

The thin man lowered the amount.

"Throw in a box of shells," Ryan said, "and you've got a deal."

Jorge smiled widely. "No problem."

"Good. I'll take it then."

***

Six hours later Ryan was driving on the Gran Via headed east. He'd already visited four of the Montoyas on the list, and for a variety of reasons ruled them out. The fifth Carlos Montoya lived near the Parque del Retiro, the city's large park on the east side. Ryan was now wearing a black uniform he'd purchased earlier, which closely resembled what FedEx delivery people wore.

He found Calle de Alfonso XII soon after, turned right and located the apartment building three blocks south. It was as an exclusive area of Madrid. The upscale residential towers overlooked the grassy, wooded park.

After parking the SEAT, he strode into the building's lobby and took the elevator to the right floor. Walking down the corridor, he saw two burly men carrying furniture out of one of the apartments. Approaching the open door, he noticed it was the right unit. He looked inside and saw stacks of moving boxes in the living room.

Ryan pressed the buzzer and waited by the door. Moments later a good-looking woman with dark hair and olive skin approached from the rear of the home.

"*Eres de la compania de mudar?*" she asked. *Are you with the moving company?*

"*No, senora, tengo un paquete para el Senor Montoya,*" Ryan replied, holding up a FedEx package. *No ma'am, I have a package for Mr. Montoya.*

"You just missed him," she said. "He had to go to the bank. He'll be back in an hour."

"I see. Does he work at a bank?"

Yes. Banco Nacional."

Realizing this was probably the right Montoya, he said, "I've got other deliveries to make, but I'll come back in an hour."

"You can leave it with me," the woman said.

"I'm sorry, but he has to sign for it." Ryan motioned to the moving boxes in the room. "You're moving?"

"Yes!" she replied with a bright smile. "We bought a new place. Much bigger."

He returned the smile. "How nice for you, *senora*. I'll stop by later."

Turning around, he walked away, passing the moving men on the corridor, obviously back to remove more of the furniture.

Ryan made his way to the street and climbed into his parked car. He had a clear view of the building's entrance, but since he didn't know what Montoya looked like, he focused instead on the moving truck parked by the entrance. He was sure Montoya would look into the truck's open cargo doors, curious how the move was going.

Just as he thought, a man dressed in a dark, three-piece suit walked up to the truck one and a half hours later. The dark-complexioned man had a short beard.

While the bearded man was speaking to the truck driver, the moving men came out of the building and closed the truck's cargo doors. The truck drove off and the bearded man went into the building.

Wasting no time, Ryan picked up the FedEx package and exited the car. Sprinting into the building, he skipped the elevator and raced up the stairs.

Moments later he pressed the buzzer at Montoya's apartment.

Once again the woman answered the door. *"Eres tu. Voy a buscar mi esposo,"* she said. *Oh, it's you. I'll go get my husband.*

Ryan stepped inside the now almost empty apartment and closed the door behind him.

The bearded man he'd seen go in the building came into the foyer a moment later. He'd shed his coat and tie, and his sleeves were rolled at the cuffs. *"Soy Carlos Montoya. Tienes un paquete para mi?"* he asked. *I'm Carlos Montoya. You have a package for me?*

"Si," Ryan replied, dropping the package to the floor and pulling out the Smith & Wesson. Pointing the revolver at the man's chest, he said, "Tell me what I want to know and you and your wife live. Don't talk and you both die."

Montoya's face turned white. "Who are you? What do you want?"

"Information. I'm looking for Angel Stone."

The bearded man froze when he heard Stone's name.

Just then the man's wife returned to the room. Seeing the gun, she halted in mid-stride. "I'm calling the police!" she shrieked.

Montoya held up a hand. "Don't Maria."

"What's going on, Carlos?" she said. "Who is this man?"

"It's business," Montoya replied.

"Business? What are you talking about?"

Montoya rubbed his beard with one hand. "Shut up, Maria. Let me think."

Ryan spotted a door in the apartment's foyer. Still training the gun on the two people, he walked to the door and opened it. It was a large coat closet.

Pointing to the woman, he said, "You. Get in the closet. And keep your mouth shut or your husband dies."

Her eyes went wide, but she complied, walking into the closet. The detective closed the door behind her and faced Carlos Montoya. "Like I said before. You tell me everything I want to know about Angel Stone and I'll let you and your wife live."

"Who are you?"

"I'm your worst nightmare, Montoya, if you don't talk."

"What do you want to know?"

"Where is she? Where is Angel Stone?"

"I don't know."

Ryan took a step towards the other man. "Talk, damn it!"

"It's true, I know Stone. I did some banking business for her, but I don't know that much about her."

"You lie," Ryan stated, anger in his voice. "I know all about you. You're the money man in the U.S. terrorist bombings. I know about you, and Stone, and Heiler."

A shocked expression crossed Montoya's face. After a moment his shoulders sagged.

"I already found Heiler," Ryan said. "He's dead. And you'll be next if you don't tell me where she is."

"If I talk you won't hurt me or my wife?"

"That's right."

"Okay," Montoya said. "She lives in Paris. She has an apartment on St. Michel boulevard. I've got the address – I'll go get it."

"Forget it. I've already been there. Where else could she be?"

"I don't know."

Ryan pressed the revolver's barrel to the man's temple. "Talk or you die. And your wife is next."

Montoya's face showed raw terror. Beads of perspiration formed on his forehead and his hands began to shake.

Ryan pulled back the trigger and cocked the gun.

"She ... owns a sailboat," Montoya stammered, "... she docks it in Jamaica ... but I don't know if she's there ..."

The detective remembered the picture of Stone and Reynolds standing on a sailboat. "Stone owns a house there?"

"No, not that I know of. When she goes down there she stays in hotels or rents apartments."

Ryan un-cocked the S & W and pulled it away from the man's head. With his free hand, Ryan took out his cell phone, turned it on, and scrolled through the photos stored there. Finding the image of the sailboat, he showed it to Montoya. "Is this it?"

"Yes, that's the boat. She named it *Liberte.*"

The name on the boat had been so small on the photo that up until now Ryan didn't know what it was. "Okay. Who's the man in the photo?"

"His name is Frank Reynolds. He's one of the partners in the operation."

That confirmed what Heiler had said, reinforcing the detective's feeling that Montoya was telling the truth. "How about the dirty bombs. How many were there?"

"I don't know," Montoya replied. "I only handled the money side."

"So you re-routed the wire transfer you received from the U.S. government?"

"Yes."

"To where?"

"I set up dozens of accounts, all over the world. They were in the name of dummy corporations."

"How about Stone? Where's her money now?"

Montoya shrugged. "Who knows. I wired her share to one of her numbered accounts in Switzerland. But she's a smart woman. I'm sure it's in some other bank by now."

"The U.S. paid one billion dollars. How was the money split?"

"I got $100 million, as did Heiler and Reynolds. There was also $100 million to another person, but I don't know who that was. It was a numbered account. Then Angel got the balance of the ransom."

"So she got $600 million?"

"That's right."

Ryan wondered who the mystery recipient was. Could that have been the Islamic connection? "Tell me more about this mystery person."

"I don't know any more than I told you. Angel told me to set up that numbered account and deposit $100 million into it."

"Who controlled that bank account?"

"Angel did."

"All right. How does the Al-Shirak group fit into this? Who are they? Where are they located?"

Montoya shook his head. "I never knew. Angel handled that part of it."

Ryan cocked the revolver again and pressed the gun to the man's forehead.

The banker's hands began to shake. "I told you! I don't know! Angel compartmentalized the whole operation. I only know the details of my part."

Satisfied the man was telling the truth, Ryan un-cocked the S & W and lowered it. "How did you communicate with Stone?"

"By e-mail and by cell phone."

"The FBI wasn't able to trace the ransom text messages. Why is that?"

"We used burner phones. Special ones I programmed that are untraceable."

Ryan nodded. "I want you to call Stone right now. I have to find out where she is."

Montoya shook his head. "It won't work. I've tried to get a hold of her for over a week, but the numbers have been disconnected."

The detective pondered this. Maybe the explosion at Stone's apartment had spooked her. "How do you communicate with her now?"

"I don't. Once the money was split, we all went our separate ways."

"So why have you been trying to call her?"

"I'm moving to a new house. I wanted to let Angel know. I've made a lot of money dealing with her and I figured she'd plan some other operation in the future."

Ryan motioned with the gun. "Call her right now."

The banker shrugged. "*Si*. But it won't do any good." He reached into his pocket, pulled out a cell phone and punched in a number.

Ryan leaned in close to the man, wanting to hear Stone when she picked up. But all he heard was a computerized voice saying the number had been disconnected.

"Try the other numbers, Montoya."

The banker did as he was told, calling them all with the same result.

Taking the cell phone from the other man, the detective put it in his own pocket. Maybe the FBI could gather some info from the device.

A frightened look crossed Montoya's face. "What happens now?"

"Don't worry. I told you I wouldn't hurt you or your wife. And I'm a man of my word."

"You'll let us go?"

"No. You're an accomplice in terrorist acts. You helped kill thousands of people. No, I'm not going to let you go. I'm going to turn you over to the local authorities. You'll pay for your crimes."

"Let me go and I'll give you all the money I have left. Over ninety million!"

"Forget it, Montoya." Ryan pointed with the gun. "Now get in the closet with your wife."

"Please!"

"Get in there before I change my mind and shoot you, you son-of-a-bitch."

The banker's shoulders slumped and he stepped over to the closet door, opened it and got in the small room.

Ryan pulled out his cell phone and punched in Erin Welch's number. The woman answered on the third ring.

"It's Ryan," he said. "I need some help."

"Who did you shoot now?" she asked.

Ryan chuckled. "Nobody. Listen, I caught Carlos Montoya. The money man in the conspiracy. I questioned him and I'm holding him for the local cops."

"That's good news," she replied, sounding relieved.

"I need you to call the Madrid police to come pick-up this piece of garbage." He read off Montoya's address. "Then you can arrange to have him extradited to the U.S."

"I'll make the call as soon as we hang up."

"There's something else, Erin. Apparently Stone has cut off communication with Montoya. I think we spooked her when I found her Paris apartment. I'll send you his cell phone – maybe one of your tech geeks can trace her from it."

"Good thinking, J.T. Were you able to find out where Al-Shirak is located?"

"Nothing on Al-Shirak. Looks like Stone handled the Islamic side of the operation on her own. But I found out that besides Stone, Heiler, Montoya and Reynolds, there was a fifth person involved."

"Who is it?"

"Montoya didn't know. But whoever it is, they got $100 million as their cut of the ransom money."

"What about Stone? Any luck on finding out where she is now?"

"I got a lead on that. I'll be going there next."

"Where's that, J.T.?"

"Jamaica."

Chapter 69

Annotto Bay, Jamaica

Frank Reynolds was driving the Land Rover slowly over the rutted, winding road. He was careful not to hit the tree branches that grew wildly over the remote, rural road. The canopy of trees overhead was so thick that although it was a sunny day, he needed the headlights to show the way.

Frank had closed on the estate earlier that day, and was on his way over there now to make sure the property's security system was working. Angel Stone had remained back at the hotel, lounging by the pool. It still stung that she hadn't wanted to share the estate's main house with him, but he was an optimist. Over time, he hoped, she would come around.

Putting those thoughts aside, he focused on the task at hand.

He slowed the Land Rover even more and put it in 4-wheel drive mode as it navigated over a particularly rough part of the road. It had rained heavily in Jamaica yesterday, and this stretch was a boggy mess, the gravel/mud combination almost completely washed out. The vehicle bounced around roughly for the next few minutes.

Then the forest area gave way to lighter vegetation and eventually to a clearing, as the road paralleled the sea. To his left, beyond the wide, sandy beach, the Caribbean was visible, its aquamarine water sparkling in the bright sun.

There were no other cars, or people, or boats that he could see. In the distance he spotted the outline of the estate's walls, a long white ribbon that seemed to go on for miles.

He turned off the vehicle's air conditioner and buzzed down the driver's window. The crisp scent of sea air filled the cabin and he relished the smell. It felt good to be here, to be alive, to be rich. He'd never had this much money. More than enough to last him a lifetime. Once again he realized how lucky he'd been to meet Angel all those years ago.

The estate's walls grew in size and soon he was driving alongside them. The 8 foot walls were topped by razor wire.

Moments later he came upon the imposing metal gate at the entrance. Stopping at the closed gate, he climbed out of the Land Rover and went to the wall-mounted keypad. He input the code the realtor had given him, and the gate began to open inward, the gears emitting a grinding noise.

Getting back in the SUV, he drove through onto a paved road, glancing in the rearview mirror to make sure the gate closed. The road wound around the lush grounds. Palm, mango, and banana trees dotted the property, along with several gardens with fountains. Passing the tennis courts and the large swimming pool, he eventually arrived at the semi-circular driveway that fronted the impressive, three-story home. The architecture was Mediterranean, and its palace-like grandeur reminded Frank of an Italian villa.

Leaving the SUV in the driveway, he strode up the marble front steps and opened the ornate front door using the key the realtor had given him. Entering the wide foyer, he input another code into the security system's keypad, turning off the system.

The marble-floor foyer led to an elaborate, arched entryway which opened up to one of the home's main living areas. Fully outfitted with imported Italian furniture, it was clear to Frank that the previous owner had spared no expense.

He went through the whole main house, all twenty-five rooms, turning on the lights and systematically searching every room. As he expected, there was no one there. That done, he went to the security room, located on the first level by the kitchen.

Unlike the rest of the house, the security room had none of the luxury so evident elsewhere. In the room was a functional metal desk, fronted by long row of TV monitors, their screens dark.

Sitting behind the desk, he pressed buttons on the console and the TV screens flickered to life. Each screen showed a different exterior part of the property. Next he checked on the motion detectors and the electrified fence that topped the high walls. All the security systems were functioning properly.

Later he would walk the whole perimeter of the estate to make sure there were no dead zones. But for now he was satisfied the security of the house was adequate. And since he'd be living in the guest quarters, he planned to build a duplicate security room there as well.

Striding out of the room, he walked the long length of the house to the large den at the rear. The den's back wall was constructed of floor-to-ceiling glass panels, allowing a breathtaking view of the gardens, the back yard, and the beach.

Opening the French doors, he stepped onto the covered patio, where he spotted Angel's sailboat, anchored in the cove. The sixty-foot boat was a beauty. And now that he and Angel lived full time in the Caribbean, they'd be able to sail at will, with nothing but time on their hands.

It was perfect, he mused.

Then he saw the modest guest house, which was set a hundred yards to his right, behind a row of palm trees. Where he would be living.

Well, maybe it wasn't perfect. But he'd still be with Angel, at least part of the time.

And when he couldn't be with her, he'd have other things to console him. Frank had been to Jamaica enough times to know there were many exotic, beautiful women on the island. Sometimes he would have to pay for the company, but so what, he was rich.

Then he turned around and began to walk back through the house.

Time to pick up Angel, and bring her home.

Chapter 70

Kingston, Jamaica

J.T. Ryan parked the rented Jeep Wrangler in the marina's visitors lot and climbed out.

It was a sunny day and he relished the warmth, a nice contrast to the cold, dreary weather he'd left in Berlin and Madrid.

Striding to the long dock, he scanned the numerous boats docked there. They were mostly powerboats, but he spotted three sailboats, although they appeared to be smaller than the *Liberte*.

Ryan had already visited a dozen marinas in Jamaica's capital city, all with no success. From her end, Erin Welch had also tried locating the sailboat, but found no record of it. Knowing Stone's history of deception, Ryan figured she had changed the name of the boat frequently to elude authorities.

He walked to the pink-and-green painted marina office and went inside. Approaching the counter, he pulled out several photos from his jacket pocket.

A black man was behind the counter and he flashed a wide, friendly smile. "Can I help you, mon?" the man said in the typical sing-song voice common on the islands.

"I hope so," Ryan replied, handing the photos to the other man. "I'm looking for some friends of mine. They keep their boat, the *Liberte*, in a marina around here, I just don't know which one."

The black man scanned the two photos. One of them was of Stone and Reynolds standing on the sailboat, and the other of Stone by herself. "Naw, mon. They don't dock here." The man tapped the picture of Stone. "Pretty girl. I'd remember her."

"The *Liberte* is a big boat. Sixty feet or so. Any idea where they might keep it?"

The other man thought about this a moment. "Are your friends Americans?"

"Yes, they are."

"Try Montego Bay or Ocho Rios, on the north side of the island. A lot of Americans go there, mon."

Ryan pulled a twenty dollar bill from his pocket and placed it on the counter. "I appreciate your help, friend."

The man flashed another bright smile. "No problem, mon." He handed back the photos and took the money.

Turning, Ryan walked out of the office and climbed back in the Jeep. Spreading out a map of Jamaica on the passenger seat, he studied the layout of the island. He'd try Montego Bay first, which he estimated was a six hour drive.

Chapter 71

Annotto Bay, Jamaica

Frank Reynolds was reclining on a lounge chair on the deck of Angel's sailboat, sipping his fifth Corona. The boat was tied up at the estate's dock and it rocked slightly from the small waves lapping the cove. The sun was beginning to set, casting a warm orange glow over the area. It's so peaceful here, he thought, taking another pull of beer. The murmur of the sea was lulling him to sleep.

Startled by a slamming noise, he glanced up at the brightly-lit main house just beyond the sandy beach. He saw Angel come out of the house and march to the dock.

Stopping in front of the boat, she crossed her arms in front of her. She was wearing shorts, a bikini top, and a hard look on her face. "What are you doing, Frank?"

He grinned, took another sip of Corona. "What does it look like I'm doing?"

Angel's face turned red. "What did I tell you to do hours ago?"

Frank tried to think, the beer buzz clouding his thoughts. "I don't remember."

"I told you to paint over the boat's name!" she spat out. "And put on the new name. It's important!"

"Oh, yeah ... I remember now." He took another swallow. "I thought I'd wait and do that tomorrow —"

"Frank, when I tell you to do something, you do it. Understood?"

"All right."

"All right what?"

"All right, I'll do it."

"Good. Now go take a cold shower and sober up. Then paint the goddamn boat!" Angel turned and marched back quickly to the house.

Shaking his head slowly, Frank placed the bottle of beer on the deck. Then he got up from the lounge chair and proceeded to the sailboat's head.

Damn, he thought, Angel could be such a cold-hearted bitch sometimes.

Chapter 72

Montego Bay, Jamaica

J.T. Ryan pulled into the seaside resort city of Montego Bay at ten in the evening.

Tired from the drive, he spotted a Marriott Hotel, checked in, and had dinner at a nearby cafe. Realizing it was too late to get anything done at that hour, he went back to the hotel to grab some sleep.

By eight the next morning he was making the rounds of the local marinas. He hit the larger ones first, but finding nothing, he widened his search to the smaller places on the outskirts of town. There were only two ways on and off Jamaica, by air or sea, so it seemed like there was no shortage of boats, nor of places to dock them on the island.

Ryan visited over a dozen places and by the end of the day he was no closer to finding Stone. Unlike in the movies, where being a detective appeared exciting, in real life detecting was repetitive, sometimes boring work. Driving around and asking the same questions over and over. But it was still better than being cooped-up in an office somewhere, doing paperwork.

At nine p.m. he headed back to the Marriott, hoping the following day in Ocho Rios would be more productive.

***

As he steered the Jeep along the main avenue of Ocho Rios, he realized this was a much smaller seaside town than Montego Bay. And the predominant commerce was tourism. All the businesses were either hotels, motels, restaurants, gift shops, or bars.

It was early February, the height of the tourist season, and the streets were full of cars. The sidewalks were packed with pedestrians, most of them in beachwear. It was a festive, animated crowd – talking, drinking, and laughing, obviously on vacation from the 9-to-5 grind back home.

Car traffic ground to a halt and he buzzed down his window. Hot air filled the cabin, as did the sound of calypso music playing somewhere nearby.

Eventually the traffic eased and he passed a small hotel on his right. Since the place was not on the beach, he hoped it would have a room available. Pulling the Jeep into the parking lot, he walked to the front office and checked in.

They had a small cafe by the lobby and he went in and ordered lunch.

When the young waitress returned with his meal later, he gave her a smile. "I'm looking for a friend of mine," he said, holding up the picture of Stone for the waitress to see.

The young woman studied the photo. "She kind of looks familiar."

"Do you think she stayed at this hotel?" he asked.

"I don't think so, but I've seen her around. Ocho Rios is not that big a place."

"She has a sailboat – maybe you saw her at a marina?"

The waitress nodded. "Maybe. There's two big marinas in town. And those places have restaurants. I think I've seen her there."

"Okay," Ryan said, finally beginning to feel like he was making some headway. "You've been a big help."

The girl smiled and moved away to another table.

Ryan ate quickly, paid, left a big tip, and went back to his vehicle.

Pulling out the map of Jamaica once again, he glanced at the inset of Ocho Rios. As the waitress indicated, the town had two large marinas, one east and the other west of downtown.

Putting away the map, he cranked up the Jeep and headed west, fighting the heavy traffic the whole way.

The first place was a bust – no one at the marina or the restaurant recognized Stone. Wasting no time, he headed east on the traffic-choked road, and pulled into the marina's parking lot an hour later.

Walking to the dock area, he scanned the boats. There was a large number, both power and sail, their chrome deck fittings glistening in the bright sun. Not spotting the *Liberte*, he strode to the office and went inside.

A middle-aged woman with curly, blonde hair was behind the counter. She sported a dragon tattoo on her neck, and wore a tight T-shirt and shorts that magnified her pudgy frame. The smell of cigarettes hung in the air.

"Hi," Ryan said, "I'm looking for someone and I was hoping you could help me."

"Do you want to rent a boat slip at the marina?" the woman asked in a tired voice.

"No, I'm just looking for a friend of mine."

"We got a sale going on this week – twenty percent off."

The detective forced a smile. "I'm just looking for information."

"What do I look like, the yellow pages?"

Ryan chuckled. Pulling out his wallet, he took out several bills and placed them on the counter. Then he removed the photo of Stone from a pocket and laid it next to the money. "I'm looking for this woman."

The pudgy blonde scanned the picture. "I might know her. Then again, I might not. I'm a little low on cash this week."

Ryan sighed, took out more money and put it on the counter.

"Yeah," the blonde said with a tobacco-stained grimace. "I know that uppity-ass bitch. Thinks she's better than the rest of us."

"Don't give me a line of bullshit, lady." He tapped the photo for emphasis. "You really know her?"

"Sure. I know her."

"You know Angel Stone?"

"That's not the name she used. She said her name was Tobias."

He took out the photo of Stone's boat and handed it to the blonde. "She has a sailboat. The *Liberte*. Does she dock it here?"

The woman glanced at the photo quickly, then picked up the money on the counter and stuffed it into a pocket of her too-tight shorts. "That boat looks familiar, but my memory's not what it used to be."

Aggravated at the blonde, but excited he'd found the first good lead in four days, Ryan fished out another bill and held it up in the air. "You've seen this boat before? The *Liberte*?"

The woman examined the photo closely. "Yeah. That's her sailboat. But it's not called the *Liberte*. It's named the *Hope*."

Ryan thought about this information. It would fit Stone's character to change the name of the sailboat frequently to avoid detection. "She docks it at this marina?"

"She used to, until a week or so ago."

His excitement faded a bit. "You know where she went?"

The blonde pointed to the money he was holding in his hand. "You give me the cash and I'll look in my files."

Ryan gave her the money and she turned and walked over to a desktop computer. Coming back moments later, she said, "I don't know where she is now, but she was staying at the Hyatt Regency here in Ocho Rios."

"Okay. Anything else you can tell me about her?"

"Just that she was a bitch, and that I couldn't stand her guts."

Ryan chuckled. "Don't hold back, lady. Tell me how you really feel."

The blonde looked perplexed, and then realized he was making a joke. "I get it."

"Anyway, thanks for your help."

***

The Hyatt Regency was a newly-constructed, thirty-story, exclusive resort located right on the beach. It had one of those glass-and-chrome open-air atriums filled with gardens, tropical plants, and native birds. The scent of flowers was cloyingly strong in the lobby, and the cacophony of bird calls competed with the voices of the hotel guests.

Ryan went to the reception desk and flashed a smile at the pretty black girl working there. Placing the photo of Stone on the desk, he said, "My friend is staying here. Can you tell me which room?"

The receptionist smiled back. "What's her name, sir?"

"She's kind of quirky. She goes by a couple of different names. Stone, Norris, and Tobias."

The girl gave him an odd look. "I'll check, sir." She began typing on the computer console in front of her. "We did have a Mr. and Mrs. Tobias at the hotel until a few days ago. They've checked out."

Ryan pointed to the photo of Stone. "Is this her?"

The young woman stared at the picture. "Yes, I remember her now. She had striking green eyes. She was staying here with her husband. A tall, blond man."

All that fit with what the detective knew about Stone and her accomplice Frank Reynolds. "You've been a big help, miss. You said they checked out. Any idea where they went?"

The girl shook her head. "No. But I remember they were talking about buying a house."

"A house? Where? In Ocho Rios?"

"I don't know, sir."

"Okay. I appreciate your help."

The black girl smiled. "No problem. Have a good day."

Turning, Ryan headed out of the hotel and had the bellhop retrieve his Jeep from the lot.

Driving to downtown Ocho Rios, he spent the next several hours visiting realtors. But he had no luck locating Stone, and after fighting the still heavy traffic, he called it a day.

Going back to his hotel, he ate a dinner of black beans and jerk chicken, with a Red Stripe beer.

Frustrated by his lack of progress in locating Stone, he went to bed and fell into a fitful sleep, punctuated by nightmares of the bombings in Honolulu and the other American cities. The TV images of the dead and wounded woke him throughout the night.

Finally, at seven a.m., he climbed out of bed. Still groggy from the lack of sleep, nevertheless he was full of resolve to find the woman and make her pay for her crimes.

After a shave and shower, he put on fresh clothes and had breakfast. Using his cell phone, he Googled realtors and wrote down the addresses of the ones he'd missed the previous day. Then he set out in the Jeep once again.

He struck out at the first three realtors he visited, and, expanding his search, decided to go to places on the outskirts of town.

The Remax office on Palm Road was small but architecturally distinctive, and from the Mercedes and BMWs parked in front of the place, probably catered to a high-end clientele.

Ryan was shown into the manager's office, an elderly man with silver hair and a clipped British accent. After introducing himself, Ryan sat in one of the guest chairs fronting his desk.

"You're looking to buy some property in Jamaica?" the realtor asked.

"That's right. Some friends of mine are buying a home here and I'm intrigued by the idea of doing the same."

"What's their name?"

"The Tobiases."

The realtor's face lit up. "Yes, of course. They just purchased a delightful home. A large estate, actually."

Ryan pulled out the photo of Stone and Reynolds on the sailboat and handed it to the man. "You recognize them?"

"Yes. That's Mr. Tobias. I never met the missus, since he handled the whole transaction. But I'm sure she's a fine person as well."

Ryan smiled. "She's a sweetheart, all right. Where did they buy?"

"Like I said, it's an incredible property. A foreclosure, so they got quite a deal. It's a mansion on ten acres. It's located right on the beach in Annotto Bay."

"Where's that?"

"East of Ocho Rios, about a three hour drive. A remote area." The realtor arched his brows. "Maybe you'd be interested in looking at properties in that area? I've got several homes in the vicinity."

Ryan feigned interest. "Yes. I would love to see them. But first I'd like to pay the Tobiases a visit. They don't know I'm here yet and I'd like to surprise them."

"Of course," the elderly man said, and gave Ryan the address and directions.

The detective stood and extended his hand. "You've been a great help. As soon as I visit them I'll call you and we can set up a time to look at some homes."

"That's lovely," the man replied and they shook hands.

Ryan put a finger to his lips. "But remember, I want to surprise them, so please don't call them."

"Mums the word. By the way, do you have an idea how much you want to spend on a home?"

"My father left me a very large trust fund," Ryan lied. "He made his money in oil. So I'm sure I'd want a place as nice as the Tobiases'."

The realtor's face lit up with a wide smile. "Excellent. Just excellent. Here's my card, please call me, and soon. I know you'll love Annotto Bay."

"I'm sure I will."

***

Back in his vehicle, the detective studied the map of the island once again, locating the general area of Stone's new house. The home was situated off a remote side road accessible only by going through a forest-like area.

Stopping for gasoline first, he took the A3 road east and about two hours later saw the small sign for Annotto Bay.

Getting off the main road, he was soon bouncing over a mostly dirt and mud trail. He put the Jeep in 4-wheel drive mode and turned on his headlights, as the heavy canopy of trees blocked out most of the sun.

A half-hour later the trail reached a clearing and the sudden brightness of open sky almost blinded him. Like the realtor had said, the area was remote. He saw no cars or people, and the nearby Caribbean was devoid of boats.

In the distance, toward the end of the road, he spotted what appeared to be a long white wall. Consulting the map, he realized this was probably the right property.

He pressed the accelerator and the Jeep shot forward.

Chapter 73

Annotto Bay, Jamaica

J.T. Ryan drove slowly past the estate's closed front gate.

The gate appeared to be constructed of heavy-gauge steel. Surveillance cameras were mounted at both sides of the entrance, and razor-wire topped the high walls that seemed to surround the entire property. The home had extensive security, reinforcing his feeling that the place would be difficult to break into undetected.

He continued driving on the secluded road, the white walls to his left. The property seemed to go on forever, but eventually the wall curved and headed in the direction of the sea, now visible in the distance. As before, he saw no people or boats.

Continuing his drive, he weighed his options. Whatever he did, he couldn't do it in broad daylight. It would have to wait until dark.

Half an hour later he reached a small village. There wasn't much there – just a gas station, motel, hardware store, and a restaurant. The residential part of town consisted of two modest houses and rows of shanties.

Pulling in front of the hardware store, he went inside and picked through their selection until he found what he was looking for. Then he headed to the restaurant, where he nursed a Red Stripe and waited for nightfall.

***

Finding a desolate wooded area about a hundred yards from the home's wall, he stopped the Jeep and climbed out. There was a full moon, and the sea, which was close and to his right, shimmered.

In front of him was a clearing, covered by low-lying vegetation, mostly wild grass. Beyond that was a remote part of the wall, a long way from the entrance. He doubted surveillance cameras had been mounted in this area.

Grabbing the backpack full of supplies from the back seat of the vehicle, he hoisted it on his shoulders. Then he pulled the Smith & Wesson revolver from his pocket and checked the load. Luckily, he'd been able bring the weapon in his checked bag on the flight into Jamaica. Unlike the U.S., airport security on the island was considerably more lax.

Crouching, he made his way slowly across the clearing.

Five feet from the wall he stopped and looked up. Like the main entrance, razor-wire covered the top edge of the wall.

Un-slinging the backpack, he took out the thick canvass tarp he'd purchased earlier, along with the compact, foldable aluminum ladder. Propping the ladder against the wall, he began to climb. Then he pitched the tarp over the razor-wire, covering several feet of it.

But immediately after the tarp made contact with the wire, sparks flew. He heard a sharp, crackling sound, and smelled a burning odor.

The wall was electrified, something he hadn't foreseen. Climbing back down, he reassessed his options.

Looking toward the sea, he realized that was the only way in.

Continuing to crouch, he made his way along the high wall, reaching a sandy beach moments later. The wall continued into the sea another one hundred feet or so.

Stuffing a few of the supplies into his pockets, he dropped the backpack and waded into the warm water.

Doing a front crawl stroke, he swam out past the wall, his wet clothes weighing him down. Swimming around the wall, he entered a sheltered cove. He spotted Stone's sailboat right away, moored on a dock along the back of the property. A powerboat was moored next to it.

The long, wide beach was deserted, but the large house that lay beyond it on the rise was well-lit. He heard the faint sound of classical music in the background.

As he treaded water, he scanned the layout of the property. The large home was impressive – a multi-level mansion, like the realtor had described.

To his left, behind a row of palm trees, was a small house, also well-lit. The caretaker's or maid's house? Probably.

He saw no one about, nor did he hear voices or dogs barking.

Swimming forward, he reached the shallow area of the beach and his feet touched bottom. He waded slowly through the calm surf, careful to be as quiet as possible.

When he reached shore, he stopped and listened closely to the night sounds – the murmur of lapping waves, the chirping of cicadas, the hum of air conditioners, and the classical music.

Pulling out the revolver, he crouched and began walking over the wet sand toward the mansion.

Chapter 74

Annotto Bay, Jamaica

Angel Stone was in the mansion's study listening to Mozart and reading a book on her iPad, when she heard a loud beep. Putting down the iPad, she got up from the leather armchair and went to the security panel mounted on the wall. The small screen on the device was flashing *'Intruder Alert'*.

Going to the teak wood cabinet at the other end of the room, she opened one of the drawers and removed a Heckler & Koch semi-automatic. Taking the safety off the pistol, she went to the partially open slider of the study. Sliding the glass partition fully open, she stepped out into the balcony.

Located on the second floor, the study overlooked the backyard garden and the sandy beach beyond. The nighttime scene outside looked the same as always – peaceful and quiet. The floodlights showed no movement, save the lapping of waves and the swaying of palm fronds.

Going back inside, she took a cell phone out of her jeans pocket and pressed one of the pre-programmed buttons.

"Hey, Angel," she heard Frank Reynolds say when he picked up on the other end. "Want ... some company?" He was slurring his words.

"Sober up, Frank. The motion detectors just went off in the backyard. We may have an intruder."

"Calm down, sugar. Probably ... another iguana."

"Get out there and look around."

"I'm sure ... it's nothing ... "

"Do it, Frank." She hung up and put the phone away. Then she turned off the lights in the study, stood by the windows and peered out.

Chapter 75

Annotto Bay, Jamaica

Frank Reynolds put his cell phone in his pocket and got up from the vinyl couch.

After taking a last swig from his Corona, he watched the TV screen for another minute as his favorite soccer team kicked a goal. But his team was still three goals behind.

Going to the coat closet of the small guest house, he pulled out the Mossberg shotgun, racked the slide and went to the front door.

Stepping outside, he began patrolling the grounds. It was a warm night. Rain as was on the way.

Holding the Mossberg in front of him, he searched the lush garden, scanning for anything suspicious. He was certain it was nothing, another false alarm.

As he continued, his thoughts drifted to two nights ago. He had spent the evening with Angel and she had been a sexual tigress, satisfying his every desire and then some. When she was in the mood, she was very, very good. Totally satiated and exhausted from the love making, by two a.m. he had fallen into a deep, tranquil sleep.

But by morning, the more typical Angel had returned – calculating and businesslike. She had the ability to turn off her emotional side like a light switch, something Frank had never been able to understand.

He shrugged, knowing that no matter what, he loved her deeply and probably always would.

Then he heard a rustling sound by the beach, jolting him back to reality.

Standing very still, he listened closely.

Chapter 76

Annotto Bay, Jamaica

J.T Ryan reached the end of the sandy beach and knelt behind a row of flowering bushes for cover. In front of him was a wide expanse of grass, bordered on both sides by elaborate gardens. He was no more than one hundred and fifty feet from the mansion, its three levels towering over the property.

Floodlights bathed the backyard, lighting up the nighttime scene as if it were daylight. There was no way he could cross the yard unseen. He'd have to go through the gardens to reach the house.

Hearing no voices, he peered over the bushes, trying to determine if anyone was nearby. He saw no one, and only heard the faint sounds of classical music from inside the home.

His sopping wet clothes clung to his body. Realizing his water-filled shoes might make a sloshing sound, he removed them and hid them under the bushes.

Clicking open the cylinder of his revolver, Ryan twirled it around to make sure no sand obstructed the mechanism. He clicked it shut and dropped to a prone position.

Then, using the low-lying bushes for cover, he crawled on his hands and knees toward the right.

Moments later he was in the sprawling garden, which was decorated with colorful tropical plants and palm trees. In the middle of the garden he noticed a fountain rising from a small pool.

In a crouch, he moved to the fountain and knelt behind it, then gazed up at the mansion. Lights were on in several of the rooms, but no one was visible. Ryan was about thirty feet from the back entrance, a wide French door. He was close enough to spot the surveillance cameras mounted on the home's exterior walls.

What was the best way in? he wondered. He still had the element of surprise, but if he broke in through the back door, he'd set-off an alarm. No doubt the windows had sensors, so going in that way was no better. Since the place had so much high-tech security, undetected access was probably impossible. His best option appeared to be speed. Sprint to the back door, kick it in, then race through the house and capture anyone he encountered.

But before Ryan could put his plan into action, he heard a voice from behind him yell, "Freeze! Or I'll shoot!"

Chapter 77

Annotto Bay, Jamaica

Angel Stone was in the mansion's security room, staring at the grainy images on the multiple TV monitors in front of her. Nine of the screens showed no activity.

But out of the corner of her eye she saw a blur of action on the tenth screen. That feed was from the surveillance camera overlooking one of the backyard gardens. She zoomed in for a closer look.

Two men were facing each other. One she recognized immediately – it was Frank, aiming a shotgun. Angel didn't recognize the second man, who had his hands up in the air but appeared to be holding a handgun. Although she couldn't make out what they were saying, it was clear they were arguing.

Frank motioned with the shotgun, but the other man shook his head.

Then it all happened in an instant.

She heard the crack of a pistol and the boom of a shotgun and both men crumpled to the ground.

Angel pulled the H&K from her waistband and raced out of the room. Sprinting to the back door, she unlocked it and went outside, holding the gun in front of her with both hands.

Cautiously, she made her way to the edge of the garden. Peering around the trunk of a palm tree, she scanned the scene. In the glare of the floodlights, two men were clearly visible. Both lay by the fountain, unmoving.

She approached, going to the stranger first. The inert man was flat on his back, his shoulder bleeding profusely. Checking his pulse, she realized he was alive, just unconscious.

A chrome revolver was next to his body. After picking up the gun, she studied the man's face. She recognized him now – he was the guy who broke into her Paris apartment. Somehow he'd survived the bomb.

With trepidation, she went to Frank and knelt by his motionless body. He was on his side, seeping from a wound in his abdomen. A large pool of blood was underneath him.

Checking his pulse, she found none.

"Frank!" she screamed, and stared at his lifeless eyes.

Then Angel sank to the ground and began to sob.

Chapter 78

Annotto Bay, Jamaica

J.T. Ryan was awakened by a stabbing pain in his shoulder.

Realizing he was strapped to a wooden chair, Ryan looked around the room. It was a storage area, full of boxes and crates. A light bulb hung from the ceiling, providing the only light. Heavy rope had been used to tie him to the chair. He struggled against it, but the bindings were too strong.

His right shoulder was bleeding and hurt like hell. But he was lucky, he knew. The shotgun shell would have blown his head off if he'd moved a second later.

In front of him was a closed door – the only way in or out.

Ryan heard the faint sound of classical music coming from outside the room, confirming his suspicion that he was in Stone's house.

Hearing a loud click, he stared at the door as it opened.

Angel Stone stood there, holding a pistol in front of her. Without saying a word, she stepped inside.

He'd only seen photos, but it was clearly her, the bright green eyes unmistakable. Dressed simply in jeans and a white polo shirt, the woman was stunning, much more beautiful in real life than in the pictures.

She approached him and checked the rope bindings. Obviously satisfied they were secure, she stuck the pistol in her waistband. Folding her arms, she stood in front of him. Her eyes were red-rimmed as if she'd been crying.

"Who the hell are you?" she spat out, her voice angry.

Knowing she'd probably found the ID in his wallet, he went with a modified version of the truth. "My name's J.T. Ryan. I'm a tourist. I was out swimming and got lost. I saw the lights from your house and came ashore. This guy tried to shoot me and I defended myself."

Stone stepped forward, closed a fist and punched him hard on his wounded shoulder.

A blinding pain shot through him, and he groaned. Blood spurted from his wound.

"Your name may be Ryan," she hissed, "but you're no tourist. Try again."

"It's true. Look, I know I was trespassing on your property. Call the cops. Let them sort it out."

Stone punched him in the shoulder again, and this time the pain was so intense he passed out.

When he opened his eyes, she was still there, her green eyes full of hate. "You killed Frank," she yelled, "and you're going to pay for that!"

She paused and lowered her voice. "You're lucky Frank was drunk and his reactions were slow, otherwise he would have blown you away. His damn drinking always got him in trouble." She shook her head slowly. "But talking about it won't bring him back. He's dead. You killed him and you're going to pay for that. But first you're going to tell me who you are. And don't give me this bullshit about being a tourist. I saw you ransacking my apartment in Paris."

Realizing she must have had surveillance cameras in her apartment, he decided there was no sense in lying. "My name is Ryan, and I'm with the FBI. I've been working the Al-Shirak terrorist plot."

Stone took a step back, an astonished look on her face. "How the hell did you find me here?"

"It's a long story, Stone. Let's just say I ran into a couple of friends of yours. Heiler in Germany and Montoya in Spain."

At the mention of the two names, her jaw dropped open. But she said nothing, her eyes flashing anger.

Once again she closed a fist and struck his shoulder. As blood spurted, he grit his teeth from the pain.

"You bastard!" she screamed. "What do you know about Al-Shirak?"

"I know ... everything," he replied, as he gasped for air. "I know all about you Stone. I know you're the ringleader, and that you got most of the ransom money." He paused and took a deep breath. "Give yourself up, tell me who else is involved, and the Attorney General will cut you a deal."

She barked out a harsh laugh. "You're full of shit, Ryan. No one's going to cut me a deal. I've killed thousands. They'll fry me in the electric chair." She crossed her arms in front of her again. "But I don't have to worry about that, do I? You're the one who should be worried. You're the one who's not leaving this room alive."

She grinned. "But first, I want payback for Frank. You killed the only man I ever loved, you fucking bastard. You're going to die a slow and painful death."

She held her index finger up in the air, then brought it to her lips and kissed it.

In a blur of motion, she stabbed her finger into Ryan's wound and twisted it around.

He groaned from the blinding pain, struggled against the ropes, and watched her jam her finger deeper into the bleeding wound. He felt her hook her finger inside his shoulder and jerk it out, tearing more of his flesh in the process.

Ryan almost blacked out, but fought it, as he desperately tried to figure out a way out of this mess.

Her hand was bloody now and she slapped him hard across the face.

"How do you feel now?" she spat out. "But I'm just getting started. This won't bring Frank back, but seeing you suffer gives me some consolation."

A cold grin spread on her face and her eyes looked feral. "What should I do to you now? Maybe I should cut off your balls and make you eat them, like drug kingpins in South America do to their enemies. How does that sound?"

"They're on their way," Ryan said.

"What? Who's on their way?"

"The FBI," Ryan lied. "I called them before I swam ashore. There's a team being choppered in from Montego Bay."

Stone frowned. "You're lying, you bastard. Yeah, you had a cell phone on you. But it got wet – that thing is dead."

Ryan shrugged. "Don't believe me. I don't care."

The frown didn't leave her face. She glanced at her watch, then back to Ryan. "Guess I'll have to cut the fun short. Too bad, I was just beginning to enjoy myself."

Pulling the pistol from her waistband, Stone leveled the weapon at Ryan's face and pressed the muzzle to his forehead.

Chapter 79

Annotto Bay, Jamaica

J.T. Ryan felt the cold steel of the gun barrel pressed against his forehead.

"Goodbye," Angel Stone growled with a wicked grin.

Ryan pushed down with his feet as hard as he could, and propelled himself backward, toppling the wooden chair to the floor. He was still tied to the chair but at least out of the line of fire.

Stone, with a look of rage on her face, stood over him and re-aimed the pistol.

Hooking one of his feet between her legs, he jerked it forward, causing her to stumble to her knees.

"Fuck you, Ryan. You'll pay for that!"

He kicked her savagely, striking the side of her face; she grunted and dropped the gun. He kicked her again, this time in the solar plexus, and she crumpled to the floor.

Breathing heavily, he stared at her unmoving body. His thoughts raced, knowing he still had to get free before the woman regained consciousness.

Another stabbing pain shot through his shoulder as he stared at the wound. It was bleeding profusely. He knew he'd lost a lot of blood. Suddenly he felt lightheaded; a wave of nausea hit him and he blacked out.

Chapter 80

Annotto Bay, Jamaica

Angel Stone regained consciousness, her face and chest throbbing in pain. Standing up quickly, she glanced around the storage room. Ryan was on the floor, his inert body still tied to the overturned chair. His wound was seeping blood, the red fluid covering much of the floor.

Spotting the Heckler & Koch semi-automatic by her feet, she picked it up and glanced at her watch. She knew she had no time to waste – the FBI would be here any moment.

Sprinting to the door, she left the room, and raced down the stairs.

Rushing to her bedroom on the second floor, she grabbed her go-bag, which was full of cash, another weapon, and several phony passports. Then she dashed outside and ran to her sailboat.

Quickly uncleating the dock lines, she stepped up to the aft deck, cranked up the engine, and steered the boat out of the cove and into open sea.

Chapter 81

Annotto Bay, Jamaica

Ryan's eyes blinked open and he saw the light bulb hanging from the ceiling. He was on his back, still tied to the overturned wooden chair. Feeling weak and nauseous, he noticed his shirt was coated with blood. The back of his head was damp, probably from the pool of blood he was laying in.

Turning his head, he looked around the storage room – Stone was gone.

He had to get loose and go after her. But how?

Pushing with his feet, he struggled against the chair, and eventually turned it on its side. Although he was still bound to the chair, he used his legs to inch his way out of the room and into the corridor. Close by was a staircase leading down.

Fighting the urge to vomit, he continued to use his legs to propel himself to the top of the staircase and once there, peered down. It was a long way to the bottom, over twenty-five feet. But it was the only way out.

Ryan thought through his options. He only had one, and it wasn't a good one. He could fling himself down the stairs, chair and all, and hope the fall would break apart the wooden chair. It was crazy, and the odds were high that he'd break his neck instead of the chair. But he had no choice. He'd bleed to death just laying there.

Using his feet, he pushed against the side wall as hard as he could, propelling himself down the stairs. He rolled down in a crazy rush, the chair crashing on every second step or so, every part of his body screaming in pain. His head swam from the disorienting movement, and he heard the chair thudding loudly against the wood of the steps.

All of a sudden he stopped moving and opened his eyes. He was at the foot of the stairs, still tied to the chair.

Struggling against the ropes with his arms, he heard a sharp cracking sound, saw one of the armrests break loose from the chair. Using his free hand, he began to untie his other arm.

Moments later he had removed all of the restraints.

Standing up slowly, he glanced around. He was in a corridor in what he figured was the second floor. There was a window at the end of the hallway and he went to it and looked out. As he had feared, Stone's sailboat was gone.

Ryan was determined to go after her, but knew he'd already lost a lot of blood. He had to patch his shoulder first. Finding a bathroom, he located a first-aid kit and bandaged the wound as best he could. In the kit was a bottle of aspirin, which he opened and dry-chewed four tablets.

Next he went to one of the lavishly appointed bedrooms. Searching the walk-in closet, he saw a metal case under a row of shoes. Opening the case, he found two Glocks. Selecting one of the pistols and an extra clip, he quickly walked out of the room.

A minute later he was out of the mansion, striding toward the dock. Reaching it, he gazed out past the cove, to the open sea. It was early morning now, and a pink and blue sky was replacing the grayness of dawn. But all he saw was open water – the sailboat was long gone.

Spotting the powerboat moored to the dock, he climbed in and tried to start the engine. Unfortunately it was a new model Chris-Craft that required a key. Dropping to his knees, he looked underneath the console. Seeing the ignition wires, he yanked them loose and within minutes hot-wired them. The inboard engine roared to life.

After untying the bow and aft lines, he steered the boat out of the cove, gunning the engine as soon as he reached open water.

Scanning the horizon, he saw only one other boat, a large oil freighter in the distance. Stone's sailboat was nowhere around.

Where the hell was she? he wondered. He tried to think like Stone. Where would it be safe to hide? Not north, toward Cuba or the U.S. Then he remembered the Cayman Islands. The first ransom demand had given a Grand Cayman bank for the wire deposit. Maybe Stone had some connection there? It was worth a shot.

After consulting the compass mounted on deck, he cut the wheel hard left and pushed the throttle wide open. The engine howled as the Chris-Craft sliced through the choppy water, headed west toward the Cayman Islands.

***

An hour later he spotted a large sailboat in the distance. It was a two-master, just like Stone's boat, running at full sail. And it was headed west.

Up to now, all he'd seen in the Caribbean had been oil freighters, a cruise ship, and a couple of large powerboats. Deciding the two-mast sailboat was probably Stone's, he steered right for it. Pulling the Glock from his waistband, he took off the safety and held it at the ready.

When he was two hundred feet from the sailboat, he saw its sails begin to furl on the masts, and the boat slowed down. Soon after he heard the roar of gunfire and saw small plumes of water shoot up all around his powerboat. Several more shots whizzed over his head, and he realized that at this distance, Stone must be using a high-powered rifle to be so accurate. Nevertheless, he leveled the Glock pistol and fired off a three-round burst.

But the salvo of incoming rounds continued, getting closer to his boat every second.

Ryan cut the wheel hard left, then quickly hard right, steering the powerboat in a zigzag pattern as he approached the larger vessel. He still heard the *cracks* of the rifle fire, but the incoming shots were wilder now, not nearly as close to the powerboat.

Fifty feet from the sailboat he stopped zigzagging and headed straight for the other boat, which was now motionless. He gunned the engine once again.

When he was twenty feet away, he fired off another three-round burst, then pulled back on the throttle. But the powerboat's momentum carried it the rest of the way, and it crashed into the side of the sailboat. He heard the *crunching* sound of metal, wood and fiberglass as the two boats collided, the sudden jarring motion almost knocking him off his feet.

Using the powerboat's console for cover, he scanned the other boat's deck. But Stone wasn't there.

Wasting no time, he stuck the pistol in his waistband and moved to the edge of the powerboat. Grabbing the side of the sailer, he hoisted himself up to the other boat with both hands, then rolled across its teak deck for several feet. Pulling out the Glock, he trained it in front of him as he surveyed the deck. Where the hell was she?

He listened closely for any sounds, but only heard the wind and the slapping of waves against the hull.

Glancing right he saw the powerboat, its front end crushed, begin to drift away in the open sea. The sailboat was not drifting, a sign that Stone had dropped anchor when she'd furled the sails earlier. He noticed all the high-tech equipment on the sailboat, including roller furling systems on both masts.

Guessing Stone had probably retreated into the cabin below deck, he considered his options. The bi-fold hatch door leading below was open. He could see the stairs headed down, but beyond that it was a dark void. It was clear she was setting a trap – waiting for him to climb down the stairs before shooting. He'd be dead in seconds.

Then he came up with an idea.

While keeping an eye on the open companionway, he searched the deck for several items. Finding a can of gasoline, a disposable lighter, and several towels, he carried them to a spot near the entrance. Pouring gasoline on one of the towels, he lit the cloth and hurled the ignited towel down the stairs. Repeating the process two more times, he watched as smoke began to billow out of the cabin entrance moments later.

Crouching closer, he gazed down the stairs, saw the lick of flames below. He heard a woman cursing and then muffled coughing. Training the gun in front of him, he waited.

A volley of shots rang out, whistling over his head, and he flattened himself prone on the deck. He heard more coughing, then the *clump* of shoes on stairs.

Angel Stone emerged from the entrance, wearing the same jeans and polo shirt as earlier. She was holding a pistol.

Ryan fired one shot, the woman groaned and dropped to the ground. Her handgun clattered to the deck as she grabbed her leg with both hands.

"Don't move," Ryan said, "or you're dead."

Stone stared at him, her green eyes full of hate. She coughed again, and then shook her head slowly. "You bastard! You fucking bastard."

The detective, still in pain from his shoulder wound, but pumped-up from adrenaline, simply nodded. "I've been called worse."

Standing, he walked over and picked up the woman's handgun and stuck it in his waistband.

"Don't move," Ryan told the woman.

"I'm bleeding!" she cried out. "You've got to help me."

"Later. Now lie down and shut up."

Stone complied, and Ryan grabbed the roll of duct tape he'd found earlier and taped her hands and feet together.

"You shot me in the leg," she yelled. "I'm going to bleed to death."

"I can only hope."

Turning away from the woman, he scanned the deck. Spotting a fire-extinguisher by the wheel, he raced toward it, unhooked it from its mount and sprinted toward the cabin entrance. Holding one hand over his nose, he climbed down the stairs.

Five minutes later he trudged up the stairs and exited the cabin. Coughing repeatedly from the smoke, he crossed the deck toward Stone, who was still there, lying on her stomach.

He rolled her over on her back and inspected her leg. Blood was seeping from an open gash in her jeans.

"I hate you, you bastard!" she screamed.

"So you said."

"I'm going to fucking bleed to death if you don't help me!"

"Kind of looks that way," he said with a wry smile.

"You son-of-a-bitch!"

He looked at her for a long moment, trying to decide what to do. The TV images of the thousands of dead Americans crossed his mind.

Finally, he decided.

Kneeling down, he reached over, unbuttoned her jeans and pulled down her zipper.

Stone's eyes flashed hatred. "You're going to rape me? You're worse than a fucking animal, Ryan!"

"Don't flatter yourself, Stone. I got better at home. Now shut up, and let me work."

She let out a long rant of obscenities, some of which he hadn't heard before. Ignoring this, he pulled down her jeans and inspected the deep wound on her leg.

Grabbing a nearby towel, he wiped the blood from the open gash. It looked like his bullet had been a through-and-through and no arteries had been hit, otherwise the woman would already be dead. Wiping away the blood once again, he tore off a large piece of duct tape and pressed it to her leg. For good measure he tore off two more pieces of tape and applied them to the wound.

Stone stared at him and said nothing, as he pulled her jeans back up and closed them.

He stood, looked down at her.

"What happens now?" she hissed.

"Now we go back to Jamaica. I call the FBI and they arrest you."

She frowned, and after a moment she gave him a suggestive smile. "Let me go and I'll make it worth your while. I know a lot of ways to please a man."

"Forget it."

The smile vanished and her eyes went cold. "I'll pay you! Whatever you want. I have more money than God!"

"Where you're going, all that money won't do you any good."

"Please, Ryan! Tell me what you want."

"Shut up."

Knowing the trip back would be insufferable if he had to listen to her, he ripped off another piece of duct tape, kneeled down, and slapped the tape across her mouth.

Turning away from her, he walked to the side of the sailboat that been damaged by the powerboat. He inspected the area, realized the boat was damaged but still seaworthy.

Then he went to the sailboat's deck controls by the wheel. After studying the controls for a few minutes, he pressed several buttons. He heard the *clanking* of the anchor's chain as it retracted into the boat. Then he heard a *whir* of motors and saw the sails begin to unfurl. The white canvass rose and reached the top of the masts a moment later.

The sails billowed as they caught the wind and the boat surged forward, cutting through the choppy water. Glancing at the compass, he turned the wheel right and headed east toward Jamaica.

Although Ryan's shoulder still throbbed like hell, he felt the best he had in months.

Lee Gimenez

One Month Later

Chapter 82

Atlanta, Georgia

J.T. Ryan walked into Erin Welch's FBI office and sat on one of the visitor's chairs fronting her desk. She was talking on the phone, had waved him in a moment earlier.

She spoke for another minute, then replaced the receiver. "Thanks for coming in, J.T. How's that shoulder?"

He rubbed it. "Almost good as new."

"Good to hear," she said. The attractive blonde was wearing a stylish Armani suit with a white blouse. Her long hair was pulled into a ponytail. "I have something for you." Opening a drawer, she took out an envelope and slid it across the desk.

"What is it?" he asked, picking it up.

"A bonus. For doing such an excellent job on the Al-Shirak case."

Ryan opened the envelope and examined the check. He let out a low whistle. "Nice."

"You earned it. What are you going to do with it?"

"Take Lauren on a long vacation."

"That girl deserves it," she said with a grin. "She's a saint for putting up with you."

He put the check in his jacket. "So how are things going on your end?"

"I got a bump in pay and a commendation from the Director."

"Good for you, Erin. By the way, I've been watching the news. The recovery efforts in the bombed cities look like they're going well."

"Yeah. They've made a lot of progress over the last month. The cleanup has been faster than expected, and some residents are beginning to move back."

"What's happening with Stone?" he asked.

"The CIA and FBI questioned her extensively while she was being held at Langley. They just transferred her to Guantanamo."

Ryan nodded. "Did she talk at all? Give up any of the other people involved?"

Erin frowned. "No. Wouldn't say a word."

"What about Al-Shirak? Has the FBI been able to locate the group?"

"No. They've vanished like a puff of smoke."

"What about the dirty bombs that weren't used? Any luck in finding them?"

The woman shook her head. "Not yet. We're still looking for them."

"And the ransom money, Erin?"

"We were able to locate about half of it, thanks to Montoya. He sang like a jaybird, gave us all the details of the banking side."

"Where's he now?"

"Guantanamo. Since he talked, he won't get the death penalty."

"What's next for Stone?" he asked.

"She's been charged with terrorism under the Patriot Act. She'll be in prison at Guantanamo until her trial."

Ryan thought about this for a moment. "I want to see her – I think I can get her to talk."

Erin laughed. "You're a cocky son-of-a-bitch. We've had teams of agents questioning her non-stop with no results. What makes you think you can do better?"

"I'll charm her with my wit."

"I doubt it, J.T. I questioned her myself – that bitch is a stone-cold killer."

Ryan shrugged. "At least let me try."

"She's under surveillance 24/7. They've got cameras tracking her every move in her prison cell. You won't be able to pull the stunt you used in Chicago."

"Humor me. What have you got to lose?"

"Okay. I'll make it happen."

He stood. "Thanks, Erin."

"But don't get shot down there," she said with a wry smile. "I need you for another case I'm working on."

Chapter 83

Prison Complex
U.S. Naval Base
Guantanamo Bay, Cuba

J.T. Ryan was led into the same interrogation room where he'd questioned Tom Harris months ago. It was a grimy, stifling-hot room with bare concrete walls. The stench of urine, feces, and mildew hung in the air.

Angel Stone was already there, seated behind a scarred metal table, her hands shackled to a loop on the table. The woman looked far different than when he'd last seen her. Now she was wearing a baggy, orange jumpsuit and her long hair was straggly and dirty.

Ryan sat across from her, and turned to the Marine guard who had escorted him in. "I'll take it from here, Sergeant."

"Sorry, sir," the marine replied, taking a post by the door. "I have to stay in the room. Orders."

The detective nodded and faced Stone.

"What the fuck do *you* want?" the woman hissed.

Ryan smiled. "What? You're not going to thank me for saving your life? I could have let you bleed to death."

"Fuck you!"

"Okay," he said with a chuckle. "I guess it was too much to expect." He glanced around the room. "How're the accommodations?"

"You're an asshole, Ryan."

"I'm guessing they're not as good as you're used to ..."

Stone glared at him, her eyes blazing with hate.

He leaned forward in the chair. "If you tell me what I want to know, I can help you."

"You're fucking crazy. I haven't had my trial yet, but I already know how it's going to turn out. I'll get the death penalty." She shrugged. "But so what. It's better than living in this shithole for the rest of my life."

He lowered his voice for emphasis. "What if I made the death penalty go away."

"Bullshit! You couldn't do that."

"You're right about that. I couldn't do it by myself. But I know people who can make it happen."

"Who?"

"The FBI. They could arrange it with the Attorney General."

"You're full of shit, Ryan."

He stood abruptly, turned away from her, and walked toward the door.

"Wait!" she called out from behind him. "Tell me more."

"Sure you're interested?"

Stone nodded and he sat back down.

"It's simple," Ryan said. "You tell me what I want to know, and I'll call the FBI and make it happen."

"I'm not an idiot. I want it in writing."

"Of course."

"I want two things, Ryan. First, take the death penalty off the table. And I want to do my time at a minimum security prison back in the States – one of those cushy places you read about."

He shook his head. "Sorry. I can promise you the death penalty thing, but I can't get you out of Guantanamo. But I can make sure you have better accommodations here – a nicer cell, good food, your own bathroom."

The woman considered this a minute. "Not good enough. I want a prison cell back in the States or it's no deal. Gitmo is a hellhole."

"It's your funeral, lady." He stood once again and turned to go.

"Wait a minute."

"My patience is wearing thin, Stone."

"Okay, okay. You're deal sounds good. But before I agree, I want to know what information you're looking for."

"Fair enough," he replied sitting back down. "First, you have to tell me all about Al-Shirak. Who they are and where they're located."

"What else?"

"Where you stashed the other dirty bombs. The ones you didn't use."

The woman went quiet. After a moment she nodded. "Okay. I agree. But no deal until I have it in writing."

"You'll get it."

"By the way, why *didn't* you let me die, back there on the boat?" she asked, a puzzled look on her face.

"I'll be honest with you, I thought about it. You deserve it. But I'm not a murderer, like you."

Stone chuckled. "Nobody's perfect, not even me. Now go get me that offer in writing, then I'll tell you what you want to know."

***

The Navy had assigned Ryan a room at the BOQ, the officers' quarters building, for his stay at the naval base in Guantanamo. The room was sparse, consisting of a small bedroom and an adjoining sitting area. It was outfitted with plain but sturdy furniture, the walls painted an industrial gray. Scuffed linoleum covered the floor. It reminded Ryan of his quarters at Fort Bragg, years ago.

He was in the sitting area now, debating what he'd tell Erin Welch. He knew it wouldn't be an easy sell.

Picking up the phone receiver, he dialed her number and waited for her to answer. "Welch," he heard the woman say a moment later.

"It's Ryan."

"J.T. How are things in Cuba?"

"Just met with Stone."

"How'd it go?"

"Good. She'll tell us what we want to know, but."

"What's the catch, J.T.?"

"We take the death penalty off the table."

"Are you crazy? The Attorney General will never go for that!"

"It's worth it, Erin. We find out about Al-Shirak and the location of the remaining bombs."

"I agree, it sounds tempting, but I'm telling you, the AG will never go for it."

"Listen, Erin. We're vulnerable right now. There are probably other conspirators out there planning attacks. There are four dirty bombs left. Do you want more dead Americans on your conscience?"

"Of course not." Then she went silent, obviously thinking. "Okay," she finally said. "I'll talk to the AG, try to get him on board."

"Don't just try, do it. I've got Stone primed for this. But she could back out if we wait too long. She's highly unstable, probably insane. Get the FBI Director involved. We can't let this deal fall through."

"I hear you, J.T. I'll call Director Stuart as soon as we hang up."

"Good. Just one other thing."

"What?"

"I also promised Stone I'd get her better accommodations at the prison here in Guantanamo."

"Well, at least you didn't tell her we'd get her a suite at the Four Seasons," she said sarcastically.

Ryan chuckled. "How soon can you get back to me?"

"Like I said, I'll call Stuart right now."

"Thanks, Erin."

The detective disconnected the call and replaced the receiver. Then he leaned back on the small couch, knowing it could be a long time before she got back to him. The wheels of justice moved slowly, especially when it depended on people in Washington D.C.

***

Ryan went back to the Guantanamo interrogation room two days later, with an official document in his hand. As before, the room was stifling hot and a foul odor was pervasive.

Angel Stone was already seated in the room, her hands shackled to the metal table. She was still wearing an orange jumpsuit but she looked even more haggard than two days before. Black smudges were under her eyes, and her hair looked filthy. The stunning beauty of a month ago was gone, replaced by a worn, tired appearance. Ryan was pleased Gitmo was taking its toll – it was well-justified payback for the deaths she'd caused.

Standing next to her was a Navy ensign, dressed in a pressed white uniform.

Ryan approached the ensign. "I'm J.T. Ryan. I assume you're the Jag officer representing Stone?"

"That's right, I'm Ensign Logan," the young officer said, extending his hand.

The two men shook and Ryan took a seat across from the woman. "Good to see you again, Stone."

She glared. "Where the hell have you been?"

"These things take time, you should know that."

"I knew you were full of shit – making promises you couldn't deliver."

Ryan placed the document on the table. "It's all here. In writing, like I said it would be."

After giving him a skeptical look, she glanced up to Ensign Logan. "Check it out – see if it's true."

Logan picked up the document and read it thoroughly, then placed it in front of Stone. "It's all there, Ms Stone. It's official. They've excluded the death penalty from the charges. And you'll be moved to a better prison cell here at Gitmo. It'll have a real bathroom and you'll get better food. It won't be the Ritz, ma'am, but it's the best you can expect at Guantanamo."

Still glowering, she studied the document and read it a few times. After several minutes she faced Ryan. "Okay. I'm ready to talk."

"Good," the detective said. "I know about Heiler and Montoya, but who are the rest of the conspirators in your plot?"

"There was Frank," she sneered, "but you killed him."

"Besides him."

"There was no one else."

"What about Al-Shirak? Who are they? Where are they located?"

Stone let out a hoarse laugh. "They don't exist."

"What?"

"I made them up. There is no Al-Shirak."

"I don't believe you, Stone."

She laughed again, this time harder. "Al-Shirak was a fiction – something I made up to throw off the FBI and CIA, and keep them going in circles."

"What about the imam in Chicago. Imam Rahim. You gave him $600,000. And he had a detonation device you gave him. He was part of the plot."

Stone shook her head. "I gave Rahim the money and the device to create the aura of this mysterious Islamic terrorist organization. Rahim was a fall guy. He's a very greedy and stupid man, but no, he wasn't involved in the bombings."

Ryan was shocked. "So there is no Al-Shirak. That's why the FBI could never find them."

Stone chuckled again. "Pretty clever, huh?"

"Not really. You're the one stuck in this hellhole."

She frowned. "What else do you want to know?"

He leaned forward in the chair. "Tell me about the dirty bombs. Heiler manufactured eight, and you exploded four. Where are the rest?"

"Heiler was lying," she replied with a shrug. "He only made four and I used them all."

Ryan reached over, picked up the document and stood up. "It's you who's lying, Stone. Tell me the truth or I tear this up right now."

A worried look crossed her face. "All right, all right. Don't be such a fucking ass. I'll tell you."

He sat back down and stared at her. "Talk, bitch."

"There were eight bombs in total. I exploded four of them. The four left over are in the States. Frank and I buried them at a farmhouse outside of Savannah, Georgia."

"I need the address."

She told him and Ryan wrote it down. "Okay. The FBI will go there and look for them. If your info checks out, then we've got a deal."

He continued interrogating her for another hour, asking specific questions about her operation. Finally satisfied she had told him everything, he stood up and turned to go.

"Hey, Ryan," Stone said with a laugh. "Don't you want a goodbye kiss before you go? Or a goodbye fuck? After all we've been through together?"

He gave her a hard look. "You make me sick, lady."

She laughed again.

Maybe she *is* insane, he thought.

Then he turned and left the room.

***

Six hours later Ryan boarded the FBI Lear jet that had brought him to Guantanamo. Within minutes the jet took off and he settled back on the leather seat.

He was pleased that the FBI had located the dirty bombs in Savannah, and relieved that the case was over. He was also glad to be headed home, and looked forward to his vacation with Lauren.

But in the back of his mind, he was already thinking about the new case Erin Welch had mentioned. Wonder what that was about?

***

Look for Lee Gimenez's other novels at Amazon, Barnes & Noble.com, Apple, and many other retailers. He invites you to visit him at www.LeeGimenez.com.